HISSES&
HONEY

ALSO BY SHANNON MAYER

The Venom Trilogy

Venom and Vanilla (Book 1)

Fangs and Fennel (Book 2)

The Rylee Adamson Series

Priceless (Book 1)

Immune (Book 2)

Raising Innocence (Book 3)

Shadowed Threads (Book 4)

Blind Salvage (Book 5)

Tracker (Book 6)

Veiled Threat (Book 7)

Wounded (Book 8)

Rising Darkness (Book 9)

Blood of the Lost (Book 10)

Elementally Priceless (A Rylee Adamson Novella 0.5)

Alex (A Rylee Adamson Short Story)

Tracking Magic (A Rylee Adamson Novella)

Guardian (A Rylee Adamson Novella 6.5)

Stitched (A Rylee Adamson Novella 8.5)

RYLEE (The Rylee Adamson Epilogues Book 1)

LIAM (The Rylee Adamson Epilogues Book 2)

HISSES&
HONEY

THE VENOM TRILOGY BOOK 3

SHANNON
MAYER

47N RTH

Text copyright © 2017 Shannon Mayer

Published by 47North, Seattle

www.apub.com

Amazon, the Amazon logo, and 47North are trademarks of Amazon.com, Inc., or its affiliates.

ISBN-13: 9781477818138
ISBN-10: 1477818138

Cover design by Jason Blackburn

Printed in the United States of America

CHAPTER 1

A vampire mob boss and a reluctant Drakaina—a.k.a. a siren who can shift into a two-story snake—walk into a bar in downtown Seattle followed by said Drakaina's very human ex-husband as he begs on his knees for forgiveness. Unfortunately it was not a silly opening to a joke but my actual life. Burnt cookies coating my mouth couldn't have been more unpleasant.

"Alena, please take me back, please, please, *please*." Roger clutched at my right hand, seeing as my left was firmly caught up in Remo's tight grip.

Remo raised a single eyebrow, and a corner of his lips turned up, showing off a glint of one fang. When the light caught his eyes right, the violet color that rimmed his dark iris all but glowed. I rather liked the look of him, from those strange eyes of his, to his lovely mouth, to his hand on mine, and right on down to . . . well, to other parts that I fantasized about far more than I would ever admit.

"You want me to do something about him?" Remo flicked his eyes in Roger's direction. A sigh slid out of me as I shook my head. Remo dealing with Roger would likely mean more than Roger being picked up and tossed back out the door. And as much as I disliked my ex-husband and all he'd put me through, I didn't want Remo to hurt him.

"No, I'll deal with him." I let go of Remo's hand and turned to face Roger, who still clung to my other hand. He stared up at me from down on his knees, clammy fingers squeezing mine over and over. I couldn't help but be surprised he'd even touch me. The last time we'd had dealings, he'd been terrified that I was going to give him the Aegrus virus, and that was a pretty valid reason not to want to so much as brush up against me, never mind cling to me.

The Aegrus virus was currently sweeping the world and wiping out humans left, right, and center despite the various governments and health officials doing all they could to slow it. Seeing as it originated from the Super Duper community—of which I was now a part—Roger should have been staying away from me. Which made me wonder just what he was up to.

I tried to untangle my hand from his without hurting him. Not such an easy task as it would seem now that I was a Drakaina. "Aren't you afraid you're going to get sick, Roger?"

"No, I want to get sick; I want you to get me sick." He smiled up at me, his eyes wild, like he'd been drinking heavily. But I didn't smell anything on his breath. I tried to reel back, but he clung to me like a burnt piece of stubborn banana-nut muffin clinging to the bottom of a baking tin.

"What? Are you out of your mind?" I pushed his hand off mine finally and took several steps back. I might not have carried any lasting warm feelings for the man who'd cheated on me and left me to die on my own, who'd tried to take everything from me, including my home, my bakery, and my inheritance. But that didn't mean I wanted him to die.

Okay, I had wanted to kill him myself, but still, I didn't really want him to die. Really, honest, I hadn't fallen that far from my mother's teachings.

He scrabbled across the rough floor of the bar on his hands and knees, drawing attention from all quarters. Hickory sticks, this was not how I'd thought the night was going to go when Remo asked me out for a date. A nice night out, with a . . . well, "nice" wasn't the word I'd use for Remo, because "a nice night out with a gorgeous vampire mob boss" aren't really the kind of words that go together. I shook my head, knowing Roger better now that we were no longer married. A narcissist through and through. His real colors had truly shown when my life and our marriage had been on the line.

I put my hands on my hips and stared down at him. "Roger, what are you planning this time?"

"I just want to be with you." He smiled up at me, but the smile didn't reach his eyes. I frowned and pointed one finger at him.

"We are divorced, dingle nuts." He jerked as if I'd slapped him, but I kept talking as if I hadn't seen him move. "I don't want to be with you, and why you think you being sick would mean there's any chance I would is beyond ridiculous! The only thing that getting sick would give you besides death is being turned . . ." Understanding hit me like a rack of pans falling from the top shelf and landing on my bare toes. My jaw dropped, and I had to catch myself to keep it from unhinging with the shock. Something that was entirely possible, considering what I was.

"You think that if you get sick, you can be turned into a Super Duper, don't you? You think that you can convince Merlin to make you like me?" I spit out the words as I took another step back.

Roger smiled and held a hand out to me. "Come on, baby. We've been through so much. I just want to be with you. Come on, cough on me."

I glared down at him. "You mean you want my money and inheritance. What, did Barbie put you up to this?" Barbie being the woman he'd cheated on me with. The woman he'd been about to give all *my* money because apparently she was good in bed. Or whatever his reasoning was in regards to her talents. I didn't care.

"Barbie and I broke up," he said. "I realized that I'd always loved you. She was just a phase. I'd just needed to sow some wild oats."

I snorted and put my hands on my hips. I raised my voice so the onlookers that were drawing close would hear me. "You mean a phase that lasted our entire marriage? You don't sow oats when you are *married*, Roger. You are out of your mind if you think I'd ever even consider going back to you. It's not happening. *Rog.*"

The crowd in the bar tittered, and all eyes were on us. I didn't like being the center of attention, but I was not backing down from my ex. Not even to avoid the embarrassment he was causing.

He was, unfortunately, not deterred. The growing crowd oohed as he scooted forward in a weird bunny hop off his knees in order to clutch at my hand once more. "Please, please forgive me. You made me a better man. I know that now. You've humbled me, and I can be better. I am better, but only with you at my side."

I rolled my eyes and jerked my hand away from him. "Please, the only thing you want is the money."

"No, not true." He looked away, though, unable to meet my eyes. "You are beautiful now, and I would be proud to call you my girl." He smiled up at me, and there was more than a hint of lust in the depths of his eyes.

That was the other part of this recipe he was trying to sell me. I wasn't the quiet, drab church mouse he'd married, the girl who'd been raised in the Firstamentalist church, raised to be submissive. Raised to be a doormat, to do what I was told and not question the patriarchy. Once I was turned into a Super Duper, I'd become a siren, and my beauty was a part of my deadly power to control those around me. My brown hair had darkened to a raven-wing black, my brown eyes had brightened to brilliant emerald green, and my body had lengthened and refined in every shape and curve. But none of that defined me. None of it.

I was the same Alena as before, and just happy to be alive and living my life.

I drew myself to my full height, over six feet with my heels on. "I was beautiful before."

Some of the women in the crowd hooted, and several of them hollered.

"You go, girl!"

"Give him hell!"

"Dumb ass should never have cheated on you!"

I raised an eyebrow at the man at my feet as the women in the background cheered me on. "Go away, Roger. Go away and don't bother me anymore. Ever. If my parents invite you to dinner"—yes, that *had* happened after he'd left me for Barbie—"you better decline. You are not a part of our family, and you never really were, so stay away from all of us. Understand?"

His eyes hardened, flashing with nothing short of pure rage. "You should have died in that damn hospital."

Now *there* was the Roger I was expecting. I pointed a finger at him. "And you should have never underestimated my desire to live and survive without you."

"Oh snap!" someone yelled from the crowd. The voice sounded suspiciously like Ernie, the cherub who had, for the most part, helped me in my journey as a Drakaina.

A smiled twitched over my lips as I turned away from my ex. "Leave me alone, Roger."

"You never updated your will, did you?" he shouted.

I rolled my eyes but didn't look back. "Roger, I have not had time; I've been rather busy."

"Good," he growled. "Don't forget that you had a choice—I gave you a choice—and you picked the hard way."

I didn't even flinch at his words. Didn't think anything of them, because he was full of hot air and promises that never came to fruition. That much was the same before and after our marriage collapsed. Roger was a user, and a lazy one at that.

I shouldn't have been surprised at what happened next, but it happened so fast, and, really, I didn't think he had it in him to be so ballsy—not Roger.

The crowd crying out a warning, the noise of a gun cocking, the click of the hammer falling, the boom of the weapon inside the pub, the sounds right on top of one another.

I spun to face Roger, and with my inhuman speed I turned in time to take the bullet in the right side of my chest at the top of my breast instead of my heart. The hit threw me back a few steps, and I clamped a hand over where the bullet had slammed into me. The pain was dull, and while I gasped for air, I already knew I was fine. I'd only had the wind knocked out of me. Roger, though, didn't realize the can of worms he'd just opened.

He grinned, wide enough that I could see all the way to his back teeth. "Law is law. You might have beaten me in the divorce"—he lifted the gun and waved it in the air—"but I can still kill you and not go to jail because *you* are a supernatural beast, and *I* am a human. I exist; you don't. That hasn't changed. I checked. And your will leaves everything to me, doesn't it?"

Rotten bananas couldn't have left a worse taste in my mouth. Who was this man? Had I ever really known him? And he was wrong. I did exist in the eyes of the law; that was how I'd managed the divorce.

Remo cleared his throat. "You still got this?"

God love him, he was trusting me to take care of Roger on my own. Now that was a man who respected me and my abilities.

I pulled my hand from where the wound would have been if I'd still been human. As it was now, there was just a burnt-out hole in my top that stunk like gunpowder and charred fabric. "Yes, thanks. I've got this." I held my hand out to Roger, showing him the bullet, which was squashed flat. "Roger, you should do your research before you try and kill a Super Duper, especially one like me."

His face paled, and his hand trembled on the gun. "Oh shit."

I smiled at him, and my two oversized fangs lowered. The tips dripped with a venom that would kill him if I so much as flicked a single drop into his mouth, never mind if I bit him. "Would someone call the police, please?" I asked, keeping my voice light and calm. I might not be bothered by a bullet, but Roger still had a gun with ammo in it, and the pub was full of humans.

I couldn't let any of them get hurt.

"Already done, sweet cheeks!" someone called from the direction of the bar. I took a step and snatched the gun away from Roger as fast as I could, which meant that in the blink of an eye it was out of his trigger-happy fingers. I pressed the flattened bullet into his open hand, then lifted the gun up to his eyes so he could see what I was about to do.

"Please don't shoot me," he whimpered. He truly didn't know me if he thought I could shoot him.

I put a hand on either side of the gun and bent it in half as if I were making a pretzel. The crowd oohed, and there was a distinct snicker from Ernie somewhere on the sidelines.

"Roger. If you ever come near me again, you're going to wish you were this gun. Do you understand?" I smiled at him, but I could feel that the smile was anything but pretty.

Dangerous, that's what it felt like. If that was even a thing. Could a smile feel dangerous? Well, in that moment it was.

He swallowed hard several times and gave a nod, but said nothing. The door behind him opened, and two police officers stepped in. I wasn't surprised to see that Ben Jensen was one of them, since he was one of Remo's men. Human, but bound to serve the vampire, Jensen always seemed to be around. Suspicious? Yes, but then again, Remo didn't like to let things slide. He trusted me to take care of myself, but a little backup wasn't a bad thing either. After all I'd seen in my few weeks as a Super Duper, I wouldn't turn down a friend who was good in a tight spot.

Jensen nodded at me, and within seconds he and the other officer were escorting Roger through the door while my ex babbled about being out of his mind.

"I didn't know where I was. I just thought that I should come here—the voices told me to!" Roger's legs seemed to give out from under him, forcing the two officers to hold his weight up.

"You should take him to the psych ward then," Ernie called out, helpful as always.

"Put him in a straitjacket!" someone else yelled.

"Give him a prostate exam."

My fangs retracted as I thought about that last suggestion, my lips curling up with distaste. No one should have to be exposed to Roger's private parts.

I turned away from the open door to see Remo still there. Waiting. The man had the patience of someone who was far older than he looked. Which, from what I understood of him, was exactly the reason he could manage the calm, cool look under severe pressure.

He held a hand out to me, his eyes sad. "That's some way to start a date, even for you and me."

I flicked a finger at the hole in the top of my chest. "Hole" wasn't really the right word. The bullet had torn through my human skin and revealed the brightly colored snakeskin below. Snakeskin that was harder than diamonds and had very few weaknesses. That I knew of anyway. Fennel oil was at the top of the list, and it could burn me like flames to a piece of paper, eating up the snakeskin and cutting right through bone if left on me long enough. It was my kryptonite, but I hoped I'd seen the last of it.

I combed one hand through my hair and gave Remo my other.

He led me through the room. Several people smiled at us, some even going so far as to wave, which I didn't understand at first. It was like we were royalty or something. What the heck was going on?

"They saw you on TV." Ernie floated close to my shoulder, his wings brushing against my skin. The thin straps of my tank top left my shoulders mostly bare, something I never would have worn before. Not because of a lack of confidence but because of all the rules I'd followed for so long. Which made wearing the top and matching skirt so much more enjoyable, knowing that I was finally making decisions based on what I wanted and not what was expected of me.

I glanced at him.

"So?"

"You're kinda famous now, girlfriend." He smiled, flashing his white teeth even as his blue eyes sparkled.

"I don't want to be famous," I said.

Ernie shrugged. "Could be a boon to the bakery, all this free publicity. Maybe you need to hand out cards." He shot into the air. "Ladies and gents, if you'd like to see the Drakaina in her natural habitat, be sure to stop by her bakery, Vanilla and Honey, for a taste test. Out-of-this-world baked goods!" He swept a hand toward me, and I blushed as the crowd clapped.

"Ernie, knock it off!" I whispered.

He dropped back down to my eye level. "Nah, it's more fun to watch you squirm. And let's be honest. It will grind Roger's gears to see your business really take off. If you make a crap ton of money, he will really lose his mind."

"Oh," I whispered. He had a very good point there. I smiled and held up my hand, tightening it into a fist. Ernie curled up his hand and knocked it against mine.

"Go team!" he yelled and did a backward somersault in the air.

Remo kept us moving through the bar, finally stopping at a secluded table, where he pulled a chair out for me. I slid in and smoothed my skirt down my legs. The edge of the silky, flowing material stopped at midthigh, far shorter than anything I'd ever worn before I'd been turned into a Drakaina. White with blue and green flowers speckled over it, the green brought out the color in my eyes, and the white showed off the warm tones in my olive skin. I'd worn it thinking only of how Remo would see me. Okay, that and maybe I just really liked the feel of the soft material.

Our waitress came, and I ordered a Shirley Temple. Remo raised an eyebrow. "Still not drinking?"

I shrugged. "I recall vaguely my behavior when I unintentionally imbibed at Zeus's pool party. The results were . . . not pretty." Actually the results had sent me into the lap of a god, after which his estranged wife, the goddess of love, had threatened to kill me just for looking at him. Not good all around, and I planned to avoid a repeat of that scene.

Ernie held up two fingers. "Ouzo for me." The waitress wrote it down and then hurried off when Remo waved her away.

"Really, how can you drink ouzo?" I looked at the cherub, who leaned back on the high seat of the bench.

He smiled and winked. "It makes me think of cupcakes, and you know how I love my food."

A rush of heat spread up my face. "May I remind you that my brush with poisoning others was not something I'm proud of?" I'd decided that putting my venom into a batch of cupcakes would give me a leg up on the bad guys. It had worked, with one small hitch. I'd mixed up the cupcakes and taken some of the poisoned ones to a family dinner. My parents were still complaining about the smell of vomit in their dining room.

"But it got the job done." He pulled one wing forward and ran his fingers through the white feathers.

Not really, it hadn't. The only good thing that had come from it was the satisfaction of watching Roger and Barbie barf all over each other. See, I wasn't joking about my parents inviting my ex and his girlfriend over to eat.

The waitress brought us our drinks. "You sure you don't want any-thing, honey?" She put a hand on Remo's shoulder, rubbing it gently, and I tensed, a low hiss slipping out of me before I could catch it. She didn't hear me, but I had no doubt Remo did. His eyes shot to mine, and I struggled to pull myself together. She was just getting fresh; it happened. No matter how big or the dangerous the aura he carried was, Remo was one dang sexy man, and I knew it, along with the rest of the female population of Seattle.

He shook his head and waved her away without a word. She gave a little huff and shot me a dirty look. Maybe she had heard me hiss at her. I smiled and reached across the table to take his hand. He pulled back, leaning in his chair away from me. That was . . . odd.

"We have to talk," he said, a coolness in his voice that hadn't been there just moments before. Even the first time we'd met there had been heat between us. We'd fought, but he'd never been cold with me.

Ernie flopped down on the table while my heart began to pick up its pace, a slow-burning adrenaline coursing through me. Something was wrong, and I was afraid of whatever it was that made Remo so different.

The cherub seemed oblivious to the rising tension. "What are we discussing tonight?"

Remo turned and stared at Ernie, giving him a glare that should have frozen the wings off the cherub. "Privacy for this. It is between Alena and me."

Ernie stopped in midmotion, a pretzel halfway to his mouth, his shot glass of ouzo in the other. "Oh . . . one of *those* talks. Got it. I won't be far." He popped the pretzel into his mouth and zipped into the air, flew a few booths away, and then leaned down as if he was listening in on the conversation.

My stomach twisted into a sudden knot, as if the snake in me had turned in on itself and was hiding her head. I reached across the table again and took Remo's hand, wrapping my fingers around his, but he didn't react. "What is it?"

He pulled away from me, brushing my fingers off his—as if I were dirty. Part of me wanted to smack him, and the other part of me wanted to smack him too. What was going on?

He closed his eyes. "You understand there are unspoken rules in our world? That there are not supposed to be cross-species relationships? We have discussed this before."

The coil in my belly tightened further, constricting my ability to speak well. I knew what he was talking about, but I thought we were past that issue. "Yes."

His jaw tensed. "I've told Dahlia to break it off with Tad. Their relationship is not right and is bound to fail."

"You what?" I jerked, slamming into the booth back behind me. "But they have something special. They really love each other! How could you do that?"

"I know that they care for one another." His jaw ticked again. "That doesn't negate the reality of their lives, or mine." He paused, his eyes flickering over me and then staring just over my shoulder. "I have other vampires coming in to join me in my fight against Santos. Vampires who are older than me and who are sticklers for the rules. I cannot have cross-species dating happening. If your brother were only a favored donor, that would be something else. But Tad's not, and we all know it."

I felt the prickle along the back of my neck, but I refused to cringe. I refused to beg like Roger for something I could see Remo had already decided on. I straightened in my seat and folded my hands on the table.

"You can't be with me, can you? That's what you are saying?"

His whole body tensed as he slid farther away from me and leaned back in his chair. "No, I can't."

12

CHAPTER 2

I sat there, frozen in place. I shouldn't have been bothered Remo was breaking things off with me. It wasn't like we'd been dating long, only a week or so since my divorce had been finalized, and before that we'd not really been together. Just . . . working toward it. We hadn't even had sex. I mean, I'd slept beside him more than once, but no nookie because . . . damn it, I couldn't seem to find a good enough reason now that I was losing him.

I shouldn't have been upset—this was minor in the scheme of things and all I'd faced so far—but I knew I wasn't going to find another man like Remo. One who knew when to let me fight my own battles, who let me make my own mistakes and respected me enough to let me find my own way. A man who didn't even push me into having sex, though we'd come close, each of our own accord.

"Just like that?" I was proud of how my words came out without trembling. Without a single sobbing quiver, no matter what my emotions were doing to me on the inside.

His eyes hardened ever so slightly. "You forget that I am not like you. I'm not designed to be monogamous; no vampire is. Do you really think you've been the only woman in my arms the last few weeks?"

Lies. I could almost taste the lie on the air and had to fight not to flick my tongue out to confirm the scent of it. But if he wanted the lie to make himself feel better, then there was nothing I could do about it.

"Oh, you didn't just do that, you idiot," Ernie muttered from the ceiling above us. I didn't look at him. I kept my eyes on Remo, because I knew this would be the last time I saw him.

There would be no going back after this.

The vampire mob boss stood, his whole body tense to the point that I could feel the irritation rolling off him, the heightened adrenaline and emotions strong between us. My own skin quivered, sensitive to all the tension he threw off. It twitched like mad in response.

"We have a business arrangement still," he said. "You owe me two more feedings at my discretion for helping you, as per our agreement. If you'll step outside, I'll take one now. I'll give you a few minutes to collect yourself. Don't make me come back in for you."

I flattened both my hands on the table and forced myself to raise an eyebrow. I would not let him see me cry over him. If he could be unaffected by this, then I could be too. "I don't go back on my word, and that you think I would do that is insulting."

His eyes softened, and I thought he'd say something, but he spun and walked away. I watched him go, unable to take my gaze from his retreating back, from the shape of his broad shoulders to the narrowed taper of his hips.

"Ernie," I said.

"Yeah." He floated down. "I got nothing for you. I thought he was going to go to bat for you, stand up against the world for your love . . . I'm sorry."

I rose, smoothed my skirt and top, then strode after Remo. I would not break my word with him and go back on our deal. Why he wanted to feed now was beyond me, though. Maybe he wanted to impress the new vampires with his strength? That was probably it—the stronger he was, the better when dealing with them. The business side of my brain got it. My heart, though, was struggling.

I drew in a breath as I stepped out of the bar. I held the air, rolling it over my tongue and picking up on Remo's signature scent of cinnamon and honey. I was going to miss that smell, miss the way it soothed my senses. I followed it around the corner of the building. His hands shot out of the darkness and yanked me to him. I gasped and put my hands on his chest, shocked at the aggression he was showing.

And more than a little turned on by it.

"You can't just bite me, you know that." I blurted the words out, shocked at the mix of anger and desire raging in me. The emotions were a heady mix.

"Then do it, and let's be done with this," he growled.

Be done with this, be done with me. He wasn't doing this to impress anyone; he was doing it because he wanted me out of his life as fast as he could, and that meant using up my offers of blood as soon as possible.

Ernie cleared his throat. "You still got Beth's feather on you? It'll cut through clean."

I nodded and put a hand to my purse, pulling out the silver-and-gold feather. It was from my friend Beth. A Stymphalian bird who'd died at the hands of Theseus. I kept her feather to remind me of her, and also to remind myself of the power I carried as a Drakaina. But also to remind me that I was not invulnerable to being hurt, or even killed. The feather could cut through even my snakeskin, making the innocuous-looking item deadly in the wrong hands. Remo's hands tightened on my waist as I lifted the feather to my neck.

"Your wrist will be fine," he snapped.

Of course, the wrist was far less intimate than the neck. But if he wanted my blood, he was going to do it my way. Which meant being reminded of exactly what it was he was about to give up. With a sharp motion I made a tiny cut at the base of my neck on the left-hand side. "Bite me," I said.

With a growl he slammed his mouth against the wound, all traces of the man I knew disappearing under what he really was. A vampire. A mob boss. Out for himself and no one else.

A spike of pleasure shot from his mouth, down through my chest, and pooled in between my legs. I whimpered even as I clung to him, feeling his muscles bunch and flex under my hands. His mouth slipped from the wound and up my neck, trailing kisses, trailing love bites that made my knees weak. Our lips met, and there was an explosion of hunger in our kiss, our hands seemingly unable to draw one another close enough. This was good-bye, I knew it, and I fought to make it last longer. To make him see that I was good for him.

I was good enough.

Maybe I wasn't.

He bit my lower lip, tugged it toward him, and then let go. I looked up into his eyes to see the same dazed hunger that had nothing to do with the belly and everything to do with the body.

"You are a siren; stop trying to sway me." He pushed me away from him. I clamped a hand over the wound in my neck. I had to get it stitched up right away, to close off the wound that could be used against me. That's what I focused on, that physical vulnerability. That's why it hurt so much. It had nothing to do with the pain in my heart. Nothing to do with the realization that I'd been used again by a man who professed to care about me.

Remo stumbled away from me, and as he stepped into the light in front of the bar, a woman approached him. She had short spiky blond hair and huge hooped earrings that brushed the tops of her shoulders. She threw her head back, a perfect invitation to a vampire. He caught her around the waist and picked her up, tossing her over his shoulder to take her with him.

I stared in blank, mute silence as I struggled to understand what had just happened, and more than that, why. Why was it always the blondes who stole the men in my life?

A small hand touched the top of my shoulder, and I closed my eyes. "Ernie, tell me that didn't just happen."

"Sorry, kid," he said softly. "That was . . . not expected. I thought you'd gotten through to him. I thought he saw you for all the amazingness you are."

I stood there, my heart hurting far more than it should have over a man I'd known for only a few weeks. But there was something I would not admit to anyone out loud. I'd known Remo would be in my life from the first moment I met him. That he would be pivotal—the connection between us had happened within seconds of meeting. But apparently I was wrong about that.

Again, I'd been wrong about a man I loved. I shouldn't have been surprised, not after Roger. I just thought . . . I thought Remo was different.

Shaking, I pushed myself away from the rough wall of the building. "Ernie, you want to go bake something?"

"Hell yeah!" He flew around so he was in front of me as I made my way out to the street. "What are we going to make?"

"I don't know," I said. "Anything to take me away from what just happened."

There was a small crowd waiting to get into the bar as we passed the front entrance, and a hand reached out as I passed by and touched my elbow. "Hey, could I get an autograph?"

I paused and stared into the face of a woman who was obviously a werewolf. She had gorgeous sandy-colored curls that cascaded all around her face, as though they'd been dried by the wind. She was built lean and wiry, and she barely came up to my chin. Her face was heart shaped, but it was her eyes that told me all I needed to know. The eyes of a wild animal lurked in the amber depths.

Or at least it was obvious to me what she was; the people around her, mostly human, didn't give her so much as a second glance. The smell rolling off her was of wide-open plains, the rush of a winter wind, and the feel of fur ruffling in the cold air, which only confirmed what I saw.

"An autograph?" I blinked stupidly, as if I were trying to understand a new language.

She smiled up at me, the tip of her pink tongue peeking out one side of her mouth. "Yeah, you're a hero for us, you know that, don't you? My name is Amy." She thrust a piece of paper and a pen at me.

I glanced at Ernie, and he shrugged. "Might as well."

I took the offered pen and paper, hesitant at first, then I stepped to the side of the building again and used the wall to flatten the paper. I stood there and stared at it a minute, thinking about what to say. An autograph seemed weird, but advice . . . I could give her a piece of advice. I put words to the paper after a moment of thought, then handed it back to her. She read it, her amber eyes watered, and she threw her arms around me in a tight hug, the smell of winter enveloping me for a brief moment. "Thank you . . . that was exactly what I needed."

I patted her back, and she let me go. "You're welcome."

Ernie flitted around my head. "What did you write to her?"

"None of your business," I said. "It was for her, not you."

"What, you think you can read the future now? That isn't in your range of talents, you know, girlfriend." He snapped his fingers at me, saucy as usual.

Another time I would have made a quip, would have said something silly back. But not tonight. Not while feeling as though my heart were cracking. I'd not felt like this even when I realized that Roger was leaving me to die alone in a hospital bed while he played house with his Barbie.

I slid into my new car, a sporty Dodge Charger that I'd gleefully spent a small portion of my inheritance on. It was dark blue with white racing stripes that ran up the middle of the hood, over the roof, and down to the back of the trunk. I loved it, and the smell of new car was lovely, but all of that meant very little in the moment. I reached under the passenger seat and pulled out a tiny first-aid kit. In it were a needle and thread and some butterfly bandages. "Stitches for the snakeskin, bandages for the human," I said.

I handed them to Ernie, who dutifully placed them over the wound. "Yeah, I got it," he said while he put me back together. If only my heart could be so easily patched as the wound on my neck.

He finished and tucked the kit back in its place. I put my seat belt on and leaned forward so my head pressed into the steering wheel. I stared down at my legs as the tears fell, plopping onto them. Ernie sat on the middle console, his legs dangling near my right elbow.

"I could always shoot him with an arrow, and he'd come running back," he offered.

"I don't want him if he doesn't want me. Remember Roger? I've gone that route, and it sucks donkey balls."

He grunted. "True. But Remo does care for you. I can see it, and I should know. It's kinda my job, if you'll recall."

"But he doesn't care enough to stick it out. He's . . ." I sat up and gripped the leather-wrapped steering wheel. "He's doing what I did for years. Conforming because it's easier." My shoulders slumped as fast as I'd straightened them. I knew all too well the pressure of trying to do what was right, even when it hurt. I scrubbed both hands over my eyes. "Oh no."

"What?"

"He said that he told Dahlia and Tad to break up."

I grabbed my purse from the passenger seat and pulled my cell phone out. I dialed Tad first. He answered on the second ring.

"What's up, sis?" His cheery, upbeat voice told me everything I needed to know. Dahlia hadn't broken it off with him.

"Can you meet me at Vanilla and Honey?" I asked.

"Um, aren't you supposed to be on a date with Remo?"

"Never you mind about what or where I'm supposed to be," I snapped. "I need to try out some new recipes, and I need a taste tester who isn't afraid to tell me when something tastes bad."

"Don't have to ask me twice." He hung up, and I hit the "End" button. I looked at Ernie.

His blue eyes were sad. "I'm sorry, Alena. I really am." I nodded and he flew at me, wrapping his arms around my neck. I hugged him back.

"Thanks, Ernie. You're a good friend. I think."

He snorted. "Don't go there. I'm on your side, even when it looks like I'm not. You know that."

I nodded. I did know that now. Being in the Greek pantheon, Ernie—Eros to those who knew their history—was pulled in multiple directions. And to keep his wings and skin intact, he played all sides of the field. He had ties to multiple deities, and they didn't always treat him well if they thought he was disloyal. So he'd learned to keep under the radar the best way he could, which sometimes left him right in the middle of fights and arguments among the gods and goddesses. I'd not understood at first, but I realized he really *was* on my side. For the situation he was in, he did the best he could.

I started up the Charger and pulled into traffic. Two streets down, a set of police lights flicked behind me in the early-evening light, beckoning me to pull over. I groaned. "Like I need this tonight. I wasn't even speeding!"

Ernie leaned back in the passenger seat as he went through my purse. "Yeah, but I've no doubt that Officer Jensen just found out that you and Remo are no longer an item. You should never have rolled him; that cop is more than half in love with you. Not that I blame him, even if you hadn't rolled him." He winked as if that would make his words easier to swallow.

"I didn't have a choice, and I didn't know he'd already been rolled by a vampire!" I pointed out. Officer Jensen worked for Remo, as one of his human servants, in a way. Because the good officer had been charmed, or influenced, or whatever the vamps wanted to call it, that made his mind susceptible to other forms of influence. Like, say, from a siren who had no idea what she was doing with her abilities. So he'd gotten a rather large dose of influence from me. More than enough to make him think he loved me.

I pulled over, turned the engine off, and rolled down my window. The early-February air was chilly, damp with rain waiting to fall but overall quite fresh and lovely. A perk to being a Drakaina: not being bothered by extreme heat or cold.

Officer Jensen strolled to my window and peered in, and his chocolate-brown eyes swept over me and Ernie. "License and registration."

"Seriously?" I stared up at him. "For what? I wasn't speeding."

His eyes narrowed. "You want me to take you in? I can do that, if you like."

With a grumble on my lips, I reached over to my dash, opened it, and grabbed my registration. Next came my newly minted driver's license. Okay, it was temporary, just a piece of paper with a black-and-white photo of yours truly laminated on it, while I waited on the new color-picture version to come through in the mail. But it was mine, and that was all that mattered.

I handed it to him. He looked it over, checked the registration, and handed them both back to me. "Glad to see you are following the rules now."

There was a weight to his words that made me narrow my eyes. "What's that supposed to mean?"

"You know what it means. I told you he'd hurt you. I'm glad you broke up with him," he said, not backing away from the car an inch.

I blinked several times. "Excuse me? What did you say?"

"That you broke it off with him. He said you didn't want anything to do with him." Jensen tipped his head. "He said that you were looking for your own kind."

My jaw ticked and my eyes burned. Why would Remo blame me for this? Wouldn't he want the other vampires to think he'd cut me loose? I mean, he had, but even if I *had* broken up with him, wouldn't he have wanted to look like the tough guy? I couldn't make sense of what he was doing.

"Are we done here?" I kept my voice even, without a single indication of the confusion I felt.

"Alena, we are friends. Even though I work for him, I want you to know that I will help you if you get into trouble again. I care about—"

"I'm not getting into any trouble," I snapped. Well, the truth was I knew that I had more trouble coming. Hera, Greek goddess and estranged wife of Zeus, had a serious hate-on for me. She was earnestly trying to find a way to kill me by any means necessary. I'd defeated two of her chosen heroes, Achilles and then Theseus. One I'd maimed and the other I'd killed. Now she was raising another hero to face me, and she'd already set him up with a pet to help take me down. I didn't know which hero she'd called on this time, but I did know what creature she'd had created, because Merlin had shown her to me.

A nine-headed Hydra.

I shivered and rubbed my hands over my arms. "Again, I am not getting into trouble. It keeps finding me. There's a difference, you know."

"Not from where I stand. You don't need him to help you. Trust me on this. No matter which of you broke things off, this is better for you." He stepped back. "Have a good night, ma'am."

"Ma'am. I hate that, don't call me that!" I rolled my window up as if that would keep him out. I turned the engine over and pulled away from the curb. I shot a look at Ernie. "Nothing pithy to say?"

"I was going to say that you have better help than Jensen, but it was nice of him to offer." That didn't sound like Ernie.

"Spit it out, what did you really want to say?"

The words exploded out of him like he couldn't contain them any longer. "He's got such a hard-on for you, girlfriend, it could be seen a mile off in the dark by a blind man!"

The laughter burst out of me, and I didn't stop until long after the tears rolled down my cheeks. "Thanks, I needed that."

"Well, it's true. I mean between him and Hephaestus, you at least have options." He gave me a big wink, and I did my best not to think about Smithy, a.k.a. Hephaestus. I'd met Smithy when he'd been part of the SDMP—Supernatural Division of Mounted Police—and I'd thought he was a werewolf. Turns out, he was a Greek god in hiding, Hephaestus, the cranky old blacksmith responsible for arming his fellow gods and goddesses. Except that he looked far from old, and with me, he was far from cranky. I tried not to consider just how kind he'd been, or that he'd all but said I was the kind of woman he'd want in his life. If he hadn't had to deal with his crazy wife, Aphrodite, that was.

It seemed that all the men in *my* life had an excuse why I wasn't quite good enough. The thought galled me, and at the same time made my anger flare. I was good enough.

I obviously just hadn't found the right man yet.

I turned left, using the moment to check my mirrors and give me time to think of a proper reply. "Smithy is in the middle of his own divorce, if you recall, and he only liked me because it irritated his wife."

"Oh, don't sell yourself short. I bet if you offered him a taste test, he'd run with it all the way." He waggled his eyebrows at me, which made me laugh again.

"Ernie! I'm not that kind of girl!" I spluttered.

He laughed. "I meant at your bakery, you know, the kind of taste test you just offered your brother. What kind of taste test were *you* thinking, you naughty girl?"

The heat in my face could have baked two batches of macadamia-nut cookies in under a minute. "Stop teasing me; I don't want to be laughing and joking right now."

"No, I won't stop. Because until you realize that Remo was a fool for walking away from you, I'm going to keep pointing out that you have options. Good ones too. You might not realize it, because all you can see is that smoking-hot vampire." He leaned back in his seat and ticked his fingers with each point. "Jensen is human, which means you can be with him, even if you'd have to be awful careful not to squeeze him too tight. Same as Hephaestus—except you could squeeze him all you like with those long legs, and I'm pretty sure he wouldn't be bothered in the least. Perks to being a god, you know." He winked again, and I clutched at the steering wheel.

"Smithy," I corrected him.

"Fine, Smithy." He shook his head. "Either of those men is free and clear to be at your side with no issues. And with Smithy, he is something of a powerhouse. He's strong and could really help you out with the whole hero-coming-to-kill-you business. And you're going to need help. I know you're one tough badass, but a nine-headed Hydra? All hands on deck for that big bitch."

I was silent a moment as I took in what he was saying. "So you think I should whore myself out for help?" I didn't like what he was implying.

"Isn't that what you did with Remo? In the beginning at least?" he pointed out, and I cringed. It was true, though. That had been the deal—my blood for Remo's help.

"That was just blood, not my body." I didn't want to think he was right, but maybe . . .

My bakery was ahead, and it occurred to me that, for the evening hours, the road was packed with far too many vehicles. I frowned as I did a quick count. Over twenty cars and trucks, and I knew none of the businesses were open at that late hour.

I drew closer to see people standing out front of Vanilla and Honey, my bakery, with signs in their hands and Halloween masks over their faces.

"What the fricky dicky is this?" I whispered. I pulled around to the back parking lot, turned the engine off, and glanced at Ernie. "This conversation is not done."

"Well, I hope not." He smiled and rubbed his hands together like an evil genius. "Because I've got all sorts of ammo to use against you to prove why you should just let the vamp go."

Dang it. I slid out of the car as the crowd rushed around the back of the building and surrounded my car, slapping it with their wooden signs.

"Stop it!" I yelled, trying to get them away from my new baby. The paint job was going to take a literal beating. Of course, no one listened to me.

"Humans first!"

"Cage the monsters!"

"Go back to your side of the Wall, you freak!"

The words came fast and furious as the people pressed against me, and I struggled not to lash out at them. I would hurt them badly without even trying if I wasn't careful.

"Stop it! What are you doing?" I tried to push through, but the throng of people was thick, and I couldn't make them move without hurting them.

"You're a freak, get out of here," a man in a gruesome zombie mask yelled.

There were even some children in the mix, and they were as mean as the adults as the children picked up loose stones and threw them at me. I dodged the stones, and several bounced off my car. I'd seen this before, I'd even been a part of a mob or two like this, which made the guilt all that much stronger.

"You should have died! God called your soul home, and you denied him!" That was from a woman wearing a long drab gray dress that covered her from ankle to wrist, and a witch's mask.

Her words only confirmed what I already suspected. I wasn't facing just some random crowd of people who were irritated by my existence as a Super Duper. I was facing those people I'd once called friends, people who'd been my extended family, who'd shared the same beliefs.

As a supernatural, I was facing my first mob of Firstamentalists determined to send my soul to hell.

CHAPTER 3

My initial thought about the mob of religious nuts was to wonder if my mother had organized the group. That might not sound fair; I mean, who would think that badly of her mother, right?

Me. I would, and it was warranted too. She'd denied me the second I'd been turned. She'd said it then; it would have been better that I died than to live on as a monster.

"Mom, are you here?" I stood on my tiptoes as I scanned the crowd.

"Look at her, she's calling for her mother. Your mother doesn't want you!"

"You're dead to her!"

Okay, that was not nice to hear out loud, even if it was kinda true.

They jostled me, not really hurting me, but I didn't know how to get around them without actually hurting them. How to get away from the words, to get away from the brutal truths they hurled . . . unless I scared them so badly they left. I looked up at Ernie as he flew over all our heads. "Back me up," I said.

He cocked his head to one side, confusion clouding his eyes. "What?"

I doubled over at the waist and coughed violently until I almost choked, forcing myself to gag.

"Oh no!" Ernie yelled, right on cue. "She's got the Aegrus virus!"

The crowd shifted away from me at a speed that almost made me smile. I kept coughing, forcing myself to wheeze and clutch at my belly, really putting the act out there for all I was worth. "Oh, I think I'm so, so sick. I think I'm going to vomit." I put my hands on my knees and hunched my back. Ernie cleared his throat. "Empty stage, girlfriend."

I looked up, and my eyes widened. The back alley had cleared; there wasn't a single trace of the mob that had been there. I'd not even heard them go over my coughing and gagging.

"Damn, that's a good trick." Ernie floated with his hands on his chubby hips like a miniature Peter Pan. "But don't overdo it, though, or they'll catch on."

"You say that like they'll be back." I brushed my skirt flat, knocking off a few clots of dirt from the stones that were thrown.

He grunted. "You say that like they won't."

I sighed, knowing he had a point—again—and grabbed my keys. I pushed the "Lock" button, and the beep of my Charger acknowledged that it was indeed locked. I did it a second time just to make sure.

What Ernie said, though, was truer than maybe even he realized, and it was something I didn't want to think much about. Once the Firstamentalists decided they were going to run someone out of town, they were unrelenting until they got what they wanted. I didn't know of a single case where they'd backed down. Where they'd let anyone get away with what they thought of as sinning, or evil. I knew; I'd been a part of them for so long.

It seemed fitting that I was now one of the monsters that they were trying to cast out. But I knew their tricks; I would find a way to make sure the Firstamentalists didn't get what they wanted this time.

I let us into the bakery, closed the door, and leaned against it. "Could this night get any worse?"

"Oh, don't say that out loud," Ernie groaned. "Rule number one of the pantheon, don't ask for trouble."

A loud knock on the door behind me made me cringe, and Ernie flew backward. "Don't open it."

"It's probably Tad." Mind you, I whispered that. Just in case.

"Be sure," Ernie whispered back.

I nodded and then tipped my head back to listen for a heartbeat. I picked one up on the other side of the door, steady and solid. So, not a vampire at least, and I refused to acknowledge that a part of me was disappointed Remo hadn't followed me. I drew in a breath, and my mouth dried up as I recognized the smell.

I moved back away from the door as he knocked again.

Ernie drew close to me, still keeping his voice low. "Not Tad?"

I shook my head, debating if I wanted to open the door. I licked my lips, uncertainty flowing through me. No. I wouldn't buckle. I wouldn't hide from him no matter what. But I wasn't going to just open the door for him either.

"We aren't open. If you'd like some baked goods, we open at six tomorrow morning. Or you can place an order on our website for pickup." My store manager, Diana, had insisted that a website ordering service would work. She was right. In the first week, we'd almost doubled our sales.

"Alena, I'd like to speak with you," Smithy said, his resonant voice muffled slightly by the thick door.

Ernie grinned at me, his eyes going big and wide with glee. "Open it up, girlfriend. Things happen for a reason. Which means he's here for a reason, I'm sure of it."

Except I didn't know how to explain to Ernie that Smithy, as handsome as he was, and as strong as he was, didn't flip my switch like Remo did. Not by a long shot. Really, honestly. Didn't do it for me.

Liar, liar, pants on fire, a tiny voice sang to me. I recalled all too easily the feel of Smithy's rock-hard body under my hands when I'd been half-gooned on the punch at Zeus's pool party. To say he had a nice body was a serious understatement. Not that I'd noticed it.

I ignored my inner voice. "I don't want to talk to you. Talking to you got me into trouble with your wife, and now she's trying to kill me, if you'll recall."

"You were in trouble with her long before you fell into my lap drunk as a nymph at a frat party."

I blushed, thinking that I had indeed had my face all but planted in his crotch at the pool party. Dang, I had hoped he wouldn't bring that up. "That wasn't my fault. I didn't know the punch was spiked."

A low rumble of a laugh rolled through the door. "The punch is always spiked, Alena. Lesson number one of the pantheon."

"I thought lesson number one was never ask for trouble."

He laughed again. "Fine, lesson number two, then. The punch is always spiked."

I rubbed my hands over my bare arms, knocking back the goose bumps that his laugh had raised. I forced my feet to move, strode to the door, and jerked it open.

Smithy's blue eyes raked over me, and I grit my teeth against the way my body reacted. "What do you want?"

He didn't step forward, didn't push his way into my space. "I came to give you a warning. I know which hero Hera is calling up this time to face you."

I swallowed hard. "How bad is it?"

His eyebrows rose even as his jaw ticked. "Bad, worse than the other two combined. May I come in?"

I was being silly. He wasn't going to throw himself at me. He had the same issue I'd had only a short time before. He believed in his marriage vows, even though his wife, Aphrodite, had no problem working outside of them. He wouldn't make a serious move while he still had a wife. Smithy was a faithful man. Something I couldn't say for Remo.

No, do not go there, Alena.

I moved to one side and held the door open for him. He stepped through into the light, and I got a good look at him. His scars were still visible, all the marks of being a blacksmith for thousands of years burned into his forearms and even a few places on his neck and collarbone. Then again, those could be scars from fighting too; he was a warrior from way back when the pantheon was nothing but warfare and chaos. Not that things had changed much, really.

I clamped my fingers together with the sudden itch to touch those scars. What was wrong with me? Ten minutes before I'd been sobbing my heart out about Remo, and now here I was considering just how Smithy's skin would feel under my own.

A soft voice whispered to me inside my head, and I recognized it for who it was. The Drakaina side of me had been speaking up lately.

You are a siren, and that means your libido is high, and not easily quenched. Your nature recognizes that you are no longer attached to the vampire, even if your heart has not yet accepted it.

Great. Just what I needed.

Smithy walked to the far side of the room and eyed up the stove, even going so far as to flick the gas burner on. He ran his fingers through the flame twice before he flicked it back off.

"Showing off?" I reluctantly closed the door behind me. If it hadn't been for the mob of Firstamentalists out front, I would have left it open. Maybe it could air out the growing pheromone clouds in the small room. I glanced up at Ernie, who'd plunked himself on the shelf that held the spices, right next to the cupboard with the liquor. He was remaining remarkably quiet, his blue eyes watching us closely.

Smithy turned with a tight smile on his lips. "I like that you work with the flame, and not just an electric heat. A real flame has a flavor of its own."

I shrugged. "It gives a more even heat distribution, which is important for a lot of recipes."

"No spikes and drops. No ups and downs, just a steady, burning heat," he said softly.

I clamped my hands behind my back. I didn't think he really was talking about the stove. Even *I* wasn't that dense. "True enough. Then again, to get a good caramel, you need to bring the ingredients just to the edge of a burn before you get the right texture and flavor. It's the only way to bring out the sweetness."

Good grief, what was wrong with me?

His smile widened. "Caramel?"

I cleared my throat. "I'm a baker; caramel is a big part of that."

"No, you're a Drakaina."

Oh, and there was the cold water I needed to cool my jets. "Don't tell me what I am; I am more than aware of it. Besides, I am a baker at the core."

"You can't change what you are, Alena. No more than I can. No more than I will ever be free of her," he said.

There was a sadness in his voice there that I didn't want to hear. I didn't want to feel bad for him . . . because I understood all too well what it was to be married to someone who didn't love you anymore. Someone who just wanted to use you for your gifts and talents and would cast you off at the first hint of not getting their way.

I cleared my throat and moved to the cupboard where I kept my largest mixing bowls. I pulled two out and set them on the counter. "I thought you were getting a divorce? That's what Oberfluffel said."

His lips twitched. "I told *Oberfall* what he wanted to hear. There are no divorces for the pantheon."

"Well, if you ask around, there are no divorces for Super Dupers married to humans, but I've proved that wrong." I raised my eyebrows at him as I reached for some basic ingredients, laying them out on the counter next to my bowls. Flour, sugar, baking powder, vanilla, eggs. I just kept grabbing things, not really thinking about what I was going to make so much as keeping my hands busy. Anything to hold my mind on my own business and away from the man—no, god—in front of me.

"Ah, you think it would be that easy?" he asked.

I tried not to notice that he closed the distance between us step by step. I grabbed a bowl and thrust it at him. "Here, hold this."

He frowned into the empty bowl, and I started throwing ingredients in. Literally tossing them in, forcing him to move the bowl around to catch them.

"If you really wanted out, you'd find a way. Zeus said that Hera wouldn't allow him to divorce her. That he tried. So maybe you could convince your wife to let you go." I cracked three eggs and dropped them into the mix. I realized that I was making a sponge cake—at least that was the recipe going through my head. Even if I was putting it together wrong.

"And if I were free of her? What then?" He put the bowl on the counter and tried to capture my eyes with his. Nope, not going there. *Nana nana nana nana.* I ran the noise through my head, hoping for some help. I glanced at Ernie, who just grinned at me and gave me two thumbs up. Shoot, so much for counting on him to break things up.

Smithy slid around so I had my back against the counter and his hands were on either side. Trapping me even while he didn't touch me. "What then, Alena?"

"Umm." I looked over his left shoulder, and he moved so his face was in the way. Double shoot, this was not going as planned.

"Let me guess, he let you go, didn't he? The vampire ran away from you, citing irreconcilable differences?" Smithy asked softly, his voice tugging at me.

"And what if he did?" I finally locked eyes with him, noting that up close his blue eyes had tiny flecks of silver in them that glinted in the light. That had to be what gave him his trademark icy stare. "You don't really want to be free of Aphrodite. If you did, you would have found a way. There is always a way if you want something bad enough."

In a flash his body was pressed against mine, making me gasp as he pinned me to the counter, his large hands covering mine and holding me still. I may have let out a squeak, but I'm not entirely sure, because my brain went on strike as my damn heart went into overdrive with sweet, hot adrenaline.

His face came within kissing distance, his breath fluttering over my lips. "There has been no reason to go through with a divorce, no reason to stir the flames of her wrath." He drew in a breath and let it out slowly, the rush of it tickling across my lips again. "Until now."

Sugar cookies, this was not good, even though a part of me wanted it. Like really, really wanted it.

Panic reared its head, and the Drakaina in me fell away, leaving only the truth in its place. I blurted it out, desperate to stop this. "I love him. And I can't . . . I can't just jump from him to you. I can't."

Smithy closed his eyes. "Damn."

"He doesn't love her," Ernie said from his perch, helpful as always.

Smithy glanced at him, not for one second loosening his hold on me. "You sure about that, Eros? Or are you playing games for your master?"

Ernie shook his head. "Alena's my friend. Aphrodite is my boss. You tell me where my loyalties lie. If Remo loved her, he'd fight for her, wouldn't he? He gave up the second someone said he had to."

"You've played these games with others, setting people up." That icy glare was locked on Ernie, but the cherub just shrugged, seemingly unbothered by the accusation.

"I'm never wrong. I can see the truth of people's hearts. That's kind of my job, you know." Like he was going to let us forget that his job was to bring people together.

This sounded like an ongoing issue between the two men. "Um, can you ease off?"

Smithy tightened his hold on me, not looking away from Ernie. "Eros. What do you see for her?"

Okay, what was he talking about now? I glanced at Ernie, who'd closed his eyes, his wings stilling. "There is love in her future, a love that will eclipse the sun with its brightness. Aphrodite will hate her with a passion she's reserved in the past for lovers who scorned her." He opened his eyes. "You know I can't tell you details; it doesn't work that way."

"What are you two talking about?" I squirmed, but that only bumped my hips up against Smithy. He turned, his eyes latching onto my mouth, his hands tightening once more on mine.

"It means I'm going to break my own rules." He tugged my hands up so they were around the back of his neck. My fingers automatically curled, brushing against the base of his neck. We were nose to nose. I opened my mouth to tell him to let me go, only my hands didn't push him away. They pulled him close.

His mouth was on mine, and his tongue slid past my lips. He wrapped his arms around my waist and held me tight to his hard body, his muscles flexing against me like he was restraining himself from squeezing me tighter.

He tasted of caramel, and I fought to not enjoy his mouth on mine, because there was a reason . . . wasn't there? The Drakaina in me, though, was quite enjoying the new sensations of a Greek god running his hands over my back, hips, and butt. Power crackled where his hands traced, a slow burning fire that called to parts of me I was doing my best to bring back under control. He pulled back, his chest heaving and his eyes full of desire.

I blinked up at him, then shoved him backward hard enough that he hit the far wall with a bounce. "That was dirty pool!"

"That was desire, plain and simple." He grinned at me, all wolfy and wild. Damn, it made my blood pound, that single thing. I drew in a breath, then another, as I tried to get myself under control. Even with Remo I'd held back, and I'd wanted him from the beginning. What was going on?

"This isn't like you, Smithy. And it's not like me, even if I am a siren." The words slid out of me, and I looked up at Ernie. "Did you shoot him with one of your arrows or something?"

Smithy jerked as though he had indeed been shot. Ernie flew right up to the ceiling. "Now, what would make you say that?" There was too much innocence in his denial, and his blue eyes were far too wide. The fat-bottomed jerk!

I frowned at Ernie. "Ernie! You shot him, didn't you?"

Ernie was shaking his head, but I saw the glint in his eyes. "Aphrodite doesn't deserve him, and he's a good guy. One of the best. And you don't deserve to be jerked around by Remo. You're . . . you're a good friend. Both of you are. I want you to be happy, and there is a lot of possibility there. You two could be amazing together. This is my job, remember?"

"You don't have to keep reminding us of that. We know it's your job," I said, then swallowed hard. How could I be mad at what he was saying? He wanted us both to be happy and thought he could help us along. That's what friends did for one another.

Apparently Smithy wasn't so moved by Ernie's speech.

"You little shit! You aren't supposed to be shooting the pantheon! It's against the rules." I almost asked if it was rule number three but wisely kept my mouth shut.

He moved toward the stove and flicked one of the burners on. The flame shot up far higher than it should have.

"Don't, you'll burn my bakery down!" I yelled.

"How about he'll fry my wings off?" Ernie bit out.

Smithy ran his hand through the flame and coaxed it up into his hands. He rolled it back and forth like a baseball.

"Eros, you've gone too far this time."

"I was really trying to help. I could see that you liked her, that you wanted her. More than that, you respect her!" He held both hands out to Smithy. "I mean, you almost kissed her on your own, without me. We all know it."

Smithy threw the fireball at Ernie, and the cherub dodged it. Which meant it slammed into my ceiling.

"Stop it!" I grabbed Smithy's arm, which spun him to face me. I cupped his face with my hands and pushed my siren abilities into my voice. "Don't hate him for wanting me to be happy. He's right, this was between us before he interfered."

His blue eyes softened, then immediately hardened over again. "Don't try to control me. I've had enough of that shit."

I let him go, pushing away the urge to keep my hands on his face. "Then don't try to hurt him. He did this because he cares about you. And me."

Smithy shook his head, turned around, and flicked off the stove, then held a hand up to the ceiling, and the flames went out. He grabbed the edges of the stove and hunched his back. "When did you shoot me, Eros?"

Ernie gave an audible gulp. "This morning."

I frowned. "I was still with Remo this morning."

Ernie closed his eyes and rubbed his hands over his face. "The rumor was already out there that he was going to dump you. That the big bads coming into town wouldn't help him oust Santos if he was still seeing you. I already knew what he'd choose. I knew that he didn't really love you, Alena. I'm sorry. I'd hoped I was wrong for your sake."

The back door flung open, and Tad strode in, a grin on his face. "What have you baked up for me today?" He stared at Smithy's back. "Um . . . what's the captain doing here? You in trouble again?"

Dang it all, I'd not introduced Tad to Smithy for who he really was. "Tad, this is Hephaestus, part of the Greek pantheon. You and I know him as Smithy."

"Shit on a brick, that explains a few things." Tad breathed out.

Smithy turned, his trademark icy glare once more in his eyes as he stared at my brother, any trace of the seducer who'd kissed the bejeebers out of me gone. And then his eyes flicked over to me, softening ever so imperceptibly.

"Alena." He paused as if he didn't know what to say, shook his head, and then closed his mouth with an audible click. Not another word passed his lips as he strode out of the room. He slammed the door behind him, and I breathed a sigh of relief. Or was that regret? How much was Ernie's arrow, and how much was me feeling something for Smithy that I didn't want to feel?

Did I really want to find out? I had to admit one thing, even if it was only to myself. Maybe there was something that Ernie had pushed forward with his arrow, but . . . maybe that wasn't the whole reason I felt drawn toward the rugged Greek god of the forge.

He was handsome, and strong, and he'd been brutally honest with me. Honesty was something I valued as much as anything else. Something that I wasn't sure now that Remo had given me. Even when he'd walked away, he'd held back from being honest. So what was I doing? Wishing Remo were still with me, while considering the kiss I'd shared with Smithy? My mother would be horrified. And she would be right.

I was *soooo* going to H-E-double-hockey-sticks in a handbasket.

CHAPTER 4

"What the hell just happened there?" Tad looked at me, the closed door, and then back at me again.

"Long story." I ran a hand over my head, smoothing my hair back.

He laughed. "And? You can't say 'long story' and then not even give me a little bit of it, sis."

I rolled my eyes. "It has nothing to do with you, so I'm not telling you anything."

Still laughing, he helped me get going on the recipe. I could never be really all that mad with my younger brother. I'd lost him once when I'd thought the Aegrus virus had taken him. And then I'd almost lost him again when Achilles had used him as bait for me to walk into a trap. No matter how Tad might poke at me, no matter how we might fight from time to time, I wouldn't change it for anything. Our parents might have disowned us, but we had each other.

That was worth all the teasing in the world.

I smiled to myself, thinking about how far we'd come from the sheltered Firstamentalist lives we'd started with. I dumped the batter I'd begun and started the sponge cake over again, focusing on the ingredients instead of what had just happened. I wanted to put a buttercream frosting between the two-layer. Not the kind of frosting I'd laced my vomit-inducing cupcakes with. There would be no venom in this cake.

A thought hit me like a frying pan to the side of my head. The whole point of Smithy coming to see me was to warn me and tell me which hero Hera had raised to kill me this time. "Wait here, Tad!"

"I'm not going anywhere, but where are you going?" he called after me.

I ran out the door and into the parking lot without answering him, knowing I was probably too late. It had been a good ten minutes since Smithy had left.

But there he was on the far side of the road, across from the mob. He sat on a motorbike, gripping the handlebars, his head hanging. The low rumble of the Firstamentalists was the only sound in the night air.

I licked my lips, then sprinted across the road.

"Smithy, wait, please."

His head jerked up and turned to me, a look in his eyes I didn't want to dwell on. A look that said he'd been thinking about me and hoping I'd come after him.

The problem was, I hadn't been lying when I'd said I loved Remo.

But it was also true that Smithy's kiss had lit me up in a most unexpected way. I was in trouble no matter how I looked at things.

"Is something wrong?" He kicked the stand on his bike and stepped off. I stopped a few feet away, keeping distance between us. The closer I was, the more my libido woke up, and that was something I just didn't want to deal with at the moment.

"You said you knew who the hero was . . . or was that just a reason to see me?" I didn't really want to accuse him of lying. I didn't think he would have done that.

He grunted and looked away. "Yeah, I know who it is."

"Can you tell me? Please?"

His one hand clenched into a fist, and he was silent long enough that I wondered if he hadn't heard me. "Let me take you on a date, and I'll tell you."

"That's blackmail," I said, while a small part of me squealed eagerly.

"No, that's a trade." He smiled. "I wouldn't blackmail you."

A date. With anyone else, I'd think it was harmless. But with him, I wasn't so sure. He had some qualities that echoed what I loved about Remo, and some qualities that outshone the vampire at the moment. I shook my head, thinking fast, trying to come up with an alternative. "How about his name for a kiss?"

He arched an eyebrow and didn't even hesitate. "Hercules."

Well, that about settled that. I stepped back, feeling a bit like a jerk, knowing that he was going to be pissed when he understood what I'd done. "Thank you."

Smithy took a step toward me. "The kiss—?"

"Has already been given. A kiss you took without permission, if I may remind you." I smiled at him, incredibly pleased with myself. His jaw dropped.

"That's cheating." His eyes sparkled, though, as if he wasn't too upset.

"No, that's using what I've got to win." I threw the words over my shoulder as I walked away back across the road to the bakery. I was going to use everything I had at my disposal to win against Hera. To survive when everything was stacked against me. Smithy's laughter floated on the air.

"We aren't done yet, Alena. Not by a long shot."

I waved a hand back at him, as if to shoo him away. The sound of the bike starting up and then roaring away brought me around. He was gone, his back to me as he raced down the street.

I hurried back to the bakery. The mob booed me, of course, and I took a half step in a mock threat toward them. They all fell back, except for one bold member.

A young woman not wearing a mask stepped forward. She was about my age, maybe a little younger. She wore the typical drab colors, and her hair was pulled back in a severe braid that made her look older than she really was. But unlike the others in the crowd, she didn't hide her face.

"You aren't going to survive this. You're a monster, and you're going to be punished for that. One way or another," she said, her voice firm with her belief.

Sadness and guilt rolled through me. That had been me not so long ago. It was as if I were staring into a mirror of my past, and I didn't like what I saw. "I'm so sorry," I whispered. I turned away from her, not sure if I was apologizing to her, or to myself. That I'd let myself be taken for so long by a group that was so filled with hatred. Why couldn't they be like other churches and just love everyone?

I sighed as I hurried around the back of the bakery and let myself in. Tad was sampling the partially mixed sponge cake. I pointed at the final ingredients, he grabbed them, and I whipped them up. This, that, the other, until I had it all put together, in a pan, and in the oven. Next was the frosting. Honey filled, that's what I wanted. Maybe with a touch of cinnamon.

Tad cleared his throat. "I heard that Remo dumped you."

"I heard that Dahlia dumped you," I shot back.

"Nope, she didn't. Told me she'd rather be kicked out than break up with me."

I froze with the stand mixer half out of the bowl. "What?"

"Remo told her to dump me, that it would never work. She told him to . . . well, she told him off." He winked at me. "Wouldn't want to offend your virgin ears with the actual words she used."

I snorted, and then my heart tugged at me. Dahlia loved Tad enough to defy Remo, but Remo didn't care for me enough to defy those who were his superiors. I smiled at my brother, but I could feel the edges of it wobble. "I'm happy for you."

41

"He's an idiot, you know that?" Tad gave me a trademark one-armed hug that all brothers do when their sister is obviously on the verge of tears and they fear for their clothes. Like they think the tears of a sister are some sort of acid that will eat right through their shirt. Then again, for all I knew, mine might.

"That's what I keep telling her." Ernie flew down and wrapped his arms around my neck, squeezing me.

"You shouldn't have done . . . what you did," I said to Ernie, not willing to out him to my brother about the whole shooting-Smithy-with-an-arrow business. Tad didn't always keep his mouth shut, so it was best not to give him ammo against Ernie.

"I did what I thought was best. Smithy would be good for you in a lot of ways, and you are obviously good for him. I haven't seen him give a shit about the world in a long time," Ernie said, then patted me on top of my head.

I pulled back. "Enough of my love life or lack thereof. I have a hero to deal with."

"Who?" Tad and Ernie asked in unison.

I drew a big breath as I measured some honey into the filling. "Hercules."

Ernie let out a low whistle. "Now *that* is surprising. He hates Hera. Evil-stepmother syndrome and all that. You know, she used to make him . . . never mind."

That perked me up. "Make him what?" If I had some ammo, maybe I could convince him that I wasn't the bad guy.

The cherub frowned and scrunched up his nose. "It was a long time ago; I'm not sure it even matters anymore."

"Tell me. Please. It could help me figure out how to survive." I put my hands together, literally begging.

Ernie seemed to waver, then he finally nodded. "Well, she was jealous of the bond between him and his father, mostly because Herc's mom was human, you know? So Hera used to call him names, made him look stupid. Told him he was no good, that he was weaker than the other demigods. It went on for years and years. Every time he completed a quest or something, she talked it down. Told him it was something a simple human could have done. But she always made sure Zeus didn't see it. So it was Hercules's word against Hera's. And to keep the peace, Zeus always sided with his wife."

"She gave him a complex, you mean." Tad snorted. "He's a fool, then, if he really believed her words."

Hercules had a complex of not being good enough? That was something I understood all too well. I wanted to cringe from Tad's assessment, because it could just as easily be applied to me. Though I'd grown and moved past that kind of thinking for the most part, I understood it. And why it was such a hard cycle to break. When someone you loved or respected told you that you were weak, it tended to stick more than the words of some stranger.

"So how would she have gotten him to help her?" Tad asked. "I mean, I wouldn't help someone who treated me like dog shit. Would you?" He looked at me, and I had to look away. The silence in the room grew to an uncomfortable level. I took a breath and pushed the words out.

"Yeah, I would. Just to show them that I was worthwhile. I mean, I did for years with Mom." The words were soft, and Tad stepped over to me and slung both arms around me—a real hug, if you could believe it.

"You aren't like that now," he said.

"But I *was*. I . . . I would do anything to prove to Mom that I was good enough. Don't you remember? How she pushed me and was always telling me I could be better if only I'd tried?"

"Yeah, you more than me. I never understood why. And Dad never stood up for us. Like his silence was his way of agreeing with her." He gave me a last squeeze and then let me go. I hated that he'd said that. I'd always wanted to believe that Dad wasn't the same as Mom, that his silence was his way of defying her. Yet . . . I could see that Tad was right. Dad could have stood up for us, but he hadn't. He'd let Mom bully us—mostly me, really—into a place of no self-worth. So maybe it wasn't all her fault.

Ernie shrugged. "Like I said, Hercules has always been trying to show her he was good enough. I'd be surprised if that ever changed. She probably told him that if he could do this one last deed, she'd finally believe he was a hero."

Tad stuck a finger into the filling and paused with it halfway to his mouth, a grin spreading over his lips. "I'm not going to end up puking my guts out, am I?"

I rolled my eyes, knowing he was trying to lighten the mood. The problem was, I couldn't afford to be light about anything. Not when I had people out for my head yet again.

"Ernie"—I glanced at him, then took the mixing bowl from Tad—"Hercules is going to be working with the Hydra; that's what Merlin told me. The Hydra is the added insurance when it comes to taking me out."

The three of us stood there, silent.

"So . . . nothing I can add to that." Tad drew the last word out. "But are you going to Mom and Dad's anniversary dinner?"

I blinked several times at the sudden subject change. "Yeah, I'm making the cake, apparently."

"Awesome. No more venom, right?"

"Only if you keep asking if there's no venom in it." I slammed a hand on the counter, and a crack opened up in the marble. Dang it, now I had that to add to my list of problems. "I'm sorry, but I can't just ignore what's going on around me. I can't pretend it isn't happening, Tad."

"I know," he said softly. "I'm just trying to protect you."

I stared hard at him, thinking over his words, about his forced happy face. "Dahlia did break it off with you, didn't she?"

He closed his eyes and slowly nodded. "Yeah. I didn't want to tell you. I didn't want you to worry about me, because that's how you are . . ."

It was my turn to wrap him in a hug. He pressed his eyes against my shoulder, and his tears wet my skin. "I'm sorry," I whispered, wishing I could take the hurt away from him.

"We both fell for the wrong person," he mumbled. "I knew redheads were trouble."

I laughed, but it was anything but mean spirited. "Maybe we should have listened to everyone and stayed away from the vampires."

Ernie snorted. "Well, that goes without saying."

Except what do you do when the vampires won't stay away from you? Especially the bad ones?

I was about to find out.

A crash from the front of the shop startled all three of us. We turned and stared at the door between the front and back. "Maybe something fell off a shelf?" Tad offered. I seriously doubted it was anything as simple as that.

I ran toward the crash and slid to a stop as a torch was thrown through what had been my beautifully painted plate-glass window at the front of the shop.

"Go back over the Wall, freak!" someone shouted from outside.

"Die!"

"Burn in hell!"

Apparently the Firstamentalists had gotten bored with waiting on me to leave. I grabbed the torch before it could catch on anything and threw it back out at them. "Tad, call the police."

"Why don't you just eat them?" he grumped. "No bodies and no weapon, so it's not murder, you know."

I glared over my shoulder at him. "That only proves they are right about the whole monster business." I should have expected this escalation of things with the Firstamentalists. There was no way they were going to just leave me alone. I knew that. I just didn't think it would happen so fast.

I also did not expect the vampires that slid between the Firstamentalists and into my shop. Santos stood out above the rest both in height and attitude. I'd know him ten miles off to be fair, though. His bone structure and build were so much like Remo's, it amazed me that I hadn't figured out the family connection between them on my own. He smiled, flashing a glimmer of fangs, then wiggled his fingers in hello.

"I'm not with Remo," I said. "He dumped me, so you can just take your fight to him and leave me out of it."

Santos laughed and murmured something I couldn't quite hear, but the effect was immediately obvious. The crowd surged forward, egged on by his words, their hatred ready for any fuel to burn brighter. He grinned. "How are you going to get away this time, Alena? Humans you don't want to hurt, while facing vampires that have no problem killing anything that moves?"

The Firstamentalists pushed their way into my bakery, kicking and punching the display cases, ransacking as they went. I stood there, and they flowed around me, ignoring me while they went wild with whatever suggestion Santos had given them.

He stood on the other side of the broken plate glass. "You killed my people, you trespassed on my territory, you tried to charm me. You realize I cannot let you live now. No matter your beauty."

I smirked at him, anger making me stronger than I would have been normally. "I didn't *try* to charm you, dingle nuts. You were out like a light being flicked off. You were *easy* to take."

His face darkened, but I didn't care. He wanted to fight? I'd darn well give him a fight. I crossed my arms and stared at him while Tad yelled at the Firstamentalists to back off, to get out. I knew that the bakery could be fixed. But I had to deal with Santos before I did anything else. If he teamed up with Hercules and the Hydra, I wasn't sure I could pull that fight out of the bag and come out the winner.

Time to put on my big-girl panties and take this one head-on. "Tad, stay back."

"Not this time, sis," he said, a long, low hiss sliding out of him on the last *s* of sis. I glanced back in time to see him shift, something I'd never seen him do before.

His scales were silvery blue, and patterned so close together it was difficult to discern one color from the other. Unlike my diamond-shaped head when I was in my Drakaina form, his head was long and narrow, with elongated oval eyes that flickered red, and a long red tongue that shot out from between a mouthful of teeth. Not exactly a typical snake, then, at all. He whipped his tail around, stopping a man from going into the back of the bakery.

The Firstamentalists screamed as he rose up, hissing at them, herding them out. He darted from side to side, his speed far outmatching their attempts to dodge around him. He tipped his head and winked at me. I could almost hear him say, "I got this, sis."

No matter that it freaked me out that he was putting himself in harm's way; he was helping. With Tad dealing with the Firstamentalists, I turned my attention back to the vampires.

"You want a piece of me?" I said, and crooked a finger at Santos. "Then come and get me, doofus."

He snarled and leapt forward, sailing over the broken glass and landing in a crouch within the bakery, about ten feet in front of me. "That will be your last mistake, inviting me in, snake girl."

"I think the mistake will be yours, you bloodsucking leech." The voice that came out of my mouth was not really mine, but I recognized it. The voice belonged to the Drakaina, the monster that was very much a part of me and yet still somehow separate. When she spoke up, my voice deepened and turned all husky and dangerous. I liked it.

Santos snarled and jumped straight at me. I held my ground, bracing my legs. He slammed into me and twisted hard to one side, taking us both to the floor. Tad shot forward, his head coming within striking distance of Santos.

"No, I will deal with this!" I wrestled with Santos on the floor, rolling across the shards of broken glass and not feeling it. My human skin was pierced, but the snakeskin under it was hard as diamonds and didn't give an inch. There was the small matter of the wound on my neck.

His eyes shot to it. "Bleeding already?"

Fear lanced my heart. If he got his mouth on my neck and took even a drop of blood, I wasn't so sure the outcome of the fight would be in my favor. Around us, the vampires circled and Tad kept them off me. His bite inflicted huge gaping wounds where he literally tore flesh from their bodies. Their screams shattered the night air.

I couldn't focus on them, though. I had to keep my attention on Santos, or I wasn't going to come out of this in one piece. I jerked to the side and rolled with the vampire, my skirt getting bunched up around my hips as we fought. He wasn't trying to punch me, which I didn't understand at first. He grabbed one of my hands and yanked it up over my head. Then he grabbed the other and did the same. I could have pulled away; I could feel that he wasn't nearly as strong as I was. But I wanted—no, needed—him close, even if it brought him into proximity of my neck wound. I was going to have to be fast about this. A long, drawn-out fight with Santos was not going to end well.

"You aren't so tough." He breathed out, staring into my eyes, and for a moment I saw Remo in him, a sight that shook me. "You know I'm not the only vampire hunting for you now? You will never escape us. You're going to die begging for mercy."

"That's what everyone keeps saying, right before I kill them," I pointed out. He laughed and shot forward, his mouth open wide and his fangs bared. I turned so he would bite into the side of my neck that was not wounded.

Santos bit at me, and I let him. He gnawed on my neck, fighting to get through the snakeskin, something I knew was impossible, even with his deadly fangs. So while it was uncomfortable, I didn't fight him on that. Instead, I freed one hand from his and wrapped it around his neck, holding him close, but more than that keeping him off my wounded side.

His vampires circled around us, rooting for him, but not daring to get too close with Tad stretched out in his naga form. Every time that they took a half step forward, he hissed and bared his bloodstained teeth.

So they settled for some weird version of catcalling.

"Get her, boss!"

"Drink her down!"

"Save some for us!"

I lay there while he bit at me, and thought about how much hurt the vampire on top of me had caused. Santos had helped Theseus, he'd stolen my friends from me, and he was a huge part of the reason Beth had died. I thought about how he had hurt Remo over the years, and even if I didn't know the details, that didn't matter. Santos had bitten off more than he could chew this time.

My fangs lowered from the roof of my mouth. There was no decision left, really, barely any thought, even. It was pure instinct to strike back and hurt him for all the pain he'd caused. I hit him hard and fast, and my fangs buried into the top of his shoulder. Two pulses of venom flowed from me into him.

I opened my mouth, and my fangs retracted. He jerked once, his eyes going to mine as he stiffened. "No, that is not possible."

"Don't mess with snakes," I said. "They'll bite when you least expect it. Especially if you come into their territory."

His eyes rolled and he jerked, red foam bubbling out of his mouth. I pushed him off me and stood up, staring down at his body as he tried to fight the venom, but to no avail. I refused to turn away, knowing that I had done this. So I watched his muscles shrivel and his face twist up in agony before it went slack with a final death. The scent of licorice that had always been heavy on him dissipated, gone with whatever it was that animated a vampire. There were no big explosions, no grand finale to show that he was a foe worth fighting.

He died without a whimper, or even a last word. As every coward should.

At the edges of the room where Tad had forced them to stay, the Firstamentalists shook themselves as if waking from a deep sleep and strange dreams.

I pointed at the open window. "Firstamentalists, get out of my bakery! And if you dare come back, I will make sure you are each turned into a vampire!" My voice boomed in the small space, and the humans scrambled away at a speed that belied their frail nature.

At the window, though, the young woman who'd faced me on the street turned back. Her eyes locked with mine, and I saw there a seed of doubt. Doubt in what she was doing. I gave her a slow nod. "One day, you'll understand."

She spun, her long skirt flaring out behind her, and then she was gone.

I stood there with a dozen vampires around me, their boss dead on the floor. Tad in his naga form at my back. Remo's little brother dead at my feet. I swallowed hard, the taste of venom sliding down my throat. It burned hot, a trail of fire running down into my belly to mix with the flush of guilt and horror . . . I'd killed him. And I didn't feel bad, which made me feel bad.

One of the vamps went to his knees, and the rest slowly followed suit. "We are yours."

"Oh no, that isn't happening," I said, backing up, bumping into Tad. His scales were cool against the hot flush of my skin.

Ernie flew to my shoulder and stuck his mouth in my ear. "You could use them against Hercules; don't send them away."

I frowned. "No, that doesn't feel right."

Tad shifted back to his human form and put a hand on my shoulder. "I think you should listen to Ernie."

"Feeling right is not going to keep you alive," the cherub pointed out.

I looked over the vampires, making eye contact with each one of them as an idea was forming. I swallowed again, then took a breath and spoke with as much confidence as I could. "Go to Remo, tell him that Santos is dead. Beg forgiveness and see if that keeps you all alive."

"And if he turns us away?" one of them asked.

That was the last thing I was worried about. "If he turns you away . . . then . . . you can come back to me."

Tad grunted. "It might be too late then." I hoped he was wrong.

But the vampires all nodded one at a time.

They left quietly, but I heard one of them say something that stuck with me. "She'd make a better boss than Santos."

"No shit," his friend answered and then paused in the window. He looked about my age, but with vampires that was deceptive at the best of times. He had a dark-auburn hair, and his eyes were a deep chocolate brown that was brightened with flecks of gold. "Santos wasn't kidding about the other vampires coming for you, Drakaina."

We stared at one another, and I beckoned him back. He stepped forward.

"What do you mean?" I asked.

He swallowed hard, his throat bobbing before he answered. "He sent the last of the fennel oil to the vampire council. Along with a note that . . ." He paused and looked to where his friends—if they were friends—waited for him. One of them nodded.

"I think you should tell her."

"Wait," I said as I stepped over some broken glass so I was right in front of the one who said he'd sent the note to the vampire council. "What's your name?"

"Lee."

I held my hand out. "Alena, not Drakaina."

He gave me a twitch of a smile. "Alena, he sent a note with the oil. It said that if something should happen to him, that the council should know about you. He said that Remo was protecting you, and that he—Remo, that is—planned to take over the council with you at his side." He drew in a breath, though I knew he didn't really need it. Which meant he was probably young in vampire years. "Look, Santos basically said if he died, the council should use the fennel oil to destroy you. And Remo."

My body chilled as though the icy air sweeping through the open glass actually bothered it. "Anything else?"

Lee shook his head. "I wrote the note up for him. There was nothing else. Except a list of places you could be found."

"Where?"

Lee frowned, obviously thinking. "House number thirteen on the other side of the Wall, the bakery here, your big house by Kerry Park, and your parents' house."

Tad groaned. "Shit."

My thought exactly. If the vampire council went looking for me at my parents', how was I going to protect them?

I held a hand out to Lee again, and he took it. "I want you to tell Remo what you told me. Go quickly; the night is fading."

He bobbed his head, lifted my hand, and kissed the back of it. Maybe he wasn't as young as I thought; that was a very old gesture. I took a step back and watched them fade into the darkness.

The trampling of feet on the glass faded into nothing, and I stood there, stunned at the speed at which things had happened. A flicker of lights out front caught my eyes, and a police cruiser pulled up to the curb.

I shouldn't have been surprised. I wasn't, not really. Just more irritated. I didn't want any more ties to Remo than necessary, and Ben was his servant more than he was my friend.

Officer Jensen stepped out of the car and jogged to the smashed window. "What the hell happened?"

"Mob justice," I grumbled, irritated as a bumblebee stuck in a car. I pointed at Santos. "What do we do with him?"

"Holy mother of God, is that Santos?" Officer Jensen stared, his brown eyes wide. Of course he would wonder. The way the venom had worked, it was hard to tell that he was the same body as before. "You killed him?"

I walked around to the back of the counter and grabbed the largest garbage bin. "I didn't have a choice."

Jensen shook his head. "Yeah, but you killed him. Remo . . . I don't think he's going to be happy. I mean, you basically just—"

Tad came up beside me, a broom and dustpan in his hand, with all his clothes intact.

"Wait, how can you shift and keep your clothes, and I end up naked?" I spluttered, unable to keep the question in.

He shrugged. "Luck of the draw, I guess." Luck indeed.

Tad looked to Jensen, his eyes serious. "How could Remo not be happy? She just offed his main competition for territory. He should be on his knees thanking her."

I smiled at Tad. Dang it all, to have my brother on my side, to watch him come into his own even while he defended me. That was . . . an amazing feeling. Which with the way the rest of the night had gone was about the only bright spot.

Jensen rolled his eyes heavenward as if he would find the words there. "Ernie, help me out here. You understand power structure better than most."

Ernie swept in front of me, nodding. "Yeah, I do. Okay, here it is, girlfriend. You just made Remo look weak. You accomplished in five minutes what he's been trying to do for hundreds of years. And right in front of what I'm guessing are some of the oldest vamps out there.

I mean, they may not be right here, but they will be in the area soon. And they will find out about this."

I noticed neither Ernie nor Tad mentioned what we'd learned, about how Santos had set Remo and me up. Which meant they didn't want Jensen to know, or maybe they didn't want Remo to know?

I bent and picked up a large chunk of glass and dropped it into the garbage can with a loud crash. "Well, I guess that's Remo's issue, isn't it? Not like we're even dating anymore." The words were hard, but a tiny piece of me hoped . . . if what Lee had said was right, then Remo very well might have been protecting me by cutting me loose.

And if he was protecting me, then maybe, just maybe, he cared for me still. A sudden flash of irritation snapped through me, like the crackle of lightning on a muggy summer's night.

"What the hell, Remo?" I muttered under my breath, feeling the words spark tears in my eyes. "Push me away to keep me safe? Why wouldn't you trust me enough to hold me close?"

Why indeed was the question of the hour.

CHAPTER 5

Ernie tugged me and Tad aside while Jensen called things in, listing off the damage by the mob of Firstamentalists. They'd dropped a few masks and several placards, along with one of their pamphlets. Jensen figured that would be enough to get a restraining order against the group.

"Listen"—Ernie kept his voice low—"I don't think we should be telling anyone else what we learned from the vampire. It will give you the upper hand if people think you and Remo really are at odds."

Tad nodded. "I agree. I mean, it sounds like maybe he broke up with you, and had Dahlia break up with me because he was trying to protect us all."

Ernie nodded. "Love will make you do stupid things."

I glared at him. "I thought you said Remo didn't really love me?" Then there was the whole question of if Remo really cared; if he did, he should have been fighting for me, trusting me to be at his side.

Which he obviously didn't. So maybe he didn't respect me the way I'd thought. That only sparked my irritation with him further.

"Look . . . Dahlia is here." Ernie swept upward to the ceiling, neatly avoiding my question.

She was out of breath as though she'd been running, which is saying something for a vampire. "Is it true?" She slid to a stop, her eyes immediately going to where Santos still lay sprawled on the floor. Her jaw dropped, and she spluttered, "Holy shit, Alena, did you do it?" Almost like she didn't quite believe it.

I nodded. "Yeah, I didn't have much choice. And like always, Remo was nowhere to be found to deal with his problem."

"Whoa, bitter much?" Dahlia said.

I forced a glare at her, struggling to find the right words. "Remo didn't have the . . . the balls . . . to stick with me. Even though I know he wanted to. Just because he wants things to look right. I took him home, Dahlia. I took him to meet my parents, who already hate everything Super Duper, and he dropped me at the first sign that someone he was trying to impress might not like what I am. That's a real . . . dick move." The words spilled out of me in a jumble of hurt and truth.

I was breathing hard, and I forced myself to slow my racing heart. "And then he goes and makes you break it off with Tad."

Her eyes flashed. "That's partly why I'm here. Tad . . ." She reached over, took his hand, and yanked him to her. She planted a kiss on him and then pulled back just as suddenly. "I'm not going anywhere. Screw Remo and screw the vampire council. I don't need anyone but you."

He grinned. "Really?"

"Really. We'll go somewhere else. Anywhere else is better than being without you."

Ernie clapped and whistled. "Now *that* is how love is done."

I took a few steps back from them, giving them space.

Dahlia looked at me and frowned. "Remo doesn't deserve you. Not by a long shot."

"That's what I keep telling her," Ernie said, and I glared at him.

Jensen cleared his throat. "We all have said it at one point. Alena, you did the right thing. I shouldn't have said what I did back there about you killing Santos. If Remo can't take care of things, and you have to, then so be it. You have to protect yourself."

I couldn't even defend Remo, because Ernie and Tad were right. We needed to keep what we'd learned about Santos and his final note close to the chest. The less people who knew about what Remo was really dealing with, the better. A final plot twist thrown by Santos with his death.

With my friends helping me, we got the worst of the shattered glass dealt with and the bakery put back together. Tad and Jensen found some broken pallets out back and then used them to board up the front window.

My sponge cake was totally burnt. The smell made me wrinkle my nose and snort. I hadn't burned something this badly in years, not since I first started baking and allowed myself to get distracted by the risqué romance novels my yaya had slipped me behind my mother's back. I pulled the pan out of the oven with a huff and slammed it on the counter. This night could *not* get any worse. I opened the back door to air the room out, then went back to the pan. Charred right through. I threw the whole thing into the sink to cool off. I'd throw it out later.

Ernie sat down beside me. "What do you want to do?"

"I want to go home and sleep and start this day again," I said, feeling the fatigue right through my bones.

"Then why don't you? I think eliminating one of the baddest vampires around should surely mean you deserve a break and a soft bed," he said. "I'll go and see if I can dig up information about where Hercules is, and if there are any plans he's got in place. Okay?"

I blinked up at him, my eyes welling a bit. "You are a good friend. Thank you."

"Aw, shucks, 'tweren't nothing, ma'am." He winked, tipped an imaginary hat, and flew out the door, humming to himself what sounded like the music from *The Lone Ranger*. I smiled and shook my head. If nothing else, Ernie was good for that; he made me smile even when I felt like crying.

Tad and Dahlia followed me home in her little purple punch-buggy car, all the way to the Wall.

The Wall was over forty feet high and made of cement blocks; you'd think it wouldn't be very stable. Since I'd been turned into a Super Duper, though, I'd learned a few things. The structure was held together by a powerful spell as much as by the ordinary cement blocks and rebar. The spell was supposed to repel those who wanted to cross it, from either side, turning them away before they even reached the Wall itself. Which was interesting because I'd never felt a thing. But now many of the Super Dupers I'd met in the last couple of weeks seemed hell-bent on getting out, as if the spell was no longer working.

In addition to the Wall-repellent spell, the Supernatural Division of Mounted Police implanted every Super Duper with a tracking device. It was supposed to shock them if they crossed the Wall, like a collar on a wayward mutt who should have been contained by an Invisible Fence, unless they had permission to cross. But thanks to Remo and his gang, that was no longer the case.

The first day I'd been turned into a Drakaina, I'd been snagged by the SDMP and taken to their headquarters to be implanted with a tracking chip. Tad and I had both managed to stay clear of the whole implanting business, though—thank goodness for that small mercy. While I'd been in detention, Remo and his gang had broken into the SDMP's headquarters and destroyed whatever it was that allowed the chips to zap Super Dupers. Maybe the SDMP would get it up and running again, but they hadn't so far.

Of course, that line of thought brought me back to Remo.

He had given up on me, not even telling me what I might face, as though I couldn't handle the truth. As if I wouldn't stand by him, even if just in the background, when it came to the council of vampires. He was treating me the way everyone had my whole life—as if I were more of a burden to be taken care of than a woman who could manage on her own.

Tad had done it to me.

My mother and father had done it to me.

Even Dahlia, my best friend in the whole world, had thought me incapable of dealing with all the poop that had been thrown at me.

The more I thought about it, the more the hurt and understanding faded and the anger grew. By the time we reached house number thirteen, I was well and truly peeved.

Remo was no better than everyone else who thought I was useless in a bad situation. An unfair judgment, considering I'd faced two Greek heroes and multiple monsters, all while learning how to live as a Super Duper.

All of that combined did not bode well for the vampire standing at the front door waiting for me. Max was one of Remo's top guys. I liked him, but right at that moment, he was in a bad position to be between me and my bed. His blond hair was spiked as though he'd been running his hand through it over and over, and his blue eyes were full of concern I could see even at a distance. None of it was going to help him.

I got out of my Charger and slammed the door. Dahlia and Tad pulled in behind me. Dahlia hurried to catch up. "Alena, don't start anything."

I put a hand out to her. "No, *you* don't!" I had no idea what I was don't-ing, just that I wanted no interference.

Max made a move to take my hand, but I jerked away from him. "What do you want, Max?"

He shrugged and held out a piece of paper folded in half and closed with a wax seal. "I'm just the messenger tonight. Don't bite my head off."

I snatched the paper from him and ripped the seal open.

We need to talk. You know where to find me.

Remo

Maybe he was going to tell me about the council? I scrunched the paper back up and handed it to Max. "You can give him this, as it is, and tell him it's too darn late for begging. I think it will get my reply across clearly."

Max glanced at the balled-up piece of paper in his hand. "Seriously, he has been known to shoot the messenger."

I brushed past him. "Then don't work for him, Max."

"And who would I work for? You killed Santos," he said. Wow, word traveled faster than even I thought it would.

I glared at him and arched an eyebrow, feeling more confidence than I'd had in years. "Someone had to do it, and apparently it wasn't going to be Remo. And you can tell him that too."

His eyes popped wide, and behind me Dahlia gasped.

Well, it had to be said. Even if my stomach was tied in knots like a belly full of snakes that had wrapped around one another. "I'm not trying to be a jerk," I amended, even though I already knew it was too late. The look on Max's face said it all. Then again, what should I care? I steeled my shoulders and stood tall. "He left me on my own, so I dealt with a problem that came my way. It's not my fault he has his panties in a twist over it."

Max continued to stare. Dahlia cleared her throat. "You realize that this will put you on Remo's enemy list?"

"You don't know that," Tad said. "She just took care of a major issue for him. Hell, she saved his bacon."

"Yes," Dahlia snapped. "But right when every high-ranking vampire on the continent has shown up to see just what the hell is going on in Remo's territory. None of them wanted Santos around; he's broken too many of our laws. They would have dealt with him. But by killing Santos, Alena made Remo look weak. Worse, it could put a target on her back from the council because of her strength. They don't like not being at the top of the food chain."

Honey puffs, Dahlia was too smart for her own good. "It doesn't matter. We already know that is the case."

"What?" she shrieked. "When were you going to tell me?"

Tad took her hand. "We just found out."

She huffed several times, her green eyes flashing, but she did settle down. "So, what are you going to do?"

I raised my hand, stopping her. "Enough. I can't change things. I can't take it back. Max"—I turned to him—"you have my answer; give it to Remo in private if you can."

He looked down at the crumpled piece of paper in his hand. "Damn." With that he turned, and so did I. I pushed the door of house number thirteen open and then paused. This was one of the vampire safe houses. Which meant it belonged to Remo. Right now I needed distance from him, for both our sakes. A tiny piece of my heart broke— this had been my safe haven since I'd been turned into a Super Duper. I didn't want to leave it.

"Dahlia, I'll pack my stuff," I said.

"That might be best," she said, and it hurt to hear her echo my own thoughts. "I can't protect you from him if he is pissed, or the council, for that matter." She shook her head and brushed past me.

I made my way up the stairs to the bedrooms. I listened for a heart-beat that would tell me Sandy was around. There it was, a flutter like the beat of wings in the air, soft and at a speed that was faster than any human or other Super Duper I'd dealt with so far. I went to her room and paused before I knocked. Since Beth had been killed by Theseus, Sandy had not been herself. Then again, it hadn't been that long, only a little over a week. Most nights she cried herself to sleep; I could hear her through the thin walls, sobbing softly. I'd been reluctant to say anything. Beth had died because of Theseus; he'd taken her head in a single swipe of his sword. But I'd bitten her, my venom driving into her veins. I'm not sure she would have survived that, which meant maybe her death was my fault too.

"I can hear you out there, Alena," she said. "You can come in."

I opened the door and stepped in. "Hey. I . . . I think I made it so we can't stay here anymore."

Her eyes widened, and I swiftly filled her in on the day's events so far.

"Do we have a place to go?" she asked.

I smiled. "Yeah, it's time to go home. To my grandparents' home. I'd . . . I'd like it if you came with me. If you want to, that is." The last thing I wanted was for her to feel pressured into staying with me.

She nodded. "I don't have a lot to pack. Maybe . . . maybe we can try that new recipe when we get there? The cream cheese–filled cupcakes, the ones with the saffron icing?"

I smiled. "Yeah, let's do that."

She walked over to me and slid her arms around my waist. "Don't be hard on yourself, Alena. Please. I . . . I don't blame you for anything."

I hugged her back, doing my best not to cry. "Stop reading my mind."

She laughed and pushed me away gently. "If only it were that easy. Don't avoid me, please. You're my friend, and I know . . . I know that you were trying to save her. I know you were."

I wiped my eyes and nodded. "Thank you. I needed to hear that." I backed out of the room and headed to my own.

I didn't have a lot to pack either. I realized in that moment that I'd pretty much been living off Remo's largesse. This was his house, the clothes I wore had been bought with his money, even the food in the cupboards was bought for those victims the vampires brought in to feed on. I let out a sigh as I grabbed a few things, mostly paperwork that pertained to my actual existence as a person, even though I was a Super Duper. A few small articles of clothing, the original dress I'd worn from Merlin's. I pulled the case off a pillow and stuffed everything inside. Like I was going trick-or-treating with Tad the way we did when we were kids. I laughed to myself, the irony not lost on me. I had a built-in costume and everything now. That is, if anyone would give candy to a two-story-high snake.

I stepped out of the bedroom the same time that Sandy did. "Ready?"

She nodded and smiled. "Yes. On to the next adventure, right?"

Her words were more than a little prophetic, unfortunately. The sound of Tad yelling from downstairs had me hurrying, rushing headlong down the steep steps, the sound of arguing voices floating up to us. Tad and Dahlia were in the kitchen. He shook his head. "You can't be serious."

"I'm sorry, but you know that I have to; I have no choice." Her voice was thick with tears, and a few jeweled drops sat on the perfect smooth skin of her cheeks. "I don't want to; you have to believe me."

She took a step back but seemed to be resisting. Like she was being pulled. I reached out, and she took my hand, her green eyes swinging to me. "Remo is calling all the vampires in the area to him. I have to go; it's not something I can deny, because of the bond that is placed on all his underlings."

I tightened my grip on her. "He won't hurt you?"

She shrugged. "I don't know. I defied him by coming to you and Tad. He may have to make an example of someone to appease the council . . . and it will probably be me."

Because of her ties to me and Tad. This was my fault.

I tugged her to me, a fierce protectiveness washing over me. "Then we can't have that." I wrapped my arms around her, wanting to believe that Remo wouldn't hurt her. But what did I know? I would have sworn that he wouldn't walk away from me, but he had. I would have sworn that he cared for me more than just as a friend, or a fling, or a blood donor. And yet here we were, wondering if he would hurt my best friend because she'd followed her heart back to my brother. I swallowed hard. "You need to feed off me, then. Either it will allow you to ignore him, or you can at least protect yourself."

She shook her head, but Tad was nodding. "Alena is right. You . . . you mean too much to me. To all of us."

In my head, I cheered for him as he took her from me and hugged her tight. Silently I egged him on. Say it, Tad. Say the words. Tell her now, or you might not get another chance.

His eyes flicked to mine and then closed. "I love you, Dahlia. Please, I don't want to lose you."

Her whole body crumpled against him. "I love you too."

I sniffed, and behind me, a tiny hiccup escaped Sandy. I reached up and pulled the bandage off my neck wound. It was only partially healed. "Do it. This will heal by the morning."

Dahlia gave me a wobbly smile and leaned in close. The sensation was not like with Remo; there was no pleasure rocking through me. She drew in a few tiny swallows, but it should have been all she needed. The blood of a Drakaina was a heady thing for a vampire. Something we'd found out by accident and had since used to our benefit.

"You are family," I said. "Be careful, okay?"

Dahlia nodded, her eyes clear and her body no longer being pulled in another direction by Remo's call. At least I was guessing on that bit.

"I'll try and see if I can talk to him," she said.

I shook my head. "No, don't bother. I understand what he's facing, even if I don't like how he's handling it. We all are a team; that's how we've made it this far."

I backed up to give Tad and Dahlia some privacy. Sandy followed me out the front door to the Charger. "You think another hero is going to come at you? I mean, us, I guess, because if they go through you, I'm next, aren't I?"

She said it with complete calm. I knew why. There was a measure of fatality to our lives neither of us could escape. We'd both been chosen to be turned into Greek monsters because Hera and Merlin thought we were weak. They thought we would give up and let the heroes kill us.

They were wrong. But it still sucked rotten donkey balls, and the truth was we were going to have to fight to survive no matter how it went against our natures.

"Hercules, this time." I threw my small pillow sack into the back of the car. "And he has a nine-headed Hydra as a helper. Hera got smart this time. Monsters attacking monsters. We've seen how your feathers cut through me, and my venom does a number on other monsters."

"Very Godzilla-like." Sandy nodded. "And it makes a wicked sort of sense. You think she's doing it because of Theseus?"

I thought about her question a moment before nodding. "Yes, he showed her that we could hurt one another. I mean, where else in mythology is it monster against monster? Mostly heroes face monsters, so Theseus showed Hera a different way to do it." Another reason to be glad he was dead.

She sighed. "Do you have a plan?"

I frowned and shrugged. "Not really. Ernie is going to try and find out what he can, but you know him. He could get sucked into helping Hercules by accident. Or on purpose, depending on how he's feeling that day." I snorted and shook my head.

She laughed softly, and I slung an arm over her shoulder. She leaned into me. "I never wanted to be a monster. I just didn't want to die, you know? And now it looks like that might happen anyway."

Damn, they might have been my own words. "I know. But now we are what we are. We can do this, Sandy. I have to believe we didn't come this far just to give up."

"Beth—" She said her best friend's name and then choked up. I hugged her a little tighter. "Beth made a choice, and didn't want to believe that Theseus was using her. She wanted to belong too much; she wanted to be loved no matter the cost."

I sighed. "I wish we'd been able to get through to her before . . ."

"Yeah, me too," Sandy whispered. "I was so afraid to lose her friendship I didn't want to tell her that I thought you were right. No, I knew you were right."

We held on to each other, two monsters in the night afraid of all that could come and get us.

The door to house number thirteen opened, and I looked up at Tad. His face was tight with suppressed emotion. "She's going to keep in touch as much as she can."

I nodded and chose not to point out that he was repeating information.

We piled into the Charger, and I headed back toward the Wall. At the main gate, the SDMP slowed me down with a wave of their hands.

"You can't leave," the officer said as he leaned in the window of my car, his breath smelling remarkably like doggie biscuits. Seeing as the majority of the SDMP were werewolves, I wasn't terribly surprised at the unpleasant smell.

I cringed. "I don't have a chip implant, none of us do, and you aren't going to stop us from actually going across." I weighted my words with the strength of the siren in me before I ever thought better of it, almost as if I did it on instinct.

He blinked and shook his head twice, going so far as to tap it. "Wait, I've been warned about you."

I grimaced. "I live on both sides of the Wall, fool." I said it and realized it was true.

"No, you don't understand. It's not just us." He leaned back in, his eyes crinkling with consternation. "The Aegrus virus has exploded. The humans are falling in greater numbers than before, and some of them . . . are important people. They've declared that there will be no crossover for anyone."

Tad leaned over. "What do you mean by 'exploded'?"

The SDMP member gripped the edge of my car, and I had to keep my mouth shut tight to avoid telling him not to scratch the paint. There were other things more important than my car at the moment.

"I mean that we have a full-on pandemic, and it's spreading faster than anyone could have thought possible. It's ripping through the country; the hospitals can't keep up."

Broken hickory sticks, that was not good news, not in any way, shape, or form. But why, oh why, would the virus suddenly ramp up? For years it had just plugged along—deadly, but the hospital facilities had been able to keep it in check.

"We are all healthy," I said, "and we are going through. Talk to Smithy if you have a problem with it."

"Smithy isn't on the force anymore."

I knew that, but I had been hoping the officer didn't. I glanced at Tad and caught Sandy's eye. They both gave me a subtle nod. I hit the gas and sped past the officer, the engine roaring and the sensation flying through me. My body's sensitivity to vibrations made me feel like I was a part of the car.

"Where are we going?" Tad asked.

I thought for only a moment before answering. "Zeus's house," I said. If anyone would know why the Aegrus virus had suddenly exploded, it would be the god of thunder and lightning. He might be a dick from time to time, but the reality was he knew things. And I was going to make him spill the beans. One way or another.

CHAPTER 6

The major flaw with my plan was pretty obvious even to me. We got to Zeus's mansion on Olympic Drive, and we were let in through the main gates. So far so good.

But as my luck would have it, he wasn't there. I slammed my car door shut and stared at Narcissus, the youth's ethereal beauty no longer capturing me. "Who is here, then? If Zeus isn't, are there any other members of the pantheon hanging out at the pool?" Despite the cold chill of February, the pool in the back of the house was a balmy oasis that, from what I understood, was never short of attendants.

He swallowed hard, and I caught a look of my reflection in his eyes. A tall, fierce woman with eyes that glittered with suppressed anger. He was afraid of me, and I didn't feel one single ounce of bad. Which probably was a bad thing in and of itself. Oh, what did it matter? According to my mother, I was going to hell as it was, so why not go down in a blaze of glory?

"There are a few goddesses at the pool, yes," he said softly, just above a whisper.

I took off, my stride long, which forced Tad and Sandy to hurry in order to keep up. "What if it's Hera?" Tad asked.

"Or Aphrodite?" pointed out Sandy.

I kept moving. "Then I will deal with them." I almost didn't recognize my own voice. It had to be the Drakaina in me. She was making me stronger than I'd ever hoped. Or maybe, just maybe, I was finding my own voice.

We swept through the house and out the French doors that led to the pool area. Palm trees, flowering bushes, and a fountain that spouted into the pool dominated the eyes first. The warmth of the oasis was humid and instantly made sweat bead up on Tad and Sandy. I liked the heat, but it didn't do anything to me.

The people and creatures lounging around the pool had changed. But one thing hadn't; most of them were completely naked. Including a particular someone I knew very well.

"Yaya?" I gasped as our grandmother swam through the pool toward us. Completely naked, as in not a single stitch of even a bikini on her. Tad grunted and spun around so his back was to her.

"My eyes! I can't unsee this, Alena," he yelped.

I couldn't help laughing, and Yaya winked at me as she swam to the edge of the pool. I looked around for a towel, grabbed one off a chair, and tossed it to her. "Yaya, what are you doing here?"

I looked around, thinking that the men were getting a show, but I saw only women at the pool. That was the difference I'd noticed but not realized. Women who all looked to be of the same age as my grandmother. I frowned and narrowed my eyes at her. "Yaya, what are you up to?"

"Things are changing, Alena. Tad"—she swatted him as she wrapped the towel under her arms—"stop being a ninny; a nude body is a beautiful thing."

Sandy laughed softly. "Yeah, Tad. Don't be such a prude."

He shot her a dirty look, and she just smiled back, her eyes twinkling. It was the most life I'd seen in her since Beth had been killed. I didn't want her to flirt with my brother . . . but for now I'd let it go.

Tad flinched and peeked over his shoulder. "You can't blame me. There are certain things a man should never be exposed to. First on the list is his grandmother prancing around naked."

I put a hand on him, stopping him. We weren't here to trade funny quips. I needed information. "The Aegrus virus has exploded, Yaya. What do you know?"

Her eyes widened, too wide, too innocent, and she shook her head. "I've heard nothing. Ladies, have you heard anything?"

There was something different about her, and then I slowly saw what it was. She looked young. She looked like . . . like she'd gone backward at least fifteen years. The other women around the pool looked like they should be hanging out in the retirement home discussing which adult diaper was preferred, not swimming in Zeus's pool in the nude. They watched us with sharp, intelligent eyes that seemed . . . vaguely predatory.

I suddenly had no doubt who they were. "Yaya, are these your priestesses?"

"See"—she smiled up at me and patted my cheek—"I told you all she was a clever girl."

They cooed and waved at me.

All priestesses of Zeus. And none of the pantheon? I looked back into the house just as Narcissus stepped out of the French doors, a platter of fruits dipped in chocolate in his hand. "Narcissus. I thought you said there were some of the pantheon here?" I asked.

"There are," came a soft voice from the cabana I'd spent some time in with Smithy. My face flushed with *that* memory, and I headed toward the voice, leaving Yaya where she was. I would deal with her later, and yes, I felt like it was going to be dealing with and not just talking to.

I stepped into the shadows of the tent and saw two women I'd met before, Panacea and Artemis.

I didn't bow, but I did tip my head.

"Drakaina, it is good to see you." Panacea smiled at me. "You have healed well."

"Thanks to you." After my fight with Theseus, I'd been covered in fennel oil, and it had been burning through me. Panacea had healed my wounds, allowing me to walk away from the fight on my own two legs. I took a deep breath. "You are a healer, Panacea. Can you tell me what's going on with the Aegrus virus?"

"We do not know it as that, but I will tell you what I can," she said.

"What do you mean you don't know the virus as that?" I was confused as to just what else they might know it as.

She smiled. "It is not a virus but a curse, a curse that has been cast on the water now. A curse that will help a few of the pantheon gain control of the world once more."

I didn't like the sounds of that. "But you mean, then, that it was manufactured by like a lab or something?"

She frowned, not a single line marring her brow. "What I do know is that it is not found in nature; it is not something that the world, or the humans, have created. Someone from the pantheon has created this . . . curse."

"Can you stop it?" I could hope, but I suspected I already knew the answer to my question.

She shook her head, her eyes sad. "No, only the one who created this sickness can call it off."

I was willing to bet that there was one queen of the pantheon who had brought this about. Dang it all. Then again, maybe I was being hasty. Right.

"Who made it? Do you know?"

Again another headshake, her blue eyes downcast, her perfect blond ringlets falling over her bare shoulders. "No. Only one would know the answer to your question, and as you can see, he is not here."

Artemis, who'd been completely silent up until then, snorted. "You have a . . . forgive the pun . . . monstrous task ahead of you, Drakaina.

You *must* find Zeus. Not only will he know who has created this virus you speak of, but he must be the one to bring the pantheon back into order. If he would do that, the world would settle. There is no doubt in my mind that if he would take the reins like a true god, then all would be well once more."

I rather doubted that last bit, but knowing that Zeus held the key to actually helping me find what I needed was a start. "Any idea where he might be?"

Panacea gave a slow nod. "He always goes north when he runs away. Always north; it is the direction that calls to him."

North was the Wall. "How far north? Like in the mountains north?"

They both nodded. "Look for the snow; where the snow flies and the mountain kisses the sky, that is where he will hide. It will bring him closest to his power and strength that way, so be wary. He will not hold back if he feels threatened."

Awesome, that was just what I needed. Zeus with a twitchy trigger finger. "Thank you, both of you."

They smiled at me in tandem, but it was Artemis I found myself staring at. Like Smithy, she had scars on her body, scars that obviously she was not upset about showing if the amount of skin that was on view was any indication. Her eyes locked with mine. "Let me tell you something, Alena."

I stared at her. She used my name instead of my designation, and that caught my attention. "Yes?"

The huntress stood and was as tall as me, so we were eye to eye. "You have it in you to bring Zeus back to his senses. Trust your instincts. Trust your heart. I believe that is what went wrong when they thought to turn you into a monster. They believed your heart was weak." She placed her hand over my left breast, not in a sexual way at all. "Your heart is that of a god."

I wasn't so sure about having the heart of a god. Artemis laughed. "Your face says it all. I do not mean that you *are* a god, Alena. But in the old days, we had the hearts that people would follow into war. We fought for those we loved the best, and we laid our lives on the line. You are that person. And when Merlin turned you, I don't believe that he knew just how strong you were."

Being that Artemis was a goddess of courage and strength, I wanted to believe her that I was strong enough. Of course, the last bit about Merlin being wrong was no real surprise. That I could easily believe. So maybe the rest was true too. Yaya came up beside me.

"It's because she comes from good stock," Yaya said.

"And I'm a Super Duper," I pointed out. Part of the mystery around my life was that we still hadn't figured out just what kind of Super Duper my father was. No one had. Having one parent with supernatural lineage was the only way I'd have been susceptible to the Aegrus virus or curse or whatever you wanted to call it in the first place. And of course, good old Dad wasn't saying a word. Acting like he was a plain old human. Ha.

"I guess we'll head north, then. Thank you for your help." I took a step back before turning away.

With Yaya at my side, we worked our way around the pool to where Tad still had his back to the water. Sandy was at the edge, crouched, chatting with one of the priestesses.

I put a hand on my grandmother. "Yaya. What are you up to anyway?"

She smiled up at me, the skin around her eyes far smoother than I'd seen in years. Years. "Alena, you need to keep at this. The world is changing, and it is because of you. So don't stop what you're doing. We are gaining back our power; people are believing again in the old gods. That is a good thing. It is weakening the Firstamentalists' hold."

I pulled away from her, my mouth suddenly dry. What she was saying wasn't all that horrible, but it sounded an awful lot like the reasoning Hera had. The goddess wanted to make people believe in her again so she would get her power back to rule as she wanted. I had no idea it would be true for Yaya as well as all her priestesses. Maybe as the gods and goddesses they chose to follow rose in power, they too gained strength. As much as I wanted to be happy for Yaya, I just wasn't sure how I felt. The whole thing was just too close to Hera's version of things for my liking.

I let her go and gave her a quick peck on the cheek. She grasped my hand, though, holding me tight. "Don't forget, you have your parents' anniversary coming up. And you are supposed to be making the cake, as well as the small desserts."

I groaned softly. "I know, Tad reminded me. Mom is coming tomorrow to taste test."

Yaya's eyebrows shot up. "She is?"

I nodded. "Yeah. But . . . I don't know how that's going to go over for her." I wasn't about to explain the mob of Firstamentalists that had been outside my bakery. Crazy like a bowl full of nuts, they had no idea what was going on in the world. And I wasn't sure how Mom would handle seeing her daughter being picketed and mobbed by people she called her friends. Maybe she'd join them and add her voice to their shaming. I think that was what I was most afraid of. That once again we'd be back at the beginning of our relationship. That I would disappoint her yet again, and maybe worse, that I'd embarrass her.

I sighed. "Will you come for the taste testing? Just to have a bit of a buffer?"

"Nope." Her denial shocked me, and she smiled to soften it. "You and your mother need to work this out. And you can, I know you can. She's coming around. The fact that she's coming to your bakery says a great deal about how she's feeling. Don't deny her. And don't be late for the party either; you know I hate tardiness."

I slumped and then nodded. "I'll try."

I grabbed Tad as I walked by, and Sandy hurried to catch up to my side. "Where to now?"

"I think we all need to get some sleep, and then we're on a hunt for Zeus," I said. The night was coming to a close, and I was exhausted. I'd learned the hard way that taking care of myself amid the battles for my life was important if I wanted to be at my best.

"You know where he is?" Tad peeked at me, then relaxed as he realized there were no naked old ladies near to us. He mumbled something about grabby hands and sugar mamas not happening.

"Kind of."

"That's not what I want to hear." He groaned and slid into the passenger side of the Charger. Narcissus smiled at us, waving as we left. Funny how I'd found him so attractive the first time I'd met him, blindingly so. And this time it was like he didn't even register on my radar. Maybe the libido of a siren wasn't all that bad.

You will be drawn to men of power, and Narcissus is anything but, the Drakaina said inside my head. *He is nothing more than a pretty face. It's what got him in trouble in the first place. Pretty. But dumb as a rock.*

"Great," I mumbled to myself.

I drove back into the city proper and to the old house that had belonged to my grandparents on my dad's side before I'd inherited it. Tad and Sandy chatted back and forth, and I listened with only half an ear. My mind was too busy trying to make sense of things.

The side where we got our Super Duper blood from, by all accounts. "Tad, do you think Grandma and Gramps might have left some sort of hint in their house about their past? I mean, one of them was a Super Duper. Maybe both."

Sandy took her bag and slung it over her shoulder as she stepped out of the car. "But you said that there didn't actually have to be that much Super Duper blood involved for someone to be susceptible to infection. What was it, like a sixteenth?"

I nodded. She was right; that was what Ernie had said. Call it a gut instinct, but I had a funny feeling our family had done more than just dip their toes into the edges of the pool of Super Duper blood out there.

"Maybe we can look after a few hours of sleep?" Tad asked, almost begging. "I'm totally bagged."

I yawned, my jaw cracking, it went so wide. "Yeah, okay."

I let us into the two-story house. I'd had a renovation company come in and repair the hole in the stairs, change out the decor, and give the whole place a complete and deep cleaning. The last thing I wanted was to smell Barbie or Roger in my home.

Which was all I *could* smell the first time I'd come and checked on the building with the contractor the week before. I took a deep breath. Nothing but the heavy smell of sharp lemon cleaner and the odd wisp of a person from the renovation company. Good enough for me. Tad went straight for the back bedroom. That was where he'd always slept when we stayed overnight with our grandparents.

I beckoned to Sandy. "Come on, you can sleep upstairs with me in the master."

She followed me up the stairs to the second-floor bedroom, where I'd put two queen beds.

"Why did you do that? Didn't you think you would be here with Remo?" Sandy threw her stuff onto the bed against the far wall.

I blushed and turned away. "I don't know. I . . . I think maybe I knew it wasn't going to turn out the way I wanted." Lies, lies. But I didn't know what to say. I'd decided to put the two beds in on a whim when the contractor asked me. Maybe I had known something was going to happen underneath it all.

Sandy just nodded at my explanation before stripping down and climbing into bed. "You going to try and sleep?"

Though I'd been yawning only moments before, I knew there would be no sleep for me. I shook my head. The idea of finding something— maybe a clue to what kind of blood ran through my veins—in my grandparents' house tugged at me, and I knew there was no point in trying to deny it. "In a bit, maybe. I'll try to be quiet."

She didn't answer, and I cocked my head to one side. Her heart rate had already slowed into a flutter that barely moved. She was asleep, passed out in a matter of seconds. If only I could fall asleep so quickly and so soundly.

I shook my head and went back downstairs, thinking about the possibilities of where something might be hidden—a clue, a note, anything.

The kitchen was my favorite place—no surprise there—and we'd had it completely renovated when Roger and I had first moved in.

Of course there hadn't been much question about that, as it had been old and totally outdated, but I'd left a few things that had reminded me of my grandparents—family pieces that had been around as long as the house had stood.

The kitchen had been the place my grandfather loved best too. He wasn't a cook or a baker; he just said he'd liked the ambiance of the room, the way the light fell in through the window onto the table. I could almost see him sitting on his straight-backed chair, leaning over a cup of tea as he read one of his handwritten journals.

It made sense to me that the kitchen was as good a place as any to start searching for clues. During the renovation we'd not found anything in the walls or under the floors, but like I said, we hadn't changed everything.

I ran my hands over countertops, the cool granite soothing me, showing me just how frazzled I was really feeling. The few things I'd left unrenovated were staples in the big old house. A dumbwaiter that we'd made to look like part of the kitchen cabinets, a cool pantry off to one side that still had the original walls, and one tall cupboard that wasn't really attached to the wall. More like an old armoire than a kitchen cupboard, but I loved the way it looked.

I checked the dumbwaiter first and peered in, breathing deeply. The smell of aged wood and musky earthy things rolled up through my nose. I rubbed at it, trying to pinpoint the smells. There was nothing that I could discern, though. I pulled the dumbwaiter up and then lowered it back down a couple of times. Nothing different came about, and there was no way I was climbing in. Even if I could have fit.

Footsteps behind me, and then Tad was at my shoulder. "Couldn't sleep either?"

"No. I think . . . I think that whatever Dad is, it's important somehow, you know? Or maybe I just want it to be. Like we could understand things better if we knew," I said.

"I got the same feeling. Why would he keep hiding? We know he's a Supe, and Mom has to know he's a Supe, even if she's pretending otherwise. What's he got going on?" Tad rubbed a hand on his forehead.

I nodded. "Sandy is asleep. Let's pull this place apart."

He grunted. "A bit extreme?"

"What if it's life or death? We have no idea. Maybe something of Dad comes through with us? Maybe it could help us?" Or maybe I really just wanted to understand my family better, and this was one way to do it.

He sighed. "I think you're letting your imagination get away with you, but at the same time, I have to agree. It could be important."

We headed to the cool pantry. It would seem like the most obvious place with all the walls still intact. We knocked on the sides of the pantry, tapped on the floorboards. I smelled for all I was worth, hoping I would pick up the scent of something, anything. Nothing there, though, or at least, nothing that I could see or sense. Nothing that I could pick up on. We even pulled a few slats off the pantry walls and peered behind them. Empty except for dust and spiders.

"Snickerdoodles, this stinks." I put my hands on my hips, irritated that we hadn't found anything yet.

Without another word of complaint, we went to the tall detached cupboard next, pulling it open, knocking on the wood. I smacked the side of it. "There isn't much left in the way of things from before the renovations, and the company we used showed us anything that they found."

"What do you mean?" Tad frowned at me and leaned on the cupboard. Which shifted a little. I stared at it.

"Wait, it moved; I know it's detached, but I thought it was too heavy . . ."

We grabbed the sides of the cupboard and heaved it together, the wood scraping along the floorboards, screeching like a surprised blue jay as it went. I hoped it didn't wake up Sandy, but even if it did, I knew we were onto something. A waft of smells rolled out from behind the cupboard as air touched it for the first time in years.

"What the hell is that?" Tad breathed out.

I drew in a big breath and held it, trying to decipher just what it was I was smelling. The first image was that of my Gramps, his smiling face, the twinkle in his eye, the shape of his nose . . . the shape of his . . . nose was just like . . . I could see the picture in front of me. The picture in a hallway that I'd walked down only three times, but still the resemblance was undeniable.

"Holy shit, you aren't going to believe this."

Yes, *that* came out of my mouth. The *S* word. But in this instance I felt that I was warranted a cuss word or two. Or three. Because . . . because I had to be wrong. I just had to be.

CHAPTER 7

Tad grabbed at me as I grabbed at the papers buried in the wall in a tiny alcove that was dusty with spiderwebs and age. "What is it? What did you smell?"

I tore at the papers, yanking them to my face, the man I'd known as Gramps blurring and making me question everything I'd ever known. Because it couldn't be true. It just couldn't. Tad shook me, and I snapped my eyes up to him. "I think . . . I have to think about this. I could be wrong."

"Spit it the hell out, you're scaring me." His eyes were wide as they searched my face.

"His nose, his nose is just like that of every person I saw in pictures, on the wall, and I can't believe it, but it makes a twisted sort of sense about how strong I am and why he would help me, and I can't believe it."

Tad hauled off and slapped me, hard enough to stop my rambling. "Spit it *out*."

I blinked up at him as I held a hand to my cheek. "Merlin. The portraits in Merlin's house. I think Merlin is Gramps."

Tad reeled back. "No. Shit no. Hell no. That can't be right. Gramps wouldn't have treated us like this. And Merlin is way too young; he can't be Gramps." He paused.

"What about Yaya? She doesn't look old enough to be our grand-mother anymore, yet she is."

I held up the papers, and the scrawled words on them.

"Are you sure?" Tad stared at the papers in my hand.

The words looked like a diabolical recipe, and Gramps's love for the kitchen took on a new light. He'd been a cook of a different kind.

A grain of brains, an ounce of blood of troll, fire from a green-bellied lizard. I flipped through the papers, fanning them out in front of me. The script was all Gramps; I recognized his handwriting. But over and over, all I could think was why the hell hadn't Merlin—Gramps—said anything? And why would he try and get me killed? Why hadn't he helped us more? My heart clenched at the betrayal.

Yet again, someone in my life had turned on me.

"I don't think they are the same person," Tad said, flipping through a few of the sheets.

"How?"

"I've seen Merlin's handwriting. It's huge and loopy, not this tight-knit scrawl of Gramps's. But maybe . . . could they just be related?"

I wasn't sure if that was better or worse. No, it was better. Better that I didn't have to think ill of Gramps, that he could possibly do something as diabolical as Merlin, in making me into a monster just to be killed. But then why would Merlin use us at all?

He rubbed at his chin. "Do you think Merlin knows we're related?"

I ran a hand over the table. "We could ask."

Tad shrugged. "But does it really matter right now? I mean, so we've got warlock blood. For all we know, warlocks don't have close family ties. A lot of Supes don't."

I knew it probably didn't matter in the long and short of things, but I couldn't push it away. "Maybe that's why Merlin wants to help now? Could he possibly have not known we were related, and now that he does, he decided that he could actually be nice to us?"

Tad snorted. "Who knows? I certainly don't."

I took the papers from him and smoothed them all out, putting them on a pile on the countertop. Well, that was one secret I wasn't sure that I could swallow whole. Like a loaf of bread going down my throat sideways. Ugh. I tapped my fingers on the counter. "Okay. So we know this means we have warlock blood. What does that tell us? Anything helpful?"

He scratched at one ear. "Well, what I know about warlocks isn't a lot. They can do spells, have magic, and are born with their abilities. They also tend to be a bit reclusive because everyone wants them to do stuff for them."

I rubbed a hand over my face. "So none of that really changes things unless we have to deal with Merlin, right? I mean, does it?"

Tad shook his head, and I went on. "We have to go back through the Wall on our way to find Zeus tomorrow, so we should stop at Merlin's place and ask him if we really are related. And what it might mean for you and me."

I wondered now if one of the pictures in the hallway between Merlin's poker room and where he turned people into Super Dupers was a portrait of a young Gramps. There had been one with a resemblance to Tad the last time I'd walked down the hall. Perhaps it was possible I'd just missed the one of Gramps. I was so fogged in that moment of waking up a Super Duper I wouldn't be surprised if I'd missed something as obvious as my own grandfather staring back at me.

Tad yawned and, with a wave of his hand, disappeared back down the hall. "Fine, whatever."

I was too jazzed up, though, my body all but humming with nervous energy. A flutter of wings snapped me around, and Ernie held up his hands. "Easy, no biting the messenger."

"You aren't a messenger." I smiled, but the smile fell quickly. "I'm going to bake. What do you want?"

"Ooh, I get to choose?" He rubbed his hands together.

"If you're here with information about Hercules, you'd better believe you get to choose," I said.

He flew across the room and landed on the top of my stand mixer. "I ate this dessert once. It was amazing. Graham-cracker crust, different fruit-flavored gelatin, and whipped-cream filling. Not what I'd call high end, but it was delicious. Think you can reproduce something like that?"

I moved through the kitchen, grabbing the few packs of flavored gelatin I had, and got them started with hot water to dissolve. Then I grabbed a can of Sprite to give a bit more texture in the mouth. I put three colors, blue, red, and green, in separate bowls in the fridge and then started on a crust.

"How do you know how to make this?" Ernie asked, moving to sit on the counter right in front of me. I smiled at him.

"I'm a baker, and I collect recipes like some people collect baseball cards. I remember seeing something like what you are talking about a couple of years ago; I never made it, but it's a straightforward idea." I mixed the crust together with a good amount of melted butter and pressed it into a springform pan, then put it into the oven. I turned, wiped my hands on my apron, and gave him a look. "Now, that's got about fifteen minutes to bake, which gives you time to spill the magic beans."

He snickered. "You're getting good at the puns."

I winked. "You better believe it."

He leaned back, no longer smiling. "Here's the deal. Herc is holed up in a downtown building that is set to be demolished. The girl—the Hydra, I should say—is with him."

"The Hydra," I repeated, and he nodded.

"Yeah, she's damn hot, and she's all over Herc, pawing at his belt, and he's trying hard to be all gentlemanly." He snickered. "He always was a Goody Two-Shoes."

"Any plans you could get out of them?" If I didn't keep him on track, this conversation would go out the window in no time. He loved gossip almost as much as he loved baked goods.

"Only that they are planning a surprise attack in the next few days. They were pretty cagey, almost like they knew I was there."

"Wait, you were spying on him?" That surprised me.

Ernie grinned. "You're my home girl. I'm fully invested in team Drakaina now. No more Hera. No more Zeus. Team Alena through and through." He pulled a shimmering piece of cloth from behind him (where he kept it when he was wearing a simple loincloth is beyond me), but the cloth . . . it glittered and sparkled with the same color and pattern as my scales. I took it from him, laughing. "You aren't serious?"

He wound it around the upper part of his left arm. "Yup, I am. Just means that whatever your fate is, I'm tied into it. And . . . for the first time in years, I don't feel torn. I don't wonder if my boss is going to kill me for telling the truth."

"You don't have a boss," I pointed out. "If you backed away from Aphrodite, Hera, and Zeus."

"No, that's true. But I don't think I have to worry about you killing me either." He smiled and the oven dinged. I went and pulled the springform pan out and set it on the counter to cool. "This isn't a quick dessert; it could take a while."

"That's okay. Maybe we could have it for breakfast?"

He had a point; breakfast was only a short time away. I grabbed a bowl and put together some whipped filling mixed with a bit of pineapple juice that would be folded through the chunks of gelatin. I think, if I remembered right, it was called a broken-glass cake, the final product somewhat resembling a stained-glass window.

I put everything in the fridge and wiped the counters down while I tried to formulate a question. I had my doubts about Yaya, and I wondered if somehow she was playing me the way others had, or if she was just taking advantage of the situation as it presented itself to her. But there was no easy way to ask if my yaya was really on my side.

Finally I just blurted it out. "Do you think my yaya might be working with Hera somehow?"

Ernie flew backward, his hands over his mouth. "Girlfriend! Tell me you are shitting in my drinking water."

I cringed at the image. "No, I'm not. Yaya is getting . . . younger. And so are her priestesses. They were all at Zeus's today, at a pool party of sorts, and . . . she said that with the world changing, people were beginning to believe again. And that meant she was coming back into her own power in a way." Left unsaid was that it was in her best interest for Hera's plan to continue as it was. But Ernie was no fool, and he'd been at this game of the pantheon for far longer than I had. I rubbed at my face with both hands. "I just don't know what to think anymore."

"You really think she could be . . . using you?" Ernie shook his head, his eyes thoughtful. "I suppose it is possible, but really, she hasn't given any indication before you were turned that she wanted you to be a Super Duper, right?"

He had a point, and I slowly nodded. "You're right. She joined the Firstamentalists to keep our family away from all this." I slid my hand to the back of my neck. "I guess she's just making the best of her situation."

"That would be my guess too," Ernie said, but he didn't sound all that confident. I glanced at him.

"What are you thinking?"

"That things change, people change. It wouldn't hurt to be careful around her. Or maybe avoid her for the next little while." He grimaced as he spoke, as if he didn't like it any more than I did.

My heart lurched at the thought of not being around Yaya. She was a bright light in my life, a support I hadn't found elsewhere. But I couldn't be a fool and deny that there were things that benefited her the more I challenged the current system. I blew out a sigh, and with it came a jaw-cracking yawn I felt all the way down to my toes.

"I think it's time you go have a sleep." Ernie waved at me with his hands, herding me toward the stairs. He flicked the light out as we left the kitchen, and followed me up to the second floor, the brush of his wings against my back gently urging me forward.

He was right, I was exhausted. There were only a few hours till dawn, but a little sleep now would do me good. My brain felt like a soggy oatmeal cookie. I fell into bed, and Ernie floated beside me. "I'll keep watch over you both." He tipped his head toward Sandy, who slept soundly in the bed across from me. "No fear. Nothing will get past me."

"Thank you, Ernie," I mumbled into my pillow as exhaustion pulled me down.

I woke to the back and forth of soft voices chattering. Sandy's bed was empty, the sheets neatly folded, and the bed made neat as a pin.

I picked up her voice and then Tad's out of the discussion going on below. I rolled over to see Ernie sitting on the edge of my bookshelf, his chin on his chest as he snored, sounding like an oversized bumblebee, of all things. "Some guard he is." I kept the words quiet, though. He needed his sleep too. If Hercules was as hard to face as everyone was making him out to be, then I needed to be on my toes. And I needed to be at my best, along with my friends. I grabbed some clean clothes and hurried into the bathroom. I showered in record time and pulled my hair up into a high ponytail. I stared into the fogged mirror, my face distorted with the steam, and for a moment I didn't know who I was looking at. Alena. Drakaina. Baker. Lover. Fighter.

I shook myself and headed down the stairs. Sandy was smiling at Tad, and he was oblivious to what I saw in her eyes. A bit of a crush going on there apparently. I cleared my throat, and she glanced at me, blushed, and looked away. "Have you talked to Dahlia?" I pointedly asked Tad.

He snorted and frowned at me. "She's asleep right now. Did you suddenly forget that she's a vamp?"

"Nope, I didn't forget, just making sure I'm not the only one who remembers she's a vampire." I glanced at Sandy, and she gave me a quick bob of her head. Good, she was picking up what I was putting down.

I pulled out the pans from the fridge and started to combine the gelatin and whipped filling, then spooned it all into the springform pan with the graham-cracker crust. *"What is that?"* Tad breathed over my shoulder.

"Out of my way, it's mine!" Ernie came flying—literally—into the room and grabbed at the pan. I spun sideways to keep him from snatching it right out of my hands.

"It needs to set still! I told you it wasn't a quick dessert." I laughed around the words while I continued to dodge both Tad and Ernie.

The cherub made a *gimme* gesture at me. I rolled my eyes and spooned him out some of the filling into a small bowl. He shoved it in his mouth, slurping at the different colored cubes and whipped cream, smearing it on his face. He let out a long groan as his eyes closed. "Oooh, that's even better than I remember. Orgasmic."

"I hope not, dude." Tad snorted.

I sighed, gave up, and handed out spoons to everyone. The four of us dug into the dessert, silent while we stuffed our faces. Ernie was right, the cake, if it could be called that, was amazing. Soft and fluffy and sweet, with the buttery graham-cracker crust holding it all together. Not high end, not French baked goods, but I knew already I'd be getting requests to make it again.

"You need to make this in the bakery," Tad mumbled around a mouthful, and it was my turn to groan. I looked up at the clock above the sink. Ten in the morning.

"Poop, thanks for the reminder. I have to go. I have to meet Mom at the bakery," I said.

Tad grimaced. "You want me to come?" We both knew he didn't really want to. While I had taken the share of mom's ire over the years, Tad hadn't been immune to it either.

More than once I remember lying in my bed and listening to Mom tell Tad that he was going to go to hell for his taste in music. That it was rotting his soul, and she'd lose him. The strange mix of condemnation and fear she put together and used on us growing up left both of us reluctant to be with her.

I shook my head. "No, it's just a taste test. Diana will be there, along with the two new girls she hired last week. They'll run things, and I'll deal with Mom in the back." At least that was what I was hoping for. I sighed again, swigged back a big glass of water, and headed to the front door, but then stopped. "You two don't have a car here."

Tad shook his head. "I'm going to keep searching the house. Maybe Sandy can help me?"

She nodded a bit too eagerly. I narrowed my eyes at her, and she blushed again.

Sandy was my friend, but she'd sided with Beth when Beth had lost her marbles and gone after Theseus. I trusted Sandy, but at the same time I would put Dahlia and Tad above her every time. It was a hard truth, but one I recognized. I loved them all, but some were closer to me than others in our group.

It only took me about ten minutes to get to the bakery. Such a nice change from driving all the way in from the Wall, which was a good two-hour drive even without border clogs. I didn't want to think about the reasons why I'd continued to live in house number thirteen after I legally regained possession of my grandparents' house. Probably had to do with Remo. I snorted to myself, and Ernie raised an eyebrow at me. I shook my head. "Never mind."

"Didn't say a word." He mumbled and stroked one of his wings forward. "What is going on with the vamps, then?"

"Nothing," I said. "I told Remo I didn't need him."

Ernie laughed, and I glanced at him as I pulled onto the road where my bakery was. The place was remarkably quiet. Like I wasn't liking how quiet it was. There should have been customers for the bakery, or at least a few cars parked here and there for the other businesses in the area. There wasn't even a single picketing Firstamentalist.

I parked in the back lot and stepped out of the Charger. I took a breath, and a tingle of apprehension went through me. Then again, it could have simply been my mother's tiny Camry parked there, waiting for me.

My mom wasn't what I'd call the most open-minded when it came to me and Tad being Super Dupers. She wasn't excited that we hadn't died. In fact, she'd said more than once it would have been better if we had, because as it was we were going to hell, and any association we had with her would damn her as well. She was as Firstamentalist as one could get, hard core through and through. But she was my mother, and I loved her, and like always I hoped for the best while expecting the worst.

· I squared my shoulders and headed in through the back door, Ernie right behind me. A sudden thought hit me. I had no idea how my mom would react to seeing a physical manifestation of a mythology she always said was stupid. I pointed to the ceiling, and Ernie shot up and out of the way. To be sure, I made a zipping motion across my mouth. Ernie grinned and crossed a finger over his heart. As if that would truly seal the deal.

I looked away from him. My mom was bent over a recipe book that had pictures next to each flavor. Her hair was pulled back in a tight bun without a single hair escaping it. She was dressed in black slacks and a long-sleeved dark-gray blouse that actually highlighted her slim figure. That was a first. Normally she wore clothes that hid her body.

Diana was beside her, pointing things out. "So you can see that we can do the cream-filled cakes pretty much with any flavor you'd like. We can do red velvet, chocolate, pecan, vanilla, anything you can come up with, and we can pair it with any flavor of filling too, from fruit to . . ." She glanced up and saw me, then smiled. "Well, Alena is here, so I'll let her show you the different choices and some of the bakery's best options."

Diana winked at me, and I pleaded with her with my eyes, but she just hurried out to the front counter as I groaned quietly to myself. "Hi, Mom."

She didn't turn around but pointed at the page. "This red velvet, what does it taste like, Alena?"

I went to the fridge and pulled out the samples I'd asked Diana to make up for me first thing that morning. "Here, you can try all the different flavors."

I brought the plate over to her and set it down, labels in front of each little bite. She didn't make eye contact with me, and my heart tightened further, the muscles in my chest contracting with growing anxiety. "This one here is the red velvet."

She plucked it up and took a bite. A surprised sound slid out of her. "It's chocolatey. I didn't expect that."

"Yes." Good grief, this was about as stilted as it came. Here we go, I needed to just grab this conversation by the spatula and start whipping things together. I took a big breath and said the words before I changed my mind. "Mom, you know Dad is a Super Duper, right?"

Her shoulders slumped, and I thought for a good minute she wasn't going to answer me. The word that escaped her was quiet, barely above a whisper. "Yes."

Okay, to say I was surprised she actually admitted it was an understatement.

I took a step back, leaning against the counter. "How long have you known about Dad? Before or after you became a Firstamentalist? Before or after you were married? I don't understand how you could stay in the church when he's a Super Duper."

Slowly she turned toward me, like she was turning to face a firing squad, her body stiff and reluctant. "You already know about your grandmother's part of it."

I lifted both eyebrows. "You mean how Yaya and Zeus . . . ?"

She nodded. "Yes, that affair between my mother and the king of the gods caused the curse that I didn't believe in at first. But it was true, and once I realized that . . ." She closed her eyes so tight the edges were pinched. "I was married before I met your father."

The words hung between us, and all I could do was stare at the woman who was my mother, but who I wasn't sure I knew at all.

"What?" I blurted out, unable to keep the word to myself. "What? Who?"

She frowned but didn't open her eyes, as if she couldn't bear to look at me. "The doctors . . . they couldn't figure out what the problem was, but I wasn't able to carry babies to term. Something about my uterus being heart shaped. I couldn't do it. We tried all sorts of things. My marriage was falling apart; it doesn't matter who he was either. He's been gone a long time." I realized suddenly that I was about to get the confession of the century. I held on to the edge of the counter for all I was worth.

"I'm so sorry, Mom."

She finally opened her eyes and gave me a tired smile. "I knew about the supernatural world; how could I not with my mother being who she was? She suggested I go to a warlock for help. Your father . . . he had some . . . small abilities. He was a minor warlock at the time." Which meant he was a minor warlock now too.

Holy shit, holy shit, holy shit. She'd said it out loud. I thought my heart and lungs would burst with the adrenaline. From the ceiling came a soft sound of a breath being sucked in. I glared sideways at Ernie, and he clamped both hands over his mouth, his blue eyes wide.

"Okay," I said. "What happened then?"

"He said he could help me carry to term. Except that my husband at the time, he didn't want anything to do with me anymore. He said I was broken." She put a hand to her head and closed her eyes. "Clark was so sweet, so kind. And I . . . I kissed him when I was still married."

Double holy shit. I could think of nothing else but holy shit. Suddenly her treatment of me when I'd not officially been done with Roger but I'd brought Remo around made a bit more sense. Guilt being foisted onto me from her past. "You fell in love with him while you were still married."

She smiled now, the first real smile I'd seen on her since I'd been turned. "Yes, I got a divorce, and a week later Clark and I eloped. He promised me babies, and after some time and trials with the magic, we had you and your brother. Of course, being that happy terrified me. The curse was still in effect, you know. Just like it is for you and your brother. Haven't you noticed your love lives have been less than . . . normal?"

I thought about Roger, Dahlia, and Tad, and of course the fiasco with Remo and Smithy. I sighed and nodded. "Yeah. I know it. But all of that . . . Why did you join the church of the Firsts, then?"

She slumped into a chair. "I joined the church not long after it was started, when you and your brother were still very young. Because your grandmother pointed out that I wasn't supposed to have a successful marriage. That if Hera caught wind that maybe her curse wasn't working, she might decide to do something to you and Tad. I joined the Firsts because they are so—"

"Awful?" Ernie tried to help, and she shook her head. He floated down so that he sat on the counter beside her. She gave him a tired smile, seemingly unbothered by his appearance.

"No, that isn't why I joined. While that can be true, they are zealous. If I was to make it look like I truly believed in what they taught, I had to be zealous too. I was trying to protect you all. I was trying to keep my marriage intact, and Clark understood. The antagonism between us was all an act, but . . . I got caught up in the false belief that I could truly stop a curse on my own. When in reality I've been as miserable as I made the rest of you, so I guess the curse worked still." She shook her head but couldn't seem to meet my eyes.

"I never stopped loving you all, but I . . . the Firstamentalists felt safe, but I know that it was a false comfort. I knew it when you and Tad got sick and were turned, and I didn't know how else to keep you safe but to keep acting like the Firsts were right." She reached out and touched my face, and I realized I was crying. My mom . . . she walked up to me and swept me into a hug. I pressed my face against her neck and sobbed.

"I thought you hated me. You said you would rather I die than become a Super Duper."

"I was trying so hard to protect you." She squeezed me harder, a sob escaping her. "I would rather you think I hated you than watch you die with something Hera would cook up. She is so very dangerous, and I couldn't live with the thought that she would torture you and make your life a living nightmare. I didn't think I could bear to see you under her rule. But the truth . . ." She stepped back and cupped my face with her hands. "The truth is you are strong enough, my beautiful girl. You are more than strong enough, and I should have seen that you have had that strength all along. That your bloodlines run true, that the power in your grandmother went right through us both. I should have believed that I was strong enough too." That last was said so softly, I wasn't sure I was meant to hear it. But I did, and it cemented something between us. Her fears were not so different than my own.

Shaking, I hugged her again, relishing the feel of her hugging me back. Really holding me for the first time in what felt like forever. "I love you, Mom."

"I love you too, but ease off a bit. I'm not a Super Duper like you," she whispered. I laughed and stepped back.

"Sorry . . . wait." I let her go and ran to the phone and called my house. Tad picked up, and before he could say anything, I blurted out, "You've got to come to the bakery, right now. You have to."

He didn't ask why, just hung the phone up, and I knew he was on his way. "Tad, he's missed you too."

She nodded. "I was wrong. You are both so much more than I could have ever hoped for in children." She clapped her hands together and smiled at me, really smiled. "I think we need to start again with so many things. But let's begin with this anniversary. I don't want to hide how much I love your father anymore." She patted my face again, smiling as she pointed at the samples. "Which one do you think Clark will like best?"

Still sniffing and wiping at my face, I bent over and pointed at the red velvet. "He loves chocolate, and it's a nice twist. We could fill the center with raspberry and then do fresh raspberries as part of the toppings."

"Please tell me I'm invited," Ernie stage-whispered, and my mom laughed.

"Eros, you are invited. Seems fitting, don't you think?" My mom lifted an eyebrow at me, and I grinned, my heart all but floating. This day . . . this day would stay with me for the rest of my life. The day my mother and I finally were honest with each other.

The day I saw that, while she'd gone about it the wrong way, she'd been trying to protect us, because she loved us.

She nodded. "Now, what else do we need for the platters?"

I opened my mouth to tell her that I had a few ideas, but no words came out. I froze, hearing the heartbeat of something far bigger than any person. The beat was like a section of drums echoing one another. A heartbeat that big could mean only one thing. I stared at Ernie. His face paled.

He flipped around in a sudden circle, his eyes worried. "Alena. I think we have a problem."

The ground shook, and I put my hand on my mom's back. "Mom, stay here." I ran out into the main part of the bakery. The plate glass had been replaced, and through it I saw a thick, hard skin that looked like pebbled gray leather. The image filled the plate glass as it moved. "Diana, get my mom and the girls and get out!" I pointed to the back even as I ran to the front door.

And right into the monstrous danger that waited for me.

CHAPTER 8

I stood on the front step of my bakery and stared up at a creature that was easily the same size as me in my Drakaina form. I thought about shifting, and smoke curled up around me, leaving me blind for a split second, and then I was staring down at the top of my bakery from two stories up. I whipped around and faced the creature in front of me. Her body was that solid gray that came from overdoing the mixture of too many food colorings as you tried to swirl them together. Pasty gray and ugly, it covered her entire body except for a strip of black down the center of her back. Her body was thick, and she had four legs, the front two tipped with three claws each that dug into the cement with a screech. Nine long necks topped with nine heads wove and bobbed in front of me. Sitting on the center head was a man dressed in solid black body armor. It looked to be a blend of old and new with the bright, shiny brass buckles tightened over black hard-shelled armor that reminded me of a SWAT team. A golden shield rested on his left arm, and a sword was gripped in his right hand. He slowly pointed it at me.

"Drakaina. Your death is here." His words were firm, and he was obviously strong in his belief. That didn't bode well.

"Don't count on it, chump!" Ernie yelled as he flew up next to me. He had a wee tiny bow that he pulled taut. "Don't think she's doing this alone."

Hercules sighed. "Eros, get lost, you little bugger. I don't want to hurt you."

"Then go away! Alena is not the one you should be fighting!" Ernie yelled.

The Hydra's nine heads hissed together, the noise echoing back and forth. I opened my mouth and hissed right back, the rumble of my voice deeper and far more deadly sounding. At least to me.

Without warning, she launched herself at me, claws outstretched along with her heads. I dove down, sliding under her belly and wrapping myself around her middle. I squeezed, and she roared, then didn't roar again as she struggled to get air. Of course, she wasn't alone.

Hercules leapt off the back of her head and sailed toward me almost in slow motion. His sword was angled downward, straight for my coils. I stared at him, tried to strike, and was cut short. My coils around the Hydra's body kept me from completing the blow. He landed, and his sword drove down through my hide. I roared, my head thrown back with the pain, but I didn't let go of the Hydra. I knew how this worked. If I let her go, then she'd attack again. I wasn't going to make that mistake. Not if I wanted to come out on top.

Ernie zipped into view, and I locked eyes with him and shook my head. He couldn't help me with this. Or maybe I just wanted to do it on my own.

"Alena, let me help!" Ernie shouted, and again I shook my head. He flew out of sight. Good enough for me.

"Strength of character was not something I thought you would have," Hercules mumbled as he pulled his sword out and prepared to drive it in again. From his left side, a flutter of wings, and then Ernie was there, slamming into his head and knocking him sideways.

"Get her, Alena. I've got him."

If I could have smiled I would have. The thought of Ernie taking on Hercules? Nothing short of brilliant, even if I'd told him not to. I had to loosen my hold on the Hydra to get the room to strike, but as soon as I did that, she wriggled away from me. Two of her heads whipped around and bit into my side, pinning me to the ground, cutting right through the diamond-hard snakeskin. Fighting through the pain, I flicked my tail up and slammed it into her side, sending her sideways and into an empty building across the street from my bakery. The structured crumbled under her weight, and the rubble dust billowed up. I took stock of my injuries. I was hurt, but nothing was a mortal wound. I would heal. I lurched forward to see where Ernie and Hercules had disappeared.

Hercules held the cherub by his foot in one hand, his bow and arrows in the other. "Look, Eros, I'm not exactly happy working for Hera, but we can't have a monster like the Drakaina floating about. We can't. It's bad for the people."

"She's not like the others, you idiot!" Ernie screeched. "Put me down, fool hero! You're making a mistake! She protected people from Theseus!"

I hesitated, thinking that Hercules didn't seem like Achilles or Theseus. Maybe I could talk to him and convince him not to go through with all this. I had to try. I let the shift take me down in size.

I was completely naked, as per the usual shift out of Drakaina and back to human. "Don't hurt him!" I yelled as I scrambled toward Hercules and Eros. Hercules turned to me, a frown on his face.

"I'm not going to hurt him. But what would it matter to you?"

I glanced over my shoulder to where the Hydra was scrambling back to her feet. I didn't have long. "He's my friend, please don't hurt him."

My words only seemed to confuse him further, but he did let Ernie go. "You aren't . . . I don't understand why you would care. You're a monster."

I rubbed my hands up and down my arms and all but danced in place. Hercules seemed to be coming around, and unlike Theseus and even Achilles, his eyes didn't rove over my body like a kid with his face pressed against the glass display case in my bakery.

A roar from behind us snapped me around. The Hydra was back up on her feet, all nine heads swinging my way. All with wide-open mouths. Sugar doodles, this was going to be close. I dove out of the way, rolling across the street, my bare skin ripping from me in bits and pieces, showing off my snakeskin underneath. I stood. "Over here, you big dumb jerk."

She whipped her heads around and snarled at me. I lifted one hand slowly, and then one middle finger. "That's from my yaya."

The Hydra screeched and launched at me, but she was so big I could avoid her . . . I dove between her legs and then rolled back to my feet behind her. She smelled like an oil slick, and the Drakaina in me did not like being this close and this small. The desire to shift caught me unawares, and I struggled to fight it off. *Not yet, not yet!*

I wrapped my arms around my upper body and squeezed tight. "Not yet, she can't find us." Us. Like we were two entities. Time to think about that later. Not right now.

I ducked between the Hydra's stomping legs, grabbing onto her fat ankles and spinning around them. She screeched, and above us Hercules called out, "That's enough, Angel. Time to go."

Angel. What a name for a monster with nine heads. She roared, and the grinding noise of teeth cracking together one after another, like an echoing rumble, ripped through the air. I dodged out from under a stomping foot and ran to the front of the bakery. Ernie zipped over, floating by my shoulder.

"Holy shit," he muttered. "If you don't have to fight him, don't. I'm not . . . I'm not sure you can beat the two of them now that I've seen them together."

I nodded, thinking he was right. I stared as the Hydra and Hercules conversed. I didn't disagree with Ernie. Not for a second. The wounds the Hydra had given me finally made themselves known. Aching, throbbing as they announced themselves on my hip and upper rib cage. I pressed my hand to the worst of them. "Ernie. Go get Damara. I'm going to need her help."

He saluted me and zipped off. I shouldn't have sent him. I know that now, but . . . hindsight being twenty-twenty and all that jazz, I'd done what I thought was best.

I pressed my back against the bakery, and the door opened. I spun sideways. "Mom, get out of here." I kept my voice down so that Hercules and the Hydra wouldn't hear me.

Apparently the Hydra had excellent hearing, though. Angel whipped around, away from Hercules. On all nine heads a grin spread from one corner of her wicked sharp-fanged faces to the other. I pushed Mom back into the bakery. "Go, out the back, run!" Her eyes widened as she stared up at the Hydra, which seemed to freeze her in place. I shoved her again. The Hydra was after me. I could draw her away, that's what I told myself. I yanked the bakery door shut, praying my mom would listen to me and run for the back. I bolted toward Angel and ducked between her legs, trying to draw her away. Away from my mom.

She lurched forward. Hercules yelled at her.

"Angel, stop! That is a command!"

I grabbed at her legs, smacking her with my hands. "Come on, you're after me, aren't you?"

She ignored us both.

The Hydra bunched her leg muscles, leapt up . . . and came crashing down on top of Vanilla and Honey. The roof collapsed in a heap of cement and dust that swirled around her, hiding her for a brief moment. The roar of a dying building rushed through the air, but none of that mattered, the bakery didn't matter.

My mom was in there. My mom was in the bakery. The shift happened faster than ever before. I was on the Hydra in a split second, wrapping around her and jerking her off the building. I bit her over and over again, driving my fangs and my venom into her hide as she roared, screeching.

We tumbled sideways into two more buildings, bringing them down around us in more dust and cement. I felt none of it. I was not there—my heart was in the bakery, and it had nothing to do with my business. My mom was in there; the thought hit me over and over. She was human, so there was no way she could have survived. Terror drove me in a way I had never felt before. Sheer and absolute panic at the thought that Mom had been inside the bakery when it collapsed. It had happened so fast I couldn't have stopped it.

I uncoiled from around the suddenly still form of the Hydra, not caring if she was alive or dead, and slithered away as fast as I could. Distantly I knew I was hurt badly. That Angel had inflicted at least as many wounds on me as I had on her. I didn't care; the pain meant nothing compared to the fear that coursed through my heart.

I reached the rubble of the bakery and shifted down. Shaking, blood dripping off my body from multiple gaping wounds, I stumbled up onto the still shivering rubble. "Mom!"

There was no reply as I fought my way to the top of the heap, coughing on the dust, waving it away to try to see through. Oh, God, what if she was in there? What if she didn't make it out? I couldn't help the cry that slipped past my lips. "MOM!"

I spun around, caught a glimpse of Hercules watching me, a look of confusion on his face, before I spun away again, continuing to look for my mom. "Mom, please answer me!" I went to my knees and forced myself to take a deep breath. I could find her. If she was in the rubble, I could find her by her scent. I was strong enough to dig her out on my own too; I knew I could. Of course, I was discounting the fact that I was hurt badly. Really badly. There were broken bones in me that were just starting to register, wounds that had begun to fester with a green ooze from Angel's bite.

I ignored it all and drew in a deep breath. Through the dust and the faint whisper of baking ingredients was the hint of my mom. The one who'd smoothed my tears away as a child, the one who'd chased away the fear of the dark, the one who'd pushed me away in what I knew now was a desperate hope to protect me, the one I'd held just an hour before, finally finding safety and peace in her arms. There, deep under the debris, the smell of her floated up to me. Her unique scent, and with it, blood—a lot of blood.

I grabbed the first block and heaved it sideways. "Hang on, Mom, I'm coming." The words were hitched, and I couldn't help the tears as they slipped down my cheeks. This was not happening. It couldn't be. Another set of hands heaved stone on the other side of me. I didn't care who it was, didn't care as long as we got to my mom. I had to get to her; there had to be time yet to save her. I caught a glimpse of blond hair and distantly knew Hercules was helping me. Why, I couldn't say, and I didn't want to guess. "Mom, talk to me. Please!"

There was no answer, no cry that she was okay. I heaved the last chunk of cement off my mom, and there she was, lying on the floor of what had been the back of my bakery. I slithered down over the rocks, my blood making it easy to slide. I listened hard for her heart, but already I knew . . . her heart wasn't beating; it had stopped completely.

"No, no, no!" I scooped her up and clutched her to my chest. This was not happening. This couldn't be the end. Not when she'd finally reached out to me, not when we were finally mending the wounds of the past. "Mom, wake up. Please wake up. You can't be gone. Not now, not when I need you the most." I buried my face against her neck and sobbed, my shoulders hunched, unable to care that Hercules stood over me. Probably with a sword that could run me through. I couldn't make myself care, not for a split second.

"Do it, if you're going to," I whispered to him, my whole body shaking with grief. With disbelief. If I were gone, the fights would be over. Hera would win, but no more of my family would die. Tad and my father would be safe, and that would have to be enough. I had to believe that. I didn't look over my shoulder.

"I'm sorry. She wasn't supposed to die," Hercules said, and then he was gone, the sound of wreckage falling around him as he climbed out of the hole we'd made. I brushed my mom's hair back from her face. The first time in years she and I had finally understood one another, and then . . . I couldn't help the cry that erupted from me. The loss that was everything in the world. The bakery was nothing, I could rebuild that, but this . . .

Voices flowed around me, emergency workers, police officers, ambulance attendants. Someone tried to take her away from me, and I snapped my teeth at them, every bit of me willing to fight them off if I had to. With shaking legs, I stood, still holding her to me. The uniformed people stepped back and let me carry her out. More than one looked away, tears of their own slipping down their faces. Too much, this was too much. Somehow I was out of the hole and standing on the road in front of an ambulance. "You have to give her up," a voice said.

I turned my face to see Smithy standing there. Tad was beside him, his face pale and his cheeks stained with tears. "I'll go with her, Alena. She won't be alone." My brother choked on the words, and that brought another round of tears from my own eyes.

Smithy had a hand on my arm, and he squeezed it gently. "Alena, you have to let them take her, and I need to get you some help. You're dying, sweetheart."

"I don't care," I whispered.

"I do." His blue eyes were intense, and I fought not to sob.

"You shouldn't." Because what I had in me was nothing short of revenge. I wasn't sure I could hold the Drakaina in me back anymore.

Maybe worse was that I wasn't sure I wanted to. I wanted to let her loose and watch Hera and her pets run for cover while I rained down venom and destruction.

Smithy held his arms out to me, indicating I should give him my mother. "They need to take her, Alena. You can't help her now."

Another voice, one that was as dear to me as my mother's, called out. "That's not true, Hephaestus, and you know it."

CHAPTER 9

My distraction with what my grandmother said allowed Smithy to take my mother from my arms and hand her body off to Tad. I stared at Yaya, not caring that I was naked and covered in blood. "What are you talking about?"

Yaya's blue eyes were soft with tears, but under that was a determination that I'd seen in her before. "Death is never the end, Alena. Your mother is not gone forever, not if you're brave enough. Look to Orpheus."

I reached for Yaya, and my knees buckled. A pair of strong arms swept under my legs and scooped me up. My head lolled back, and Smithy stared down at me.

"Let me go," I said. "If I'm dead, this all ends. Hera wins. No more fighting."

He frowned. "No, you need to heal before you can even begin to consider what Flora is saying."

What Flora was saying? What was my yaya saying? That I could save my mother somehow from death? Who was Orpheus, and what did he have to do with anything? If it was possible, I would do it, I would bring my mother back. I would. I struggled, but the struggle was small and weak. I doubted that Smithy even felt me twitch. He held his arms a little tighter around me. "I'm taking Alena to my place. I'll have Panacea meet us there."

Panacea, the healer. I didn't mean to close my eyes, but I couldn't help it. There was something pulling the lids closed, something I couldn't fight, couldn't deny. My mother was dead, gone, killed in a battle with another monster. This was all . . . "My fault." the words slipped, slurred past my lips like I'd been dipping into the ouzo while baking. I reached up, touching someone's face, feeling ridged scars along a thick neck.

"Hush, Alena. Just hang on, we're almost there."

"Almost where?" was what I wanted to ask, but what did it matter? I'd killed my mother. Tad . . . he'd find out it was my fault soon enough, and then he'd hate me too. He'd hate me. Oh, God. I groaned. Dad. I still had to talk to Dad, to tell him. I whimpered, unable to keep the pitiful sound back, and I closed my eyes, suddenly exhausted.

Voices floated around me, and time passed. I knew because the voices kept saying it. "Too much time, we're going to lose her. Too much time."

I didn't really care. The dark of unconsciousness was blissful and I hid in it, a part of me hoping that I never fully escaped it.

I woke up as I was being set down on something soft and cushiony, like a marshmallow filling. I sank into it, and water slipped over my head. Smithy was drowning me, that was the only thing I could think, and I didn't want to fight it. All along he'd been working for Hera, working for her. Damn him. But I didn't damn him, not really. What was the point? I'd asked him to let me go, so he was. A voice slid through the water. "Breathe it in, Alena; it will flush the toxins out of your system."

I recognized the voice as Panacea's, and my body lurched as I opened my mouth to do as I was told. To breathe in the water. I sucked a lungful in deep, and the water didn't taste of water but of flowers and herbs, spices I could recognize, and then their names floated away on my thoughts like the bubbles escaping my lips. Lavender and eucalyptus, sage, rose petals, saffron, and honey, the honey so thick it coated my tongue. In and out I breathed, as though the water were air, and slowly my senses came back to me, and I was staring up at two people above me through a clouded glass. No, I was in a tub, a big tub, staring up through pale-green liquid. I recognized Smithy and Panacea.

"You can't be serious," Panacea whispered, her words amplified through the water.

"She's going to get herself killed if she goes after her mother. Not to mention I don't think she's strong enough to face the Hydra or Hercules on their own, never mind together. The Hydra got up and walked away from that fight; Alena has been unconscious for days after being carried out."

Panacea shook her head. "You give her too little credit because you have feelings for her. That was always your way. It's why you fell out with Aphrodite, you know, you didn't allow her to own her own strength."

"I don't need a marital lesson from you, someone who's never even been married," Smithy snapped. "And I'm saying this because it's the truth. Alena has come a long way, but look at her. Look at the damage she took, and that was without Hercules doing much. How can anyone expect her to survive the both of them if they come against her in full force?"

"Because she has more heart than anyone else I have ever met. And she fought while fearing for her mother's life. That was not a fair fight, not in the least, you big, dumb ox," Yaya said, stepping into view. "She will find a way to defeat Hercules and the Hydra. We have to let her find her own way; that is the only thing to do. Do you understand?"

I kept breathing the fluid in and out, and the water grew deeper green in color until their faces were obscured. I realized it was the toxins filtering into the water. Toxins that the Hydra carried in her bite. I pushed myself up, liquid streaming down my face, dribbling out past my lips and out my nose. I coughed, clearing my lungs. Large chunks of green came up, thick and heavy with blood as well as the poison. I held the edges of the tub and drew in a big breath. "I'm going after my mom."

Smithy shook his head. "No."

I glared at him. "You think I'm weak, just like everyone else."

He shook his head. "You are weak, compared to what you face. You've been unconscious for days, and barely survived. The Drakaina can only take you so far, Alena. Part of being strong is knowing when you can't accomplish a task on your own. I know you want to prove yourself, but I don't want to see you get killed because of pride." He crouched beside the tub and reached one hand out to me. I batted it away.

"I may be weak, but I can bend. I can bounce back. I am not going to go down without a fight. And I will ask for help. If I need it." My muscles protested as I pushed myself into a standing position. Smithy's eyes never left mine.

"I don't want you to die, Alena," he said.

I held a hand out to Yaya, and she took it, balancing me as I stepped out of the tub. I glanced at her. "We all die, Smithy. Even the gods, isn't that right?"

I caught a look from Panacea, a soft smile and a twinkle in her eyes. She gave me the barest of nods. "You are correct. We all die, at some point. But perhaps you will show us a new way to live, yes?"

Smithy grunted. "I'm not going to encourage you to do this. I'm not going to watch you throw yourself into the flames." He turned his back on me, shoulders and movement stiff. Hard. Unyielding.

"Thank you for your help," I said. He didn't turn around, and I knew that we'd crossed some barrier that was yet unseen to him. And maybe it always would be. In another life, another time . . . he would have been a match for me in so many ways. Maybe if I hadn't met Remo first, if I hadn't felt the strength of a man who believed in me, who let me find my own way for right or for wrong. A man who saw my weakness as strength, and my strength for what it was. I put a hand to my face. "I didn't mean to hurt him. Or lead him on."

A thick towel was swung over my shoulders and wrapped tight around me. "You woke him up," Panacea said. "To the possibilities that lie out there. Just as you've woken Zeus up. Just as you've woken all the gods up."

"That's not what Hera wanted, is it?" I asked. Better to ask questions than think about what had happened at the bakery. My mind skittered away from that, from the memories that were so fresh I could still smell them. Could still taste the scent of my mom's blood on the back of my throat if I let my mind go there.

"No, I believe Hera thought to only wake up her own followers. But she forgot that the pantheon is a whole, that we are all connected. In waking up her believers, she also made it so that there were people waking up to the rest of us. Remembering that there is a plethora of gods to be seen."

I shivered, and Yaya rubbed my arms as she stared up at me. "You must find Zeus. He holds the key to all of this; he holds it completely. Do you understand? If you can convince him to come back, to actually become the leader he is meant to be, he can stop the virus. And he can bring your mother back."

I stared at her, seeing the shape of her mouth, the gentle plump skin of her cheeks. She looked to be in her late fifties now. Maybe younger, even. I glanced at Panacea, who had a frown on her face. That did not give me confidence in my grandmother's words. At the same time, she was probably at least partially right. If I could convince Zeus to pull his cookies out of the oven before they burned to a crisp and get his butt in gear, maybe he could slow things down. Maybe he would have a way to bring my mother back from the dead.

Then there was Orpheus. Yaya shook her head, almost as if she knew what I was thinking. "Not here."

The twinge in my heart almost brought me to my knees. I focused on the here and now. "Where is Zeus? I thought maybe Whistler when you said he went north, Panacea."

The goddess shook her head. "No, that is too close, even for him. I would go farther north yet. Hermes could lead the way if you could convince him."

There was a flutter of wings that was far too loud for a single set. Behind Panacea appeared Hermes and Ernie. The two tiny winged men argued back and forth like siblings as they flew through the window. I wondered for a moment if that was actually the case.

"You have to help us," Ernie pleaded. "We have to find Zeus if we're going to stop the mess Hera is making of things."

"No, no, that's not how it works, and you know it." Hermes shook his head, his lean body shaking. "I'll get my messenger license revoked if I do that."

I took a deep breath and slowly let it out. "And if everyone dies because you aren't willing to break a rule, what then? The virus is sweeping the world, Hermes. My mother was killed"—oh, those words hurt, and I struggled to keep going, but I forged on—"and I need you to take me to Zeus. Please, he's the only one who can help us stop this madness."

Hermes cringed and shook his head. "It's not that easy."

Panacea made a soothing motion with her hands, as if to calm him down. "Hermes, these are desperate times. You can take a single person with you. That is allowed with your messenger license, you know that."

Hermes cringed further. "But what if Hera finds out?"

"No buts, and Hera won't find out," Panacea said. "Artemis, Hephaestus, and I will stand with you if there is any backlash. But I doubt there will be once Zeus understands how bad things have gotten. Alena will show him what he has to do, and Hera will be dealt with."

"He's a coward," I said, and Hermes flinched as if I'd struck him. I wasn't going to apologize.

"No, he's a survivor," Yaya said. "As we all are to some degree or another."

I didn't like her defending him, mostly because I didn't think he was anything of the sort. "More like an opportunist," I muttered, but Yaya still heard me and gave me a dirty look.

Panacea motioned for me to follow her, but a figure in the doorway stopped us. Smithy stood with a handful of clothes. "Here, they are my wife's, but I believe they will fit you."

I nodded, somehow feeling like I'd betrayed him. "Thank you." I took the clothes, and our hands brushed. He paused, and his eye searched mine, intense and serious.

"Are you sure?" He asked the question, and it had so many layers, three simple words.

Was I sure? Not really, but I knew that I'd been held back my whole life. The last thing I needed was another person telling me I wasn't capable. That I couldn't do what I set out to accomplish.

"Yes, I'm sure. You . . . You've been a good friend, Smithy. I can't thank you enough for that." I knew he deserved more than that. I closed the distance and looked up at him, close enough to kiss. He stared down but didn't touch me. "Another place, another time . . . I think . . . I think it would have worked. But not here, not now with the cards we've both been dealt."

He nodded, the whisper of a smile on his lips. "Yes, I think you're right. The vampire, do you think he will come for you?"

I closed my eyes, my heart tugging at me with the thought of Remo. "I don't know. I can't count on it. I can't. Not when so many lives depend on me making the right choices."

Smithy's mouth twitched again, but his eyes were sad. "Well, I think you're going to have to decide."

"Not for a while." I stepped back, clutching the clothes to me.

The smell of cinnamon and honey floated to my nose, and I closed my eyes. Not now, not here. No wonder Smithy had looked at me that way.

A soft footstep, and then a hand I knew all too well turned me around gently. I kept my eyes closed. "Remo, what are you doing here?"

"Begging forgiveness, for you to understand I was trying to keep you and your family safe."

I still didn't open my eyes. I knew what would happen. I'd forgive him, and he'd have gotten away with treating me like a second-class citizen. "Not good enough."

Panacea and my yaya gasped together, and Smithy chuckled. "That a girl, make him suffer."

Remo grunted as if I'd hit him. I opened my eyes and backed up, right into Smithy. He didn't touch me, but he was at my back. He had my back, just as any good friend would. I stared at Remo, drinking him in.

Remo looked like he hadn't slept in a week. I mean, if vampires really slept, something I wasn't sure of entirely. I took in his dark eyes rimmed in violet flickers, the curve of his lips, the silver fangs he had pierced through his chin, the short cropped dark hair; I took it all in and tried not to think about how much I wanted him to hold me. How much I wanted him to tell me that I could do it, that he believed in me. He'd been the only person in my life since I'd been turned who'd not doubted me. And I wanted him to hold me so I could cry and grieve my mother, truly letting out the sobs that even now built in my chest.

Remo was a safe place, and I'd lost it. All because he didn't want to tell me the truth about the vampire council, because he thought to keep me safe by hiding the truth. I steeled my back, dropped my towel, and jerked the clothes on a piece at a time. "What do you want, Remo?"

"You killed my brother."

Well, there was that. "It was a busy day. I baked a cake too," I said.

Behind me Smithy groaned. "Maybe don't piss off the vampire. I know you could take him, but do you really want to go there today?"

Smithy had a point, but then again *that* wasn't the point I was trying to make. If Remo had been with me, then I wouldn't have been the one to kill his brother. He could have done it himself and ended the territorial dispute *and* sent the vampire council back without having them get involved. Maybe.

I pulled my shirt over my head and poked my head out through the top. "Are you here to avenge his death? Because I'm on a bit of a time crunch. You can avenge it later, after I deal with Hercules, Zeus, the Hydra, and somehow bring my mom back from the dead—and don't forget I'm supposed to be baking for my parents' anniversary party, which is going to be difficult seeing as my bakery has been flattened and my mom is currently dead." That image stuck with me, and I bit my lower lip to keep the tears back.

Remo took three strides and grabbed me, pulling me tight against him, his lips on mine as I squeaked. The touch and taste of his mouth smoothed away some of the fear, some of the hurt. He pulled back a little and pressed his forehead against mine. "I pushed you away to protect you from the vampires, to protect you from Santos. It had nothing to do with appearances; I could care less what species you are."

"You sure about that?" Smithy asked, voicing the question I had rumbling around in my head.

Remo nodded. "Yes, I'm sure. I walked away thinking you would be safer without me. That it was my fault you were having to face Santos. He was the one who called the council, not me. They could have come and decided you are a bigger threat than even Santos, and they would have actively gone after your head. Do you understand?"

Crap on a stack of crispy crackers, he didn't know? "Did Santos's vampires not come to you?"

He frowned. "They did, but I turned them away."

I grabbed his arms. "Tell me you at least let them speak to you. That you let Lee speak to you."

He shook his head. "No. If I'd taken them into my gang in front of the council . . . it would not have gone well for anyone. Wait, how do you know any of their names?"

I groaned. "The council . . . Santos sent them the fennel oil and said I was the threat, that they should come after me because if I could kill him, I could wipe out vampires."

"Sweet mother of—" Remo swayed where he stood. "Alena, we have to get you out of here. We have to get you out of the country."

"No, I can't leave." I shook my head. "I have a responsibility to this city, to my family."

Pain seemed to lance through him, his face twisting up with it.

Yaya cleared her throat. "I think I can help with this."

We all turned to look at her, and I fully admit I was skeptical. "How?"

"I will go to the vampire council; I've dealt with them in the past. We will negotiate the terms of their stay."

My jaw dropped. "What *exactly* do you mean you've 'dealt' with them before?"

"Not like that, you bratty girl." She waved a hand at me. "There have been altercations between vampires and the pantheon before, though they aren't well documented." She nodded as if it was decided. "I may not be able to stop them, Alena. But I can hold them off you for a space of time."

She cupped my face and then kissed my cheeks. "Be careful, and be brave. *And remember Orpheus.*" Those last three words were not even spoken out loud, just mouthed against my cheek.

I hugged her, and then she stepped away from me and went out the door.

The others pulled back and slipped out of the room and closed the door behind them.

I stared at Remo, wondering if he was going to walk out on me again. "Why didn't you just tell me about the council?"

"They were watching me, and they had already pegged you for elimination. I was desperate to keep you safe."

Remo tugged me closer as if he could make us a single flesh. "I truly was trying to protect you. The council can have my vampires beheaded for standing with you against Santos. They don't understand that he stopped being my brother the second he chose to become a monster."

I blinked up at him, his words echoing through me. *"He chose to become a monster."* I nodded, understanding.

Remo kissed me softly, and I let him, tears falling. "I don't want you to be beheaded, or Dahlia, or any of my people."

I gasped. "Tell me you didn't punish her."

"I locked her up, but they don't know that there is a way out of the cell that Dahlia is more than aware of." He smiled and laughed softly. "I don't want to lose my head either."

"Do you think Yaya will be able to keep them busy?" I asked, doing my best to keep my mind on the situation at hand and not on the hands on my body.

He nodded. "I have no doubt that if anyone can, she can. Besides that, the city over the Wall seems to be at the epicenter of the Aegrus virus. The council is turning people away left and right, but even they are not strong enough to keep up the pace."

I shivered, thinking of a world that had more vampires than humans in it. That would be a bad day for all involved. Remo nodded.

"Yes, it's a bad idea, but they think they are going to get the upper hand. We have to stop the virus, Alena. We have to. It will halt the turning of humans into vampires on top of all the other problems it is causing."

"We have to get to Zeus, then. Or at least I do." I pulled away from him a little. "Hermes, I'm ready to go."

Remo wove his fingers through mine. "I'm coming with you."

"You can't," I said with a frown. "Hermes can only take one person with him. Trust me to get Zeus. I will be back as soon as I can, and then . . . we will face this together. All of it. But only if you stop treating me like I can't fight on my own. There are enough people in my life who believe me incapable. The last person I expected to fall into that category was you."

He nodded. "I never thought you incapable, Alena. I thought I was going to lose you. There is a difference."

He kissed me a third time, hard, as though he would drink me down. I kissed him back with everything I had in me, fierce emotions flowing hot between us, every desire and pent-up emotion breaking through into our lips and tongues as they tangled with one another. He pushed me back gently, and my knees hit the edge of the bed, and I fell backward, him on top of me. His body was hard and muscled, strong and safe. The fear that I wouldn't have him in my life whispered at my heels, urged me to make him mine.

"I don't want to lose you again, Alena. These last few days . . . it felt like a piece of my soul had wandered away from me, taking the best of me with it." He nuzzled against my neck, kissing and nipping, pulling soft sounds from me. I swallowed hard and gently pushed him back. This was Smithy's bed. I couldn't . . . "I can't. Not here, not now."

He shook himself and pulled back. "I lose myself when I am with you."

"The feeling is mutual." I smiled and then swallowed hard. If I was going to do this, I needed to do it now. The more time I spent in Remo's arms, the more the rest of the world disappeared.

"Hermes, I'm ready to go," I said again.

Remo helped me stand as Hermes zipped into the room, wringing his hands. "You're going to get me killed. Or worse, fired," he spluttered out.

Ernie ducked through the door. I pointed at Remo. "You two stick together."

"Wait, I can come with you," Ernie said, but I was already shaking my head.

"Not this time. I need to do this by myself, or Zeus will never believe I can take Hera on. He needs to see that I'm strong enough all on my own."

Remo nodded. "Go, and come back to me." He raised my hand to his mouth and kissed the back of it, his tongue flicking along my skin in a shiver of promise.

Remo had me. He'd always had me, and I couldn't deny it any more than I could deny myself my next breath of air.

I looked at Hermes, and he held out his hand. "Okay, if we're really going to do this, then hang on and don't let go. Got it?"

I tightened my fingers around his. "I'm ready."

CHAPTER 10

There was a lurching jerk, and the room around me was gone as Hermes and I sped through the window and above Seattle with a single whoosh of his tiny wings. The cold air didn't bite, but I could feel it course along my skin as Hermes towed me along behind him, like he was trying to get a kite high into the air. "You are going to get me in trouble, Drakaina."

"We can just say I threatened you, that you were afraid I would hurt you." I couldn't help staring down as we skimmed along, above the city and then above the Wall. For a moment I thought maybe I could see Tad at house thirteen, but then we were gone from that section so fast I was probably seeing things.

"Hermes." I squeezed his hand. "I need you to take me somewhere else first before we go to Zeus."

"What, did you forget a change of underwear?"

I thought he was teasing at first, and then he glanced down at me, completely serious.

"No! I'm not sleeping with Zeus. But I need to find someone else first."

He groaned. "Seriously?"

"Please, it could mean saving my mother."

His wings slowed and with them so did our speed. "Damn it, I'm a sucker for a sob story. But who do you think can help you save your mom?"

"Orpheus?" I said it like a question because I wasn't entirely sure that the information I was getting from Yaya was right. Or good.

But I had to try, and Orpheus was the only name I'd been given.

Hermes spluttered, and we drifted downward. "Orpheus? What in Hades do you want with that nutcase?"

Nutcase? Yaya hadn't said anything about him being crazy. I swallowed hard before I answered. "Just . . . can you take me to him?" I was going to trust Yaya, even if Orpheus *was* crazy. Even if I wasn't sure I could trust her. I had to believe she would do what she could to help me bring my mom back.

Hermes tread air, his wings barely moving. He didn't look down. "Why, Alena?"

"Because." I had nothing else. Because it might be a total waste of time. Because I wanted my mom back now that we had finally started to move beyond the past. Because I wanted to believe my yaya wouldn't steer me wrong.

Because.

His head drooped. "He's on the way." He turned west and zipped along at a good clip once more. In no time we were out over open water and approaching a large island. We skimmed the trees as the rain fell around us, soaking my hair and clothes.

"I really hope you know what you're doing," Hermes muttered.

Of course I didn't, but he didn't need to know that.

He began to lower us through the spitting clouds, and a midsize lake came into view. I thought I caught a glimpse of a name on a battered wooden sign. "Westwood Lake."

"He's there on the dock," Hermes said, dropping me off in the sand of the beach. I stumbled in the wet footing until my feet were at the edge of the water. The dock was only about fifty feet out and bobbed here and there, the water sloshing around it. On the rickety wooden planks stood a man with long grizzled hair that was twisted up in dreadlocks, though I suspected they weren't done that way for fashion so much as for lack of care. There was the sound of singing from all around him, but I wasn't sure if it was just him or not.

"Excuse me, Orpheus?" I called out. The singing stopped, and the sound of several fish jumping splashed through the air. I could have dove in and swam to him, but the dark water didn't look all that inviting. Something about it made me shiver and back out of the gently lapping edge of it.

Slowly, Orpheus turned to face me. "Who calls to me?"

I opened my mouth to say my name, but what came out was not me. "Drakaina. I seek your help."

Nope, that was not me at all.

Orpheus stepped to the edge of the dock, tipping it so that I could see the holes in the deck of it. "What help need you of me, siren?"

I pulled my words together, feeling the importance of this moment. If I said things wrong, I had no doubt I would lose whatever hold I had here. "A priestess of Zeus sent me to you."

He grunted. "Damn interfering busybodies. Why would a priestess send you to me, though?"

"My mother was killed, and I want to bring her back from Hades," I said, and he began to laugh softly.

"Oh, gods. Not that again. It's not possible. They tempted me with a possibility, that my sweet wife would sleep in my arms again. But they lied; they never intended to give her back." He spoke as though the volume of his voice were on a roller coaster up and down so that he went from shouting to whispers all in a single sentence. I frowned and clenched my hands into fists.

Around us the softest of singing started up again, and I couldn't help but startle. There, around the edge of the dock, were eyes peering out of the water. Eyes attached to heads that maybe were attached to mermaids . . . but I'd met a mermaid before. They had teeth like sharks, and I had no doubt not all of them were nice.

The creatures slid through the water toward me, and I almost took a step back. I opened my mouth and let my fangs drop down as a hiss rolled out of me, coursing along the water's surface. "Do not push me. I bite," I said. The mermaids stopped moving in my direction and instead slid under the dark water. By the ripples, it looked like they went back the way they'd come, but I could not be sure.

"Be careful," Hermes said from behind my right shoulder. I didn't need him to tell me that, but I did appreciate his concern.

I raised my voice. "How do I bring my mother back, Orpheus?"

"A simple thing, so simple you will not believe, and that is why you will fail." He sobbed a moment and shook his head.

Around me I could feel time slipping away. I weighted what came out of my mouth with the power of a siren, knowing that Orpheus did want to help. I could see it in him, only he was afraid.

"Tell me what I must do to save my mother from Hades."

His head rolled back. "A flower, offer her a flower from the land of the living. She must take it from you and hold it all the way out. If one petal should fall, she will not . . ." He sobbed again and went to his knees. The singing began again, and Hermes dropped so that he was next to my head.

"I think we should go. When he's like this there is no talking to him."

I nodded and held my hand up to Hermes. He grabbed hold of me, and once more we swept into the sky. Orpheus was right; I didn't believe him. A flower? I had to offer my mother a flower in order to bring her back from the dead. That was . . . ridiculous.

But no matter how strange, I would do it. For now, though, I would put it from my mind and focus on Zeus. Zeus and the virus first, and then I could go after Mom.

We flew up through the edges of the Rocky Mountains, staying on their western side. An hour slipped by, and as the time flew, so did the snow. Snowflakes swirled around us as we skimmed through the air. I didn't close my eyes, but stared, unable to believe the speed at which we traveled. I said as much to Hermes. He laughed. "This is slow. You're slowing me down, Drakaina. Normally it would take me maybe a few minutes, not a couple of hours."

An hour and a half brought us to the outskirts of a large forest, covered in snow, silent and ominous, but my mind was still back on a dark lake, hearing Orpheus sob. I focused on what was in front of me. The trees were clumped together and held the snow above them in a white canopy that looked like a painting, it was all so still. I couldn't see the ground, even as we raced toward it. I held my breath, thinking we were going to slam into the trees, but Hermes ducked down and wove us through them easily.

"This time I have to drop you farther back. We go our separate ways here, and then you can find your way to his cabin. That will keep me out of this. He'll just think you found him on your own."

He let go of me before I could protest that he hadn't been bothered by Orpheus knowing that he'd helped me. Then again, who would believe a crazy old man? Not me. I hit the snow and sank up to my midthigh in the thick white cold. Hermes was gone in a flash of wings. "Wait!"

He ignored me and kept going. Dang it all. This was not what I'd been hoping for. I struggled to get out of the snow, grabbed a small tree, and used it to pry myself free. The top of the snow was actually hard enough I could walk on it if I was careful. Like a pie crust done to the perfect crispness and coated in sugar, it didn't break unless I really pushed hard or stumbled.

I stared around me as I walked, noting that the birds fell silent as I approached. I grimaced. "I'm not that kind of snake."

Of course, there was no answer. They didn't know that I wasn't going to eat them in one jaw-unhinged bite. I moved from tree to tree, using the trunks as props to keep from sliding back into the snow, and the snow around the trees was thinner too. The cold and wet soaked through my jeans and made each step that much more difficult, only raising my ire. My breath misted and fogged in front of my face, freezing in the air in tiny droplets. Maybe I could survive the extreme cold, but that didn't mean I liked it. Not for one dang second. I rubbed my hands over my arms and drew in a big breath. The smell of woodsmoke pulled me forward. Hermes had said that Zeus had a cabin, so it made sense to head in the direction of the smoke.

I hurried my steps, wanting the warmth, but wanting to get to Zeus more. How I was going to convince him, I had no idea, but I *was* going to convince him. One way or another.

"There is no try. There is do or do not," I whispered to myself, warming to the words. Yoda had it right. There was no try; I could do this. I was *going* to do this.

I wove my way through a thicket of frozen brambles and trees, and stepped out into a clearing where a cabin stood. Okay, "cabin" might have been an understatement. The structure was two stories high, and from what I could see it was probably five thousand square feet on each floor, and that was being conservative. I shook my head. "Hardly a hideout, Zeus."

There was a grunt to my right, and I spun away out of sheer instinct as a spear slid right through where I'd been standing. A Bull Boy stared back at me, his eyes slowly widening as recognition settled in. I'd faced his kind when I'd first been turned into a Drakaina. Half man, half bull, they'd been Achilles's thugs and a major pain in the patoot.

"Don't kill me!" He threw his hands over his head and went to his furred knees.

At least he wasn't going to try to fight me. "What are you doing here? Helping Zeus?" I asked.

"He gave me a job. I needed one after Achilles went down." He shook where he knelt. "You aren't going to kill me?"

"Not unless you give me reason to," I snapped, using my best kick-the-kids'-butts-into-eating-veggies Yaya voice. "I need to speak with Zeus."

"He's not going to like that you're here," Bull Boy muttered.

I put my hands on my hips and stared down at him. "I don't care. Take me to him."

He got off his knees and stumbled away from me for the first few steps. His wide eyes kept flicking back to me, as if he expected me to shift into my snake form and eat him right there. "I was at the stadium," he said. Well, that made the weird looks make sense. The stadium had been the place of my showdown with Achilles, and the Bull Boys there had taken a pretty good beating. Mind you, I had too. But I'd put Achilles out of commission in front of everyone. Something that no monster had ever done before.

I hunched my shoulders. "I hate fighting."

He blinked several times. "Me too. It's why I held back. You're good at it, though. You have a good instinct. I don't. As you can maybe tell." He laughed, the pitch high and wobbly. He swallowed the last of his laughter down in a large gulp.

I followed him through the open area and up onto the front porch of the cabin mansion. I thanked him and then waved him away. I could do this part on my own at least. I thought about knocking on the door. No, not this time; I needed Zeus to see me as strong, as strong enough to give me some credit. I put my hand on the doorknob and twisted it hard. It wasn't even locked. I shook my head and stepped in.

"Well, we were wondering when you were going to get here," Zeus called out, and I blinked at the oversized bed that dominated the main entrance of the house. There were limbs in every direction, and lots of skin. Lots and lots of skin. Oh my Lord in heaven. I'd walked in on an orgy.

I stilled my squeamish side, tried to soothe the fire burning in my cheeks. I cleared my throat. "I highly doubt that you were waiting on me, Zeus."

His head jerked up out of the pile of bodies, his eyes as wide as the Bull Boy's had been. "Drakaina? What are you doing here?"

How was I going to play this? How was I going to convince him that he had to help? His ego was the size of the entire world . . . *the world* . . . The thoughts rumbled around, bouncing in my skull like tiny Ping-Pong balls as they fought to show me the idea. And there it was. The way to convince him.

I put my hands on my hips. "I'm here to . . . to kick your ass into gear. The world needs you, Zeus. The world. Not me. Not Hera, not Seattle. The world."

Zeus stared at me, then frowned, his brows creasing. "How did you find me?"

"I was told you'd head for the hills. Panacea said you always go north." I didn't want to implicate poor Hermes in this if I didn't have to, but Panacea could take care of herself. I hoped. Surprising me, the messenger floated to my shoulder.

"I brought her. She's right, boss. The world needs you. Not like this, humping anything that moves and managing the Blue Box Store. We need the Zeus that defeated the Titans to show back up and kick ass," Hermes said.

I wanted to hug him for standing up with me. I had a feeling his words as a neutral party held more weight than Ernie's would have if he'd been with me. Zeus shoved a few bodies off him and stood up. His potbelly was gone, and I didn't look lower than that. It took an effort not to blush, to pretend only that I needed his help and he wasn't standing there completely naked with a mass of hands and mouths working their way up his legs.

"As you can see, I'm on . . . vacation." He pointed at the bed and then swept his hand outward. "I don't think the world needs me at all."

That was what he said, but I heard the doubt in his voice. I forged on, as if I were making a ten-tiered cake that threatened to topple. If I got it right, I'd have a masterpiece, and if I balanced it wrong, the entire thing would come toppling down. I strode forward and met him as he stepped off the bed.

"You *do* care about this world, don't act otherwise. I know you do. And we both know I'm not wrong."

He smiled, but it was tired and more than a bit cynical with the way his lips twisted off to one side. "You are so young and stupid, Drakaina. This world wants nothing more than to be coddled. I don't do coddling. None of the pantheon does."

I dared to grab his arm, right around the biceps, and dig my fingers in hard. "Here's the thing: you would be in charge of the Super Dupers. They are the ones who need you. And besides that, if you don't come back, Hera is going to win. She'll take the throne of Olympus, and where will you be then? Just a sorry excuse of an ex-husband begging for scraps from her table."

He pointed at the floor, and I mistakenly followed the motion before snapping my eyes back up to his grinning face, though his eyes sparkled with anger. "I will be right here, enjoying the favors of whoever would like to be in my bed. Would you care to test out the mattress with me? I bet I could show you a thing or two that vampire hasn't."

I rolled my eyes. "Zeus. You are better than all this. You were a god once, so why are you running from it now?"

He yanked out of my hand. "Because no one wants the gods alive. We ruled hard and fast, we took as we pleased, and I won't go back to wanting that and not having it."

I didn't understand. "Why can there not be a middle ground? We can find a balance, Zeus. If I can find a way to be a good monster, you can be a good and fair god. Right?"

He laughed and rubbed his hand over his face. "Let me be very clear, then. I need more of the pantheon on my side. Hera has been building this plan of hers for far longer than I even realized. I am too . . . late to turn the tables on her."

I grabbed him again, and Hermes groaned. I yanked Zeus so we were nose to nose. "You have some of the pantheon on your side, you fool. And you have me on your side."

His eyes flickered with lightning, and the air around us charged. "And my son?"

I blinked, wondering who he meant for a split second. "Hercules?"

"That would be the one," he drawled.

"He seems . . . conflicted." I tried to blink away the sudden tears. "He helped dig my mother out of the bakery."

As if that would explain everything. I fought the growing onslaught of tears, the image of my mother suddenly right in front of me, and I was unable to shake it. I tried to turn away from Zeus, but he caught me by the arms. "Tell me what happened, Drakaina."

The story spilled out in spits and starts until the end, when I told him that his son had helped me move the cement blocks, that Hercules had apologized for my mother's death.

"I don't think he wants to help Hera, but he's in charge of the Hydra. Why would he help her after all she's done to him?" I wiped at my face, and someone handed me a tissue. I blew my nose and used a clean edge of my shirt to wipe away the last of my tears.

Zeus sighed. "Hercules . . . he is complicated. He wants everyone to like him, and that isn't possible. But mostly, he wanted his stepmother to like him."

"But why would that be so important? You know that hating your stepmother is a normal thing in the human world, right?" I wiped my nose and clutched the tissue in my hand.

"Because he never knew his birth mother. She died, and Hera was all he had. I didn't see what she was doing, how she was hurting him, until it was far too late." He shook his head. "She played us against one another for years, all because . . ."

126

"Because she was angry at you," I finished for him. He grunted.

"Yes. Bitter. She's been bitter for far longer than I ever realized."

My heart hurt for Hercules. I couldn't help it, and I could see now why helping me dig my mother out of the rubble had been something he would do. If he couldn't hold his own mother and say good-bye, then he could help me. None of that changed what I was facing, though. What Zeus was facing.

I reached out and put a hand on his bare shoulder. "Will you step up, Zeus? Will you help me stop Hera?"

He was quiet, something so unlike him I almost wondered if I'd pushed him too far.

"Who all do you believe is on my side?" Zeus strolled away from me, clenching his butt cheeks several times, changing the mood in an instant. I glanced at Hermes, who shrugged.

"Nothing I can do about it," the flying messenger said.

Zeus bypassed the bed and went to a large dining room table I'd not seen beyond the mass of still-writhing and occasionally groaning bodies. He took a wooden chair, spun it around, and sat on it. He spread his legs and leaned forward to put his elbows on his knees.

I didn't look away; instead I just raised an eyebrow and answered his question. "Artemis. Panacea. Smithy."

"You mean Hephaestus?" Zeus's lips quirked, and I ignored the subtle implication.

"I mean Smithy. Ernie. Me. Sandy."

He frowned. "Who is Sandy? You say her name like I should know her."

"The surviving Stymphalian bird." I took a breath and tried to think who else there was. Not too many more. "Remo, and his vampires if we need them. I'm sure I could get the SDMP on board."

Hermes zipped forward. "You know, you need Hades on your side. Your brother could help you turn the tide. The rest of the pantheon is just watching, waiting to see who will take the throne before they declare their allegiance."

"Why?" I blurted out even as I put the ingredients together. "So they won't fall with whoever loses?"

Zeus nodded. "Yes. But . . . Hermes is right. If Hades would side with me, the others would fall into line."

"Then talk to him."

"Well, that's not going to happen," Hermes muttered.

"Why not?" I wished I had paid more attention to my Greek mythology.

Zeus rubbed a hand over his chin. "Simple. I'm the one who bound him to the underworld."

Hermes nodded. "And if the rumors are true, Hera has promised him the one thing he craves."

Zeus's blue eyes were as serious as I'd ever seen them.

"Let me guess," I said. "She's offered him freedom?"

Zeus nodded and pointed a finger at me. "Bingo."

CHAPTER 11

"Do you think you could put some clothes on? I'm getting a crick in my neck staring at the ceiling," I said. Zeus strolled by me, and I stepped back. "Seriously? I thought you didn't like the cold."

He shook his head. "I don't."

"Then why do you always run north when things get ugly?" I bent and grabbed a pair of pants from the floor and flung them at Zeus. He caught them in midair, then slowly put them on. I wasn't sure if he was being reluctant or still trying to put on a show. The last hop he took to get his butt into them made me think it was more the latter. Typical Zeus.

The wink over his shoulder sealed it. "I run north because, while I don't like the cold, it's an incentive to stay inside and out of view. Of course, I didn't think I'd have to worry about Hermes invoking his messenger license to bring me a visitor."

Hermes flew backward, and I immediately put myself between them. "I forced his hand, Zeus."

He gave me a dismissive wave. "I'll deal with him later, seeing as technically he didn't break any rules. Right now, we need to get you to the underworld."

"What?" I squawked. "I don't know anything about the underworld. Or Hades. I can't go." Wait . . . my mom was there. And Orpheus had said that if I took a flower, maybe I could get her back. I looked around the room. No flowers here. No, Orpheus was mad, out of his mind. My yaya had to have been wrong; there was no way to bring my mom back. I knew it in my heart that there was no changing what had happened.

That kind of magic didn't exist.

"I didn't ask you if you wanted to go; I said you're going. If you are on my side, you will do as I say. I will run this show, not you," Zeus drawled as he tugged a white button-down shirt over his head.

"You could have unbuttoned that," I pointed out.

"I'm lazy," he said.

I burst out laughing, unable to keep it in. "Well, that's the first honest thing I've heard come out of your mouth." He glared at me, but I didn't stop smiling. "I'm not going to the underworld. Hercules and the Hydra are the ones I'm dealing with. You deal with your brother. We need to split our forces carefully."

"Shrew," he grunted.

"Show-off," I bit back.

He glanced at Hermes. "Take her back to Seattle. I'll go chat with Hades and see what I can do. Then I will meet with those who support me at the Blue Box."

Hermes zipped to my side, and I lifted a hand and gripped his foot. There was no time for any other words, as we were off and flying through the air. The time passed quickly, and it wasn't long before we were back in Seattle, touching down at house number thirteen.

"Hermes, I need to find everyone and bring them up to speed . . ."

"They are all here. You might think you live in that big house on the other side of the Wall, but your signature is here. This is where your people are waiting for you," he said.

I let go of his foot, expecting him to zip off, but he didn't leave. "You sticking around, then?"

"Looks like a big fight is coming, Drakaina . . . and . . . you're right. I need to choose a side too." His lips twisted up. "I'm with you. Not Hera. Not Zeus. I'm with you."

My lips trembled, and I held a hand up to him. "Thank you." He took my fingers, turned my hand over, and kissed the back of it, and then he gave me a shy smile. "Don't tell anyone. I can be your spy."

I smiled back and nodded. "Just be careful. I don't want you to get hurt on my behalf."

He shot ahead of me, but something held me back from going in. At the door I stood. There were several heartbeats I recognized, and I could smell cinnamon and honey, even through the door. Which meant Remo was there along with Tad, Yaya, Sandy, and Ernie.

I looked down the street toward Merlin's house. There were cars parked all over the road and his lawn, even right up to his door. Now that was weird. I jogged down the steps of number thirteen and hurried to Merlin's. Surely he wasn't having a party when there was so much going on . . . then again, it was Merlin we were talking about.

As I got closer, people started getting out of the cars, lurching toward me like B-movie zombies. A woman with dusky skin and huge brown eyes approached me. She wore a hat, but even with it I could see that her hair was falling out.

"Are you Merlin? No . . . you're the girl from the TV!" She grabbed me, her hands strong despite the obvious fragility of her body. I put my hands over hers, not afraid so much as upset.

"You have the Aegrus virus, don't you?" I asked.

She sobbed, and I caught her against my body. I knew what it was to be denied the simplest of human touch when that was all you wanted.

Around me, people circled, all of them in various stages of the virus. I realized then that I could smell it hovering around me, like a burnt caramel, sickly sweet, death curling its grasp tight around them. "Merlin isn't here?"

"We can't get in. The door is steel," someone said.

Of course it was. I gently took the woman's hands from me. "Let me see if I can get it open." Damn Merlin. I thought he was better than this. And what the H-E-double-hockey-sticks had happened that all these people were not only sick, but not in quarantine?

I ran to the door and with one well-placed kick busted it down. The door banged open, the handle and lock torn from it. I stormed inside, ready to drag Merlin out by his heels to help . . . but the second I stepped inside I knew the place was empty except for one person, and it wasn't Merlin. I could smell her. She sat at the table, her blond-and-black ringlets cascading down her back as she played with a deck of cards.

I jerked to a stop and immediately braced myself for her to launch at me.

"Oh, please. Don't act like you know how to fight." She snorted and carefully dealt out a hand of solitaire. "You know, everyone is laughing at you."

"I don't know your name, unless Hercules was right," I said, eyeing her up and down. I'd seen her in her human form only once, when Merlin had shown her to me, to warn me that he'd raised a Hydra.

Her eyes flicked to me, black as night, as though there was no soul in her. Maybe that was just my imagination.

"You can call me Angel, that's my prison name." She flicked a card over and slid it into a pile. I didn't dare take my eyes from her. She had a strange heartbeat; it sounded like there were multiple hearts in her chest . . . nine, to be exact.

"Why aren't you attacking me?"

"I underestimated you. It won't happen again. I want to talk. I want you to know that I am going to enjoy killing you." She grinned at me, flashing a mouthful of sharp teeth. The Drakaina rolled through me, and I couldn't help flashing my own set of hardware, the fangs curling down from the top of my mouth and hanging low past my chin.

Angel laughed and shook her head. "Your venom is powerful shit. I'm still healing, if you must know. Hercules thinks he's in charge of me, but he's a tool." She leaned back in her chair. "I was born to be a killer; I'm good at it. If you hadn't noticed." She winked. "Dear Mommy went down in a heap, didn't she?"

I didn't relax my stance, anger growing. "You will—"

"Pay for that? Oh, please. We both know you're a weakling. You would have died if your friends hadn't helped you. I, on the other hand, healed on my own. I'm a survivor, Drakaina. Unlike you. Do you know I killed my whole family?"

I clenched my fists, doubt riding me hard. Could I take her? I wasn't sure. "Is that why you were in prison?"

She grinned. "No, I never got caught for that. I fed them to the pigs and buried their teeth after they were shit out."

Cold chills swept through me, and for the first time I was afraid. Angel wasn't like Achilles or Theseus, or even Hercules. She was a true psychopath.

She was nodding to herself. "Yes, that was fun. I meant to kill your mom too, if you must know. It was no accident." She winked at me and grinned again. Her eyes . . . wobbled, for lack of a better word. Like they all of a sudden couldn't look at the cards, or me, or anything completely as they sought out something that wasn't there. All the monsters had their weaknesses, and it hit me suddenly what Angel's was.

"Having trouble with nine sets of eyes stuck in one head, huh?" I knew I would have a chance, if I was brave enough to take it. I knew her weakness, and in her human form, I would have a chance to take her.

She glared at me, or tried to with her wobbling eyes. I flicked my left hand out to the side, and she followed the movement. I took the opening. I leapt at her, smashing into her body and taking us both crashing to the floor.

She screeched as we went down, and I jammed a hand up and under her jaw, pinning her head back to the floor. Her legs wrapped around my waist as her hands scrabbled at my arms, huge gouges drawn through both layers of skin. I hissed at her, and her bottomless black eyes met mine.

"You don't deserve to live," I whispered. "You killed my mom." I choked on the words.

"I'd do it again," she snarled back at me.

I saw her start to shift, and I pulled her head up. If I could knock her out, I could keep her from—

Something slammed into *my* head from the side, sending me flying off Angel. I hit the wall and slid down as I struggled to get my bearings. The world spun as though I'd been on a carnival ride for days.

"Get up, Angel. I told you we weren't attacking her until I was sure it was the right thing to do."

Hercules. That was Hercules. And his shield.

I blinked in time to see him yanking her off the floor and putting her over his shoulders. His eyes met mine and he nodded. "We will meet on the battlefield, Drakaina. But not today. I need to be sure of things before we fight again. Two days from now, we will face each other to decide the fate of the world."

I pushed myself up and stumbled after them. They disappeared into the crowd of sick people . . . and protestors.

"Oh my God, what are you all doing?" I put a hand to my head. Hercules's shield had rung my bell something fierce. Something about heroes' weapons really hit home hard.

I recognized the protestors in front of Merlin's because of the petite leader with the dark curls and Irish lilt to her voice as she distributed water, food, and blankets. I'd met her at the Wall only a week or so before and saved her from a rampaging werewolf.

"What are you doing?" I repeated as I drew closer.

She smiled up at me. "Doing what we can. This disease . . . we've all got it. It's just a matter of time."

A chill swept through me as I took in the pallor of her skin, the dullness in her eyes. "No! How?"

"It's . . . on a rampage, it seems. Drakaina . . . you said you would be the guardian of this city." Her eyes filled with tears. "That you would protect us all."

I struggled to breathe. "Yes. I did."

"Can you stop this virus? It isn't natural, is it?"

Hercules's words echoed in my head. Two days before he would come looking for me. Maybe that would be enough time to stop the virus? The options were few, but I knew I had to try. She was right; I'd claimed to be the city's guardian, and it was time to live up to it in more ways than just playing Godzilla games with the Hydra and Hercules. "Stay here. I will . . . I will stop this."

The words slipped out of me as I turned and ran down the street toward house number thirteen. I burst through the door to find my friends waiting for me. All of their faces were turned to me, surprise written all over them.

I drew a big breath. "New plan. Hercules and the Hydra will wait. I have to stop the Aegrus virus."

CHAPTER 12

My group of friends and family stared at me with collective eyebrows lifted and lips clamped shut.

"Well, don't all jump up at once and tell me I can do it." I laughed, but the sound was bitter like dark chocolate, even to my ears.

I looked around, shocked to see Yaya for more than one reason. "I thought you were going to the vampire council, Yaya?"

"I did. And they sent me away. Though I believe they are preoccupied with all those who are dying of the virus right now." She shook her head, looking younger than ever. If another ten years were taken from her, she'd be closing in on my age bracket. I frowned, thinking of all the possibilities again when it came to her motivation. The one I liked the least being that she had somehow been involved in all the things that had happened to me. No, I wasn't going there.

She took my hands in hers and stared up at me. "Alena, you are not a doctor, you're not a warlock, and as much as I want to tell you that you can stop the virus, I'm not going to lie to you." Her blue eyes were intent, without a single flicker of deceit in them. Yet the Drakaina in me whispered a single word.

Lies.

Yaya had lied to me for most of my life. I shot a look to Tad, and he nodded, urging me on. I held myself tight, coiled as if I were about to strike.

"Really? You've not had a problem lying to us in the past." I bit the words at her, and she dropped my hands.

"Yes, and as I've pointed out, that was to protect you."

"So why would this be any different?" I took a step back. The words spilled out of me in a torrent. "Yaya, of all the people in my life, you helped me find my feet at Vanilla and Honey. You told me I was worth the time and effort, you supported me in my sham of a marriage. Why would you stop supporting me now?"

She closed her eyes. "Because none of those things truly took you from me. None of them could kill you. This could, Alena. I've lost my daughter, do you think I want to lose my granddaughter too?"

I put a hand over my face and struggled through the tears. "But so many people are dying, Yaya. And letting them die won't bring Mom back." I took my hand away and stared at her. "I can't . . . I can't turn my back on them. This time . . . this time I really have to do this on my own, I think."

Sandy approached, her dark eyes searching my face. "You aren't the only monster here, Alena. You don't have to do this on your own."

They didn't understand, none of them truly did. Well, maybe one of them did. Remo's eyes met mine; those flickering violet colors made them look like cut gems. He gave me a small smile, and in it I found the backup I needed. Even now, he understood me better than anyone else did.

I swallowed hard. "Yaya, where does the virus originate? Is it Hera's doing?"

"That's just it, I don't know."

Lies. Again, I could almost taste them on the air.

"Really? You know I can tell you are lying, Flora." I used her given name for the first time, and she sucked in a sharp breath. I shook my head. "I don't know who to trust anymore."

Her eyes slowly closed, but not before I saw the hurt in them. I refused to be upset by her pain. Not today, not in that moment when she still wouldn't tell me the truth.

Trying to protect me was one thing, but not allowing me to make my own choices based on actual fact was entirely different.

My jaw ticked, and I paced into the kitchen. "I'm going to do some baking. Sandy, you want to work on a new-to-you recipe?" In other words, I needed to think.

"Yeah, let's do it," she said.

Sandy hurried in with me, and I directed her to get the ingredients I would need to make a cake I'd not put together in a long time. Not since before my father's parents had passed. They'd spent some of their earlier years in the South Pacific and had come back with a chocolate cake recipe that was to die for. But whenever I made it I thought of them and all the things they were missing out on in our lives, which made me avoid it . . .

"No eggs?" Sandy asked as she stood by the fridge.

"No eggs, no milk," I said. "Just grab the sifter; we need to run the dry ingredients through four times to get everything smooth."

She ran the hand-crank sifter as I put the flour and other ingredients through. I knew the recipe by heart despite rarely making it, and I didn't need to double-check anything. I went through the motions as we put the cake together, which allowed my mind to circle around the problem in front of me.

We knew Hera had something to do with the virus. And we knew that Merlin was also tied to her, but he was missing, apparently. There were more pieces missing than just Merlin, though. The problem was, I didn't have a clue as to what they could be. I tried not to think about the problem directly and instead just let my mind wander to see if I could stumble on the answer.

Unfortunately for me, letting my mind wander also allowed it to go to my mother's death, to holding her, pulling her from the rubble. Was she in the underworld now with Hades?

Was Orpheus right about bringing her back with a simple flower? Death. Hades. Virus. Zeus. Hera. Merlin. Everything was there, I just had to figure out how they mixed together, and then I'd know what was in the oven baking, so to speak. I stopped mixing the batter midstir, seeing the recipe in my mind begin to come together.

"Hades . . . he'll know what's going on; he's the one who is benefiting from all these people dying." I blurted the words out as I dumped the batter into a pan. Not only that, but maybe . . . maybe I could find my mom. God, I was afraid to hope for that, afraid to consider that possibility in case I failed. "Hermes, go tell Zeus I will talk to Hades after all." Hades would know something with all the souls coming his way, and maybe he'd even know how to stop it.

"You got it." He zipped away in a flash of light, and I slumped into a chair.

"But why would Hades want to stop the dead coming to him?" I asked myself softly. Why indeed? It made logical sense that the dead going to Hades would potentially benefit him, seeing that he ruled the underworld.

"Who are you talking about now, sis?" Tad jumped up so he could sit on the counter next to me. His green eyes were bright and clear of the hatred Theseus had put into them, but they were red rimmed from tears. From grief.

I took his hand and squeezed it gently. "Why would Hades want people to stop dying in droves? How am I going to convince him to help me?" I glanced up at him. "I doubt my siren abilities will work on him."

Tad scrunched up his face in thought. "I don't know. I'll come with you, if you want." He looked at me and then hurried to spit out the rest. "I think you can do it on your own. I just want you to know I'm here. If you need me."

Sweeter words couldn't have fallen from his lips. I took his other hand. "Thanks. But . . . I'm good. I'll need backup soon enough, but no point in getting us all sent to hell." I winked at him, and his mouth dropped.

"You said 'hell.'"

"That I did." I laughed, but it ended on something that was more of a sob. Hermes shot through the kitchen, sliding to a stop in midair.

His eyes were wide, and his sneakers were lit up with a faint red glow like he was literally on fire. "You aren't going to believe this," he panted. "Hades has imprisoned Zeus. The gods are flocking to Hera. If we don't get Zeus out quick, she's won. You've got to get to Hades, and fast."

The world seemed to tilt, and I clutched the table for support. This was not how it was supposed to go. "So I guess that means Hades was working with Hera all along. What do you want to bet he's behind the virus too?" The words slipped out of me, and I saw Yaya from the corner of my eye. She jerked, like I'd slapped her, confirmation that I was right. So there it was—Hades was behind the Aegrus virus. It made a twisted sort of sense, seeing as there would be power in the dead for him. He was, after all, the lord of the underworld. The more people he had in his thrall, the stronger he would be.

I pushed to my feet. "Hermes. Can you find Merlin?"

He closed his eyes, and from underneath the lids his eyes moved as if he were seeing things only he could see. "The hospital on Whidbey Island. The Aegrus ward."

Where Merlin and I had first met. I stood up and looked at my friends around me. Dahlia and Sandy stood beside one another, monsters like me and beautiful in more aspects than the view the world saw.

"I need to keep Hercules and the Hydra off me until I get back from dealing with Hades. Think you two can distract them if they show up before the two days he gave me?"

Dahlia gave me a slow, wicked grin. "Think Hercules could fend off a vampire bite?"

Sandy rolled her shoulders. "We'll draw them away from the city, maybe toward the valley?" She glanced at Remo, and he nodded.

"Out of the city would be best. Take them all the way to my compound if you can. We can hold them there. It will give the vampire council something to deal with."

I looked at Tad and Yaya. "Tad, I need you to go with me to Dad. We need him to know that we know he's a Super Duper and we need his help."

Tad's face was serious. "You think he can help?"

"I think if Mom was telling me the truth, our dad is a warlock in his own right. We need him to start turning people, because right now that is all we can do to help them. Start with those at Merlin's and then move outward from there."

There was a knock on the door, and we all froze. Everyone we knew was here. I made my way to the entrance and listened only for a split second before I flung it open. My dad stood there, his face lined with grief, his black hair sporting more than a few new strands of gray, his green eyes rimmed in red.

"Dad," I whispered, and then he was holding me, and I was sobbing, and Tad was there, and we just clung to each other. What was left of our family. For a moment I was a little girl again, and I could let my dad chase away the monsters from under my bed.

But now I was the monster, and I needed to stand up and fight for my family.

Dad patted my back and pushed me away gently. "I thought I overheard my name. I wanted to save you some trouble of coming all the way into Seattle."

I sniffed and frowned. "What? I don't understand."

He shrugged. "An old warlock trick."

My lips trembled. "I tried, Dad, I tried to save her."

He put both hands on my face, cupping it. "I know, baby girl." He drew in a big breath and nodded. "So you want me to start turning those who are sick?"

"Can you?" I was hoping.

"Yes. I'm rusty, but I can still do it. I'll use my uncle's place." He winked at me. His uncle's place. Merlin's home.

He pointed at Yaya. "Flora, you can help. Send a couple of your priestesses over to Merlin's."

She nodded and turned away. I couldn't help but notice that she'd not come to our tiny family group hug.

Tad clapped Dad on the shoulder. "I'll get Jensen. He can help round people up and keep the line moving."

Yaya came back into the room. "Alena, you are giving everyone else instructions; I assume you have something for me? Unless you distrust me that much?"

Another time I would have flinched at her words, but not anymore. "Gather the rest of your priestesses, like Dad asked, and any of the Super Dupers you can." I glanced at Remo. "Call the SDMP and see if they will listen to you. See if they will help us stand against Hera and whomever she has under her thumb."

They all nodded, and just like that, they headed out in various directions. I hurried upstairs to the bedroom, needing a moment to myself. My friends, my family, I was sending them away. I knew it was for the best, but it still was hard. Suddenly I could see their actions a little clearer. How many of them had separated themselves from me in order to keep me safe? Most of them, at one point or another.

And now I was doing the same thing. Some of the anger I'd been carrying faded with that insight. Sometimes we pushed those we loved away because it was best for them. Even when they didn't want to be saved.

I sat on the bed and took a big breath. I leaned back and closed my eyes. A few minutes of quiet was all I wanted.

A soft knock on the door brought my head up, but I already knew it was Ernie by the fast staccato of his heartbeat.

"Come in."

He opened the door and flew to sit beside me on the bed. Through the entire conversation downstairs he'd been rather quiet. Besides Remo he probably knew me the best.

"You're sending them away to protect them." He put a hand on my leg, and I nodded.

"I hate to ask, but I need something from you," I whispered.

"I wouldn't be anywhere but at your side, Drakaina." His blue eyes teared up, and I had to look away.

"Hermes."

The messenger zipped in through the open door. "What's the message?"

I opened a drawer in the dresser by the bed and pulled out a pen and pad of paper. I scribbled a note and handed it to him. "For Hercules."

The words were simple.

I'm going to try and stop the virus. I will meet you after that. Please don't hurt my friends. I know you aren't a bad guy. Don't let Hera make you do things you know are wrong.

Hermes nodded and was gone in a flash.

"How do you want to do this?" Ernie asked.

A footstep at the door snapped my head up. Remo leaned on one side of the doorframe. "Yes, Alena. How do you want to do this?"

Dang it, I was hoping I would be able to get through this without him realizing what I was up to.

143

CHAPTER 13

"I don't know what you're talking about." I lifted my chin, and Remo stepped into the room in complete defiance of what I thought was my obvious look that said, *Stay out*.

"I know what you're doing. They may not realize it, but you're sending them away to keep them safe. I should know, I did it to you," he said softly.

I kept my eyes on his. "And if I am? So what?"

"Why didn't you give me something to do? I mean, other than to make a single phone call."

He had a point. Then again, I had my own. "I knew that if anyone would guess, it would be you and Ernie." I paused. "Am I going to be able to get rid of you?"

His lips twitched. "No, you aren't."

"Then you can drive me to the hospital." I stood and went to the closet, searching for something that would be more suited to what I was going to do. Going into the underworld was no small task. I panned through until I found a pair of black jeans, knee-high black boots, and a black tank top. I took them and then glanced at Remo. "If you don't mind."

He grinned and waved a hand at me. "Not at all, you go right ahead. I'll keep an eye on you."

I blushed and pointed at the door. "Get out."

He backed out, standing in the hallway, still looking in. "Done."

The door remained open between us, and he grinned across the open space at me. I strode across the distance, grabbed the door, and slammed it in his face. Ernie snickered. "You have it so bad for him. You know he's seen you naked a number of times with your shifting."

"Shut up, Ernie. He can hear you," I said.

"That I can, beautiful, and I will amend that I have it rather bad for you too," Remo said from the hallway.

I shucked my clothes, blushing furiously, doing my best not to think about *just* how bad he had it for me. I hurriedly pulled on the black attire. It suited my mood and clung to my body without reserve.

"That's good for a fight. Means you won't get hung up on loose clothing," Ernie said. "You could use a jacket, though. See if there is anything in there that will cover your arms. If the council really has that fennel oil shit, you can peel out of a jacket before it eats through."

I looked back into the closet and found a leather jacket near the back, like it had been stuffed there and forgotten. I ran my hands over it, thinking. There were tears and cuts that had been stitched together over and over, as though it had been through its share of monsters and battles. I pulled it off the rack. Maybe wearing it would be good luck, seeing as it had obviously survived a lot. The tag at the back had two initials stitched into it. *RA.* I ran a thumb over the initials and felt a surge of confidence. Yes, this was the jacket I needed to wear. Whoever had had it before me . . . somehow I *knew* she had been a badass of epic proportions.

I slipped it on, and Ernie gave a low whistle. "Now you look like a tough-ass chick."

I laughed. "Looks can be deceiving, Ernie. Surely you know that by now."

From outside the door, Remo laughed quietly under his breath, but I heard him. I opened the door, and his eyes went wide. "Ernie is right, you look like you could take on an army of demons by yourself."

I snorted. "Let's not get crazy. How about we deal with Hades first?"

Remo led the way out to his muscle car, and I enjoyed the view of his broad shoulders tapering down to his hips and long legs. "You know you can't get his clothes off, no matter how hard you stare," Ernie stage-whispered.

I took a halfhearted swat at him. "Ernie, knock it off!" He dodged me easily, laughing.

Remo turned and winked at me, and it was the first time I saw the fatigue in his eyes. Like even he didn't want to be dealing with all the crap that came along with me.

Or maybe I was just reading into it too much.

"Come on, let's get you to Merlin." Remo slid into the driver's side, and I stepped into the passenger seat. Ernie zipped through my open door and into the back, where he sprawled in the middle, both hands behind his head.

Remo started the car, and the roll of the engine vibrated along my skin, tingling and dancing. I closed my eyes and breathed through it, quickly blocking it out so I could focus on other things. Like apologizing to Remo.

"I am sorry about Santos, and for whatever grief it caused you with your superiors." I stared straight out the window, not even daring a glance at him. "I didn't have much choice, but—"

"There is no apology needed, Alena. None whatsoever. Santos . . . the Santos who was my brother died a long time ago, and I would have done the same as you had I been in your situation." He turned the wheel, taking us onto the highway via a circling on-ramp. "As for my superiors . . . they will not allow my relationship with you to continue. That much has not changed."

146

"I thought that was already done?" I kept my tone neutral. "You dumped me, remember?"

"But I'm here now with you, and that is enough for them to realize I am anything but done with you. Until I can straighten things out with them, this will be the last time I can work with you like this."

Work. Like this was some sort of business merger, a deal gone south. The shot of pain was sharp as a knife to the finger and just as unexpected. I locked my jaw to keep it from trembling, and made myself not close my eyes; if I didn't blink, no tears would fall.

"Alena, I am sorry. I should never have . . . I knew it was taboo between us, but I truly didn't think it would ever amount to anything. You are a good girl, no matter how you think you've changed. You deserve someone better than me," he said.

I kept my mouth shut, and he seemed to think it was a good idea to keep talking. Idiot.

"Smithy cares for you, and I think he—"

"I don't love him." I cut him off. "And that's all there is to that."

"They will destroy everyone around me if I do not break ties with you."

Of course, that would be the reason. Even in my heart of hearts I knew he wouldn't just push me out of his life for no reason. Remo was not the bad boy he thought he was, not by a long shot. He was going to protect those in his care, no matter the cost to his own heart. Or mine.

There had been one girl he'd fought for, though, one that he'd lost before her time. Suddenly I needed to know about her, to know what it was that I was missing. "Tell me about the girl you went to medical school for."

He nodded. "I suppose I owe you that at least." He was silent for a few minutes while he seemed to gather himself. "I loved her. She was the one who showed me that it didn't matter what I was, or what she was, that I could still have someone who cared just for me. It didn't matter to her that I was a vampire. Or a mob boss." He glanced at me and smiled. "You're like her that way."

I smiled back, but my stomach was tense with fear of what was coming with his story. He went on. "She was human, and that made her acceptable in our world. I could pretend she was a donor and nothing more in front of the other vampires. She . . . she was very sick. And she wouldn't let me turn her. So I went to school for her, to become a doctor. I thought I could still save her. I still believed that love had that kind of power."

He shifted the car into a higher gear and then clutched at the steering wheel. "I thought I found something that would help her. That would keep her alive."

He was quiet long enough that I finally asked, "What was wrong with her?"

"Lou Gehrig's disease. Her body was wasting away."

I closed my eyes and shivered. "What happened? You said you thought you'd found something that could help her?"

"I did, it would have slowed the disease, maybe bought me enough time to find a cure. But it wasn't to be. Santos found out about her, and . . . he turned her. Not to help me; he knew she didn't want to be a vampire. She was furious because he told her I asked him to do it." He didn't look at me once. "The first morning of her new life she sat at the edge of the water as the sun rose."

I closed my eyes, grief tearing through my chest for him. "I am so sorry, Remo."

"It's not your fault. But maybe . . . you can see just how hard it is for me to see you in these situations. I lost her because I wasn't with her. I don't want to make the same mistake twice."

We drove in silence the rest of the way, hoping to get to the ferry terminal for the last sailing. Each mile drove the tension between us higher as I struggled to know what he really felt. Did he love me? Or was it just that I reminded him of a girl he'd really loved and lost?

As we drove up to the docks we were guided onto the ferry. We were one of the only cars; it was going to be a light load. That it was even still running was a surprise, but then again, it was the only way on and off Whidbey Island.

"You all know that the hospital is overrun?" The attendant peered into the car. He wore a mask over his nose and mouth, which muffled his words. "You're taking your lives into your hands by going."

"I think we'll manage just fine." Remo flashed his teeth. The attendant backed up and waved us on.

As soon as the car was parked and the blocks were set under the tires by the attendant, I was out of the vehicle and running for the stairs that would take me to the top deck. I needed fresh air, away from the intoxicating cinnamon and honey that was Remo. I hit the railing hard, bending it a little as I leaned over the edge, sucking in big lungfuls of fresh, salty ocean air. Slowly, my heart eased its rapid beat, and I stared at the water below . . .

Remo . . . his past was as messed up as mine. But where did I fit into his future? Would he defy protocol to be with me, or did he really mean it about this being the last time we worked together? Did he care at all? The questions swirled in my head like the water below the boat.

Ernie cleared his throat as he sat on the railing next to me. "You know, he's hurting too."

"It's just so stupid. Who cares if we're breaking rules? I mean, no one gets hurt, he doesn't have to feed as much if he takes my blood. I . . . I love him, Ernie. I thought love was supposed to be enough? But what if he doesn't love me?" My hair whipped up between us, a mass of black strands. Ernie sighed and shook his head.

"I'm supposed to tell you that love conquers all, but that's not always the case." He shrugged. "I mean, you'd have to convince Aphrodite to help you out if you were going to somehow get through this. She's got the kind of influence that could change the rules of the heart."

I snorted. "Even I know the chances of that are zero to none."

He grunted. "Yeah. Sorry. She can be a real twat."

I laughed, horrified at the term, but still it broke a little of the tension. "I understand his position; I wouldn't risk my family for him either. If I had to, I'd let him go to keep them safe. I do understand. I just . . . it just sucks."

Ernie laughed, but it wasn't mean. "That's because both of you are grown-ups. Idiot teenagers like Romeo and Juliet throw their lives, and their families' lives, away for supposed instant love. Grown-ups look at the reality."

"Did you really just compare us to Romeo and Juliet?" Remo said as he stepped up beside me. Damn him and his lack of a heartbeat. Between that and the sound of the waves smashing against the boat, there was no way I could hear him sneak up behind me. He leaned against me, his chest to my back, his arms circling around me. He put his chin on my shoulder, and I leaned my head into him.

"I'm sorry," he whispered.

Ernie winked at me. "I'll leave you two alone."

I put my hands over Remo's, sorting through my thoughts for the right words. "I'm not sorry. No matter what, I'll never believe that love is wrong. Even with Roger . . . it helped save me from the Firstamentalists. Even if it did end badly. And I won't regret you either. No matter what happens."

"I will never regret you either, Alena." His mouth was next to my ear, and I leaned into it, wondering if this would be our last few hours together. I could feel the end coming; I just wished I knew how it would happen.

He kissed my cheek, and we stared out at the water together. The waves rose and fell as the wind picked up, and the cry of the gulls above us seemed to echo off the water below. Minutes passed, and in that time there was a sense of peace that I knew wouldn't last. But I held on to the illusion of it anyway. I could pretend that we were on a date. That we would be okay. That we were safe.

A hump of water slipped upward in between the waves, and I stared at it, squinting. "Do you see that? Is that a killer whale?" They weren't unheard of in the water between Seattle and Whidbey Island. But I'd never seen one quite that big.

"I don't think that's a whale," Remo breathed. "I think that's trouble."

I let go of him and clutched the railing edge. "How far are we from the docks?"

Remo looked over his shoulder. "We're right in the middle of the trip."

"Oh fricky dicky, this is going to be bad, isn't it?" I whispered.

Ernie shot down beside us. "I've got bad news and worse news."

I looked at him. "Spit it out, Ernie."

He grimaced. "Bad news is that out there is someone from Hera's team. Worse news is, it's Poseidon. You know, father of Theseus, who you recently offed?"

"Fricky dicky" didn't even begin to cover things. "I don't suppose we can hide?"

"He knows you're here, and whatever he's sending is coming straight for the boat. He won't spare the people on here, Alena," Ernie said, shaking his head. "I don't know what we can do to stop him."

I looked at the boat, the humans on it. While there weren't that many, there were enough that it would be a huge loss if the god of the oceans decided to take the entire ship down.

I grabbed my jacket and pulled it off. Next came my shirt, boots, and pants. I shoved them all at Remo. "Meet me at the hospital."

"Wait, what are you doing?"

I didn't give him a chance to stop me. I scrambled over the edge of the railing, stood on the thin metal lip for a split second, and then pushed off into the open air. I hit the water feetfirst, the icy cold swirling over me. For just a moment I hung suspended in the ocean. I could almost feel the animosity from Poseidon rolling over me, making me unwelcome in his world. I kicked, propelling myself through the water as I thought of only one thing. Shifting.

CHAPTER 14

The change took me as swiftly as ever, but there was no smoke to disguise it in the water. I watched in fascination as my legs blended together, my arms stuck to my sides, and I slipped my human guise to grow into a Drakaina. I felt nothing, which made watching the shift even stranger to actually see.

Snakes could swim, I knew that much, and I'd banked my life on it.

The Drakaina in me approved, her pleasure rolling through my body. I swam to the surface, my tail propelling me as I sped away from the ferry boat. I didn't dare even glance back. I knew without looking that Poseidon and whatever he'd sent after me would follow. What I didn't expect was the creature that ripped out of the depths far below me, tentacles reaching for my multicolored scaled body.

I swam harder, the surface of the water holding me, as a multitude of suction cup–covered tentacles waved at me from every direction.

"You can swim as fast as you like, Drakaina, but in the water you are mine!" a voice roared and echoed through the water, battering against my skin with all the power of the ocean behind it.

A tentacle wrapped around my middle, and I coiled back, driving my fangs into it. It let me go, and I shot back to the surface, swimming with renewed vigor, sucking wind hard in case I got dragged under the waves. I might be strong and filled with venom, but I needed to breathe.

"Take her, kraken."

Fricky dicky, someone please tell me I heard wrong. I was grabbed by the tip of my tail and jerked, full length, into the air. All thirty or so feet of me hung upside down. I spun to see the face and parrot beak of the kraken staring back at me. Its eyes were flat black and dead, as if there were no soul inside there. For just a moment I wondered if my eyes looked the same when I was a Drakaina, but I shook it off. No time to wonder anything but how the heck I was going to get out of here alive.

I lifted myself up as fast as I could, driving my fangs into the tentacle holding me. I bit down on the squirming flesh, thinking only of undercooked calamari. Over and over again I bit the kraken until it finally let go and I was dropped. I shot down, expecting to hit the water.

But the kraken caught me in its beaked mouth and bit down. This was it, I was going to be cut in half. I flexed my muscles, braced, waiting for the slice that would kill me.

The beast didn't bear down with the full power of its jaws, but instead held me even as I could hear its heartbeat slow, death coming for it, my venom coursing through its thick flesh.

A coast guard ship zipped between us, and the kraken slowly lowered me down so I was eye to eye with the captain of the ship. Even if I hadn't known already, I would have figured he was part of the pantheon. He had the same blond hair and blue eyes and glow of power around him, not to mention a distinct resemblance to his brother, Zeus. Then there was the school of fish that swam in circles around his boat, leaping and bobbing to the surface as if trying to get his attention.

"So you are the Drakaina who killed my son?" He glared up at me and pointed a trident that was barbed on each of the three tips. If I were a betting kind of gal, I'd say that the weapon would do me some serious harm.

I squirmed, thought about shifting, and before I could change my mind, the shift took me. I yelled as I fell from the air, flailing as I headed straight toward the deck of the boat.

The kraken shot a tentacle out and caught me by one ankle, holding me right in front of Poseidon.

We were eye to eye, even though I was upside down. He glared at me, his frown kind of looking like a smile from my vantage point.

The trident wavered in front of my face. "No last words? No begging for mercy?"

I clenched my jaw several times, at war with myself before I finally spoke the truth. "Your son was a complete donkey, and you should be ashamed. I didn't want to kill him, but he was killing my friends, and I had to stop him."

Poseidon narrowed his eyes until they were mere slits. "That is not how one begs for mercy."

"You're going to kill me no matter what. I might as well go out with a little dignity."

"This from the naked woman," Ernie said, breezing in behind Poseidon. "How you doing, Fish King?"

"Knock it off, Eros. I have a monster to kill."

"Rich, coming from you with your kraken." Ernie snorted. "Look, I don't think you should be so ready to jump at killing her. You didn't even like Theseus. He was your least favorite. I seem to recall you calling him a shithead more than once."

"Eros, stop interrupting me. I know you are on her side." Poseidon spun to point the trident at Ernie. "And besides, the fact that I didn't like Theseus is not the point. If we just let the monsters do what they want without repercussions, we're going to have a clusterfuck on our hands again. Do you not recall the Titans?"

"She's hardly a Titan," Ernie pointed out. "Even if she is a big-ass snake."

"My bum isn't all that big, to be fair," I added.

Ernie nodded. "Point taken, her bum is only big when she's a snake."

"Do I even have a bum when I'm a snake?"

"Ha, good point. Just a big tail, then? A big-ass tail? Ass tail. That's funny." Ernie laughed at his own joke.

Poseidon rolled his eyes, and the kraken slid a tentacle down around my middle and squeezed me hard enough that I couldn't breathe, couldn't suck even a single gasp in. I did the only thing I could. I let my fangs drop and bit into the tentacle holding me. I didn't draw back but instead let the venom pump into the creature.

Slowly it eased off and then dropped me onto the deck. I hit with a hard thump, spinning to watch as the kraken slid away from sight, under the water, with barely a burp of air.

"Damn it, Drakaina!" Poseidon strode to the edge of the deck. "Do you know how much Hades is going to love holding that over me? It's going to cost me to get my pet back."

I slid back on the deck to the railing edge. My fangs throbbed, ached like they were empty. I reached up and touched one; not a single drop of venom fell. I guess it made sense that I could run out of venom, but it did not bode well, seeing as I hadn't even gotten to the underworld yet.

The king of the ocean spun around, his trident pointed at me once more. The CB radio crackled to life behind him, and he reached for it with one hand. "*Kraken One* here."

A voice came through, distorted and scratchy with the airwaves. "We need you back at port. We've got a ship coming in we suspect of smuggling infected people to the city."

Poseidon let out a sigh and scratched at his head with the hand holding the radio before he let out another sigh. "I'll be back ASAP."

He hung it back up. "Guess that means I need to kill you in a hurry instead of drawing it out and feeding you to the fishes piece by piece."

I scrambled backward. "You don't understand, Hera is going to take Olympus, Hades is behind the Aegrus virus, I think he has Zeus trapped, the Hydra is out of control, and people are dying, and I'm trying to help! Zeus needs you to side with him. Please."

The trident paused at my chest, and I didn't dare breathe.

"Please. I'm doing the best I can."

He rolled his eyes and pulled the trident back, his eyes thoughtful. "You're going to make Hera look like a fool."

I grimaced. "I'm not trying to."

The king of the ocean gave me a gruff laugh. "Oh no, I want you to. She's a bitch of a sister-in-law." He took a step back. "I won't help you, but I won't get in your way either. Besides, if you think to take on Hades, you have some serious balls." He glanced between my legs, and I slapped a hand over my bits as my face heated up.

He shrugged. "I will give you a piece of advice. Hades is not like the rest of us. He hasn't had to acclimate to the changing world, stuck in the underworld as he's been." He bent down low so we were eye to eye. "He's the same miserable bastard that liked to torture small animals for fun when he was a child."

He reached forward, grabbed me around the arm, and threw me overboard before I could even protest. I hit the water hard and was tumbled around in the wake of his boat speeding back the way he'd come.

"Good luck," he called back. "You're going to need it."

I swam backward, then flipped to my belly and headed toward the shoreline of Whidbey Island. Ernie flew above me. "That was close. And shit, that kraken! You totally took him out!"

"I'm out of venom." I spit out a mouthful of salt water and kept moving.

"Well, that's not good." He spoke the obvious like I wouldn't know. "You're going to need venom for the underworld for sure."

I didn't answer him, wanting to focus on getting to shore as quickly as I could. Who knew how long Merlin would actually be at the hospital? What if he took the last ferry back to Seattle?

The waves at least were pushing me in the right direction. I don't know how long I swam the dark waters, heading toward the lights on shore. My feet were just suddenly on shifting sand, and I was being helped up and out of the water by Remo. He had a towel he got from heaven knew where, and he wrapped it around me. "Had a nice dip?"

"Oh, lovely." I shook my head. "Refreshing, and I did get some good info." I told him about Poseidon and what he'd said about Hades. It wasn't a lot, but it might come in handy.

Ernie tossed me my clothes, and I struggled to get them on over my still-damp skin. I slipped the jacket back on, and Remo nodded. "Ready?"

"As long as no more of the pantheon shows up, I should be good to go," I muttered.

Ernie barked a laugh. "Optimistic, I like that about you."

The three of us hurried up the slope that led away from the water. We actually weren't far from the ferry docks and had a taxi within a few minutes. I wrapped my arms around myself as we drove, unable to keep from thinking about what was coming. I just assumed that I would be able to get to the underworld. I had to believe Merlin would help me, even if it meant I had to beg.

The taxi pulled up to the hospital, and Remo paid the fare. I was already out and ahead of him, unable to slow my feet. The first time I'd come here I'd been on a gurney, barely able to lift my head, never mind keep my feet under me. The exterior walls were the same slate-gray cement that had been hurriedly put together when the Aegrus virus had first appeared. What was different, though, were the people who were now outside the hospital.

Camped all over the sparse lawn were people lying on the ground; there were some even sitting and leaning against the building. I took my time, and with my feet slowing I strained my ears. There wasn't a single heartbeat coming from the group of bodies in front of us.

"They aren't vampires, are they?" I asked Remo. He shook his head, but I already had the confirmation I needed. The smell of death filled the air like the stench of burning fish, a scent that clung to you, one that no matter how you washed your hands and clothes, it was still there, lingering, telling me they were gone.

I hurried between the bodies and kept my eyes glued on the front doors. I pushed on them, but they were locked. I thought about just breaking them down. I took a step back and looked at the cement walls again. Here and there were cracks from the hastily made building, which, along with the rough window ledges at intervals, would make for easy grips. "I think we can climb this."

"Good call. Merlin won't expect us to come in this way," Remo said, and we started up the side of the building. Ernie flew above us, giving directions where he could. I'd done this before, climbed the CenturyLink Field wall when I went to rescue Tad from Achilles. But this was different. This didn't feel at all like the wild rush of learning how strong I was, how fast, how agile. This felt like . . . going into battle, a battle I could very well lose if I wasn't careful.

We reached the tenth floor, and I found a window that was open. I pushed it, and we slipped through, Ernie right with us. We were in a small bedroom, and there was a body covered with a sheet. I didn't need to lift the sheet back to know what was under it.

I drew in a breath, the smells in the room rolling back over my tongue, but I didn't pick up on anything but death. I shook my head and rubbed at my nose.

"Use your tongue. It is more sensitive when you flick it out," Ernie said.

I walked to the door, opened it, and found myself in the main hall. No nurses waited at the station, no lights blinked on and off. This was a true tomb now, not just one in theory.

I stopped the direction of my thoughts and flicked my tongue out. Scents flowed back to me and triggered images in my brain. The nurses who'd been on last were the one with the southern drawl that I'd suspected of being an elf—I'd been right—and the gargoyle nurse who was kind but had big clunky hands. They'd been holding out as long as they could, no doubt.

On the nurses' station was a vase of flowers, most of them drooping. Except for one. A single peony, pale pink and still tightly closed around its bud. I moved, barely realizing it. Ernie asked me something, but his voice was a buzz inside my head.

Peonies were my mom's favorite flower, and she had them planted all over the backyard. I pulled the flower out of the vase, and a shiver went through me. Maybe it was a sign.

Either way, it wouldn't hurt to hang on to it, right? I slid it through the top button hole of the leather jacket.

"You okay?" Ernie was in front of me, snapping his fingers. I nodded.

"Yeah, I'm okay. Sorry."

Remo offered me his hand. "Let's find Merlin."

I turned my face away from him and flicked my tongue out again. I picked up all the same scents as before, and now one more.

Merlin. Not that far off from my dad's own unique scent, Merlin smelled like dusty old books and the sharp tang of expensive cologne. I followed his trail down to a room number I would never forget. I pushed the door to my old room open and stepped inside.

Merlin sat on my bed, his legs stretched out and a pillow behind his head. His eyes rolled to me, and he winked. "I knew you'd find me. Too smart for your own good."

I raised an eyebrow. "Perhaps that's a problem that runs in the family, yeah?"

He snorted and rubbed the end of his nose. "Ah, so you figured that out too? See what I mean about too smart?"

"Are we seriously related?" I blurted out. Sure, the world was going down like a falling soufflé, but I wanted to know just how we were connected. Part of me was horrified because he'd tried to kill me, even though he was family. The other part was morbidly fascinated. Just why had he wanted to kill me, or been willing to have me killed, when we were related?

"I am your grandfather's brother, your great-uncle." He winked. "Which does indeed make your father a warlock too. Tell me, why do you think he didn't turn you himself?"

I'd thought about the reason why Dad hadn't turned Tad and I, even though he was a warlock. I didn't hesitate to answer Merlin; I knew the answer. "My mother."

"Ah, your mother. Right, right. I remember all that mess now. Shame. She was feisty once too, before fear got the better of her and she let Hera's supposed curse control her choices."

Ernie swept around between us. "Wait, you're actually related to this douche? He's been jerking you around the whole time, and you two are *family*?"

I shrugged. "Not any worse than the rest of the pantheon now, is it?"

That came out a bit wrong, like I was part of the Greek powerhouse, which I wasn't. But he seemed to get the gist of what I was getting at.

Merlin laughed. "Another time we can discuss the family tree and exactly why I had no problem throwing you to the wolves. That is in the past, we are here now, and we"—he pointed at me and then back at himself—"have an issue. You noticed the people dying outside?"

I shook my head. "Dead, not dying."

He grunted but didn't seem upset by the change in status. "Interesting. Most of them fell ill within the last few days. The virus has been set into overdrive, Alena. If you fell sick now, you wouldn't have weeks." He smoothed a hand back over his dark-brown hair. Looking at him, I could see the resemblance here and there to Tad, and more so to my dad. I gave myself a mental shake.

"How do we stop it? You obviously aren't bothering to turn them." I didn't hold back on the heat in my words.

"You obviously don't know what it takes to turn someone. It's draining. That's why I only turn one or two people in a month. That's the real reason why your father couldn't turn you. He's not strong enough."

I blanched, thinking of my request for Dad to go and turn as many people as he could. Merlin stared hard at me as if he could read my mind. Maybe he could. "You didn't," he growled.

I grabbed the foot of the bed to steady myself. "I didn't know. I was trying to help everyone."

He slammed his hands into the bed and pushed off. "I'd better go help him, then, before he kills himself."

"Wait, I need to get to Hades; he's behind the virus. How do I get to the underworld?" I stepped in front of him, stopping him from getting to the door.

Merlin shook his head, exasperation flowing over his face. "You don't. Zeus could have taken you there, but the rumor is that he's somehow gotten trapped. He's too cocky for his own good."

"Hermes? Could he take her?" Remo asked.

Both Ernie and Merlin shook their heads at the same time.

"Not possible, not to the underworld or Olympus," Ernie explained. "Those two places are off limits for him to carry anyone."

"Merlin, I have to try. Can you try to understand that?" I spread my hands wide in front of me, ready to beg if I had to. "I can't just let people die if I can help."

He tucked a hand into the inside of his jacket and pulled out a silver-and-gold feather. A Stymphalian bird feather, either Sandy's or Beth's, I wasn't sure. He rolled it over his hand once.

"You sure you want to go to the underworld? Because as far as I know there is only one way that is certain to get you there." His brown eyes met mine, and there wasn't a single glint of jokester in them. Nothing like the man I'd first met only a few short weeks ago who'd teased me about being a Firstamentalist.

"Yes." My voice was steady.

"There will be no do-overs, Alena. You will have one shot, and you will need more bravery than I think even you have." Merlin continued to roll the feather in his hand, over and over, the metal catching the light in flashes.

"Alena." Remo breathed my name in a soft warning as I nodded to Merlin.

"Yes, I'm ready."

"Oh, I doubt that very much." Merlin did smile then as he glanced at Remo beside me. "You don't think you're going with her, do you?"

"Yes. If anyone can handle the underworld, someone already dead should do the trick," Remo said.

Merlin shook his head. "No. She goes alone. Trust me, it is for your own good. Both of you. The undead are not what you think in the underworld."

That made no sense, but I was ready to agree to his terms. Remo, on the other hand . . .

"I'm with her, so you send us both or not at all." Remo closed the distance between Merlin and himself. The two men were almost nose to nose, or would have been if Remo hadn't had a good six inches on Merlin. He stared down at the warlock, but Merlin didn't seem bothered at all.

"I'm telling you, vampire, it's a bad idea."

Remo glared at him. "I'm going with her."

Merlin shrugged and put a hand on Remo's chest, pushing him away. "Your funeral."

"I can get there on my own," Ernie said, "but I'll be behind you if he's sending you fast."

Merlin nodded and faced me. "Fast, it will be. You ready, then?"

I swallowed, a sudden knot of anxiety filling my throat like a too-big candy gone down sideways.

"I need you to say you want to go to the underworld. That you accept the consequences as they are." Merlin took a step toward me. I held my ground, drawing myself up higher.

"I want to go to the underworld, and I accept the consequences as they are. Whatever they are."

He flicked a look at Remo. "If you're going, hang on to her and don't let go, or you'll get separated in the fall."

Remo stepped beside me and took both my hands in his. We stood like a bride and groom, Merlin as the priest beside us.

"Oh, isn't this sweet," Merlin muttered. Apparently I wasn't the only one who saw the imagery.

I held Remo's hands, thinking that this could be the last time that I'd get to do this. That I'd hold his hands while he willingly touched me.

I turned my back a little to Merlin, which meant I caught only a glimmer of movement, the flash of gold and silver, the sudden piercing pain in my chest. My heart stuttered, and the Drakaina in me tried to roar forward, tried to shift, but there was nothing to shift, no body left as I went to my knees.

That dirty rotten . . . bastard. He'd tricked me, and this time I knew there was no coming back. The feather stuck out the front of my chest, right through my heart. Monster killing monster, even now.

CHAPTER 15

Voices roared around me as the final breaths slipped from my body.

"It's the only damn way, you fool, and if you aren't holding on to her when she takes her last breath, you will be left behind."

Remo snarled, and then he was holding me, kissing my face. "I *am* a fool. Alena, I am a fool."

There were no words left in me. I wanted to lift my hand and touch his face, wanted to say good-bye properly. The other girl, the one he'd lost . . . had he held her as she died? No, that was silly thinking, she'd died in the sun. He'd not seen her, not held her. At least I'd be able to give him this closure.

Merlin bent over me, his face fading in and out of my sight. "Hades can send you back, intact. But that's the only way. Time to show if you are really a monster with guts or not, Alena. Make me proud to say we're related."

I closed my eyes, and the world around me dissolved. I was falling through space, a scream on my lips and then erupting out of me as what felt like tree branches slapped at me as I tumbled through space. I opened my eyes as a skeleton reached out and smacked my face with its bony fingers. I jerked, trying to get away from it, from the weight hanging from my right hand.

"Alena, stop, you're slipping!"

I twisted in midair to look down at Remo. He stared up at me. "They're dead, just like us. You don't have to fear them."

I shivered, and then we seemed to pick up speed. "Hang on!" he shouted as he disappeared into a black watery abyss that swallowed him whole, and me right after with barely a splash.

I held my breath as the water sucked me down in a big gulp. The liquid squeezed through my mouth, like it was fighting to get into me even while I tried to keep it out. I tugged Remo upward, kicking hard to get to the surface. The foul water that crept between my clamped lips tasted like things I didn't want to think about for fear I'd gag and open my mouth.

The seconds ticked past as I swam hard for the surface. How far down had we gone? As the need for air grew, the frantic desire to let go of Remo rose with it, so I could use both arms to propel myself upward.

No, I wasn't going to let him go. Not if I had any say in it, and even if it meant sucking in some nasty, foul water, I would hang on to him. We were dead, right? So the water couldn't hurt me, not really. I relaxed everything but my hold on Remo and let the water buoy me up. My lungs burned like an oven with an oil fire out of control, and I was a split second from opening my mouth when my head finally broke the surface. I gasped for air, and Remo broke through the black water beside me. He sucked in a big breath.

A few moments passed while we both composed ourselves, and a thought tumbled to the front of my brain. I stared at him. "I thought you didn't need to breathe?"

He shook his head and slicked back his hair with his free hand, drops of greasy black water trailing down his face. "You and me both."

Oh, that couldn't bode well for the underworld if Remo's powers were no longer the same as before. Was that what Merlin had meant about Remo not coming with me?

What if that applied to me too and I couldn't shift? I already knew I had, like, zero venom left in me. I reached with my tongue to the roof of my mouth to feel my fangs. Nothing, they weren't there. "My fangs are gone," I said.

Remo made a face that told me he was checking. "Mine too."

Yeah, that was all kinds of bad. What, then, were we just human?

I glanced around, finally taking in what I was looking at and, more importantly, what was looking back at me. We were in the center of a still lake, and we were at least a hundred feet away from the shoreline on either side of us. To the front and back of us, though, I couldn't see the end of the water. The place made me think of Orpheus once more, of the way he stood on the dock looking out.

Maybe in his madness he'd gone to a place he remembered from the underworld. I shivered.

"Maybe this is the River Styx?" I said more to myself than to Remo, but he answered me anyway.

"It would be moving," he said.

"Maybe not. I don't think the rules apply down here," I said. The River Styx was infamous in Greek mythology. I suspected we were in it, but that didn't mean it had to follow the same rules as the rivers we knew from the land of the living.

Eyes blinked all around us from the edges of the water. Big, small, narrowed, and wide open, the colors across the spectrum of light. I swirled slowly in the water, taking it all in. The eyes peered from around large stones, from behind twisted and gnarled trees, and some just peered up at us from the ground itself, each blink dusting up the dirt like a tiny windstorm. "Remo, you seeing what I'm seeing?"

"Yes. There aren't any watching us from farther down on the left side. Swim." He gave me a gentle push in the direction he pointed at with the flick of his chin. I swam, doing my best to keep all the eyes within my vision. Because I had a feeling that if I looked away for even a second, they would rush us. There wasn't animosity flowing from them, exactly, so much as . . . hunger. "They want to eat us."

"Yeah, that's what I'm worried about." Remo swam beside me, carefully. As though he didn't want to make a single splash. Silently I agreed with his tactic. Until something brushed against my leg, the lightest of touches that sent my heart rate into orbit.

"Something is in the water." I bit the words out, doing my best not to recoil completely for fear of sudden movements drawing more attention.

"I felt it too. Just keep swimming."

"This isn't a Disney movie," I whispered, my mouth hovering over the water's surface.

He grunted, and I thought it was a laugh. I turned my head, took my eyes off the eyes that followed us from the shoreline, and watched in horror as Remo disappeared under the water, sucked down like Luke Skywalker when the trash-compactor monster grabbed him.

"Remo!" I screamed his name, and all around us a cry went up like a cacophony of shrieking toddlers that couldn't be consoled. The sound reverberated against my skin and ears, sending shivers through me over and over—maybe I still had some of the Drakaina in me after all—as I spun around and around in a vain attempt to find him. I drew a deep breath and then dove under the murky depths. I forced my eyes open and blinked against the grit that filled the scummy liquid. The view was anything but clear, but I *could* make out a twisting shape, not unlike my own coils, and within it . . . Remo. I swam forward and tried to shift, knowing that I could take another serpent in my Drakaina form.

Nothing happened. Not a single puff of smoke. I didn't slow, only swam harder. A coil rammed into me as it swirled around, squeezing Remo. I caught a glimpse of his eyes, saw them flutter shut, the bubbles racing from his mouth. I reached out and grabbed a piece of the snake, digging my hands in. My strength was still with me at least. I tore a hunk of the snake's flesh off, and the serpent reared around, its face right in mine. It let go of Remo and wrapped around me. As we rolled through the water, we drew close to Remo, and I managed to push him to the surface. Or at least push him in that direction. The serpent rolled again and tightened its constriction on me, but I felt nothing. No pain. No loss of breath.

It put its head to mine, quite literally nose to nose. *Who are you, that you would defy me? That you would resist my call, my coils, and your death?*

I mouthed a single word, the bubbles escaping me finally as I stared into the glittering dark eyes. *Drakaina.*

The snake reared back, and I was released. I swam to the surface, my mouth coated with the foul water. I gagged, unable to get my bearings. A hand grabbed my arm and pulled me toward the shoreline. "Better to deal with a thousand small creatures than that." Remo's voice was filled with pain, and I looked at him. He was pale, and I realized I'd been right in my assessment. He was nothing more than a human here in the underworld. Not good, this was not good at all, and there was nothing I could do to change it. Not if I wanted to get us out of here. Our feet finally met resistance, and I slogged ashore, putting a hand behind Remo's arm and helping him to stand. He leaned heavily on me, but again, I had retained some of my strength, so it wasn't an issue.

I turned back, and the snake that had grabbed Remo reared up above the water, its mouth partially open, fangs hanging low. "Drakaina, you . . . are alive?"

A voice curled up through me and out my mouth, one that was mine and yet not quite. "She is the Drakaina now, I leave my power with her. She is your queen, and I suggest if you like your skin where it is, you help her."

I snapped my mouth shut. The big snake bobbed his head once. "As it once was, now it will be again. Are you sure, my queen?"

The voice answered with a soft chuckle. "At first, no, I was not sure. But she has the heart that it takes to hold this much strength. Strike, help her find Hades, the world is at stake."

Strike, the giant snake, tipped his head and flicked his tongue out. "Again?"

"Always. You know how it is with the damn pantheon." I cleared my throat, and the Drakaina in me faded.

"Wait!" I yelled, and Remo looked at me like I'd lost my mind. I swallowed hard. "Wait, you . . . you've been helping me." I spoke not to the snake in front of me but the one within me.

The voice of the Drakaina no longer sounded in my ears, but in my mind.

I was. But you do not need me now. You are finding your footing. Trust your instincts, trust the strength of your heart and mind.

"And if I need your help again?" I asked.

I will always be here. But I will sleep now; it has been a long time since I could trust someone with my power without having to hold their hand. Go, do what you came to do: find Hades. Her presence faded. Strike and Remo both watched me. I blew out a breath.

"I don't understand why I could hear her so clearly here." I shook my head in confusion.

Strike slid forward out of the water. He was big, but maybe only half my size when I shifted forms. "The underworld crosses barriers that are in place in the land of the living. Just like you would not hear my voice if we went back to the other side."

I looked up at him. "Why can't I shift?"

"That is one of the rules here. You are stripped of the most deadly strengths that have been bestowed on you. The shifting, the venom. You cannot use them here. Same with the vampire. Stripped of his abilities and pushed back to being only a human. You retain things you were born with."

"Well, shit," Remo breathed. I had to agree with him. Except . . .

"I still have my strength." I looked up.

"Then it must be something you had before," Strike said. "You would have had to have been born with it for it to remain."

I glanced at Remo, and he nodded. "The warlock blood. It obviously runs stronger in you than you realized."

A blessing rather than a curse this time. "Strike, you can help us get to Hades, then?"

He bobbed his head once. "I can take you partway. When we get to Cerberus, there is nothing I can do there; you must pass him on your own." He slithered ahead of us, and I got a good look at the patterning on his back. He was colored like an anaconda, shades of black, green, and brown. I hurried to catch up to him, not really wanting to be left behind in the underworld. Remo was right with me and slid a hand into mine. We walked through the underworld, as if we were on some sort of weird date with a large snake as a chaperone. I snorted to myself, and Remo lifted an eyebrow at me. "You cannot find this funny."

"Weirdest date I've ever had," I said.

Remo barked a laugh, and even Strike shook his head. "You think this is a date?"

"Probably our last one. Might as well make it memorable." I pushed the words out past the pain that hovered with them. I had a job to do, this was not the time to be moping about my love life or lack thereof.

Strike took us around the edge of the swamp and past a fast-flowing river. "We have to get to the other side." He flicked his tongue in the direction of the far side of the river.

I looked the water over. There were a lot of logs in the water, so many that I paused. "Could we not hop the logjam?"

"You really think those are logsssss?" Strike hissed the last bit at me. "Everything in here is either going to try and kill you, torture you, or hold you down until something bigger and badder can come along and torture or kill you."

"Crocodiles?"

"Not exactly," Strike said. "Throw something at them, then you'll see."

I stared out at the water, bent, and picked up a loose stone and threw it out at the logs. The "log" I hit snapped open a mouth that was . . . all mouth. There was no body I could see, just a gaping maw with row upon row of teeth that glittered with water and pieces of flesh. It snapped closed with a crash like thunder, the water rippling around it. There were no eyes, no nose that I could see, just a mouth designed for death. A giant crocodilian mouth that was so well hidden I had no idea how it couldn't have caught thousands of people. I took a step back from the water. "Maybe in my Drakaina form."

"Well, of course, but that is why you aren't allowed to shift. If you want to see Hades, then you have to want it badly enough to actually fight your way through to him. He's kind of a recluse, you know." Strike led the way once more, his body slithering easily through the soft dirt and mud.

Beside me, Remo blew out a breath. "I have not feared for my life in a great many years."

"You're welcome?" I queried with a half smile, and he shook his head.

"I look forward to getting back to the other side, where I am not weak as a newborn kitten," he grumbled, and I took his hand once more. If not for the occasional creature we came across, it would have seemed like just a very dark and gothic stroll. Weird but not terrible. Or maybe it was just that I was with Remo. I glanced at him, knowing that was the answer. Damn him, he even made the underworld seem like a place I wanted to be, as long as it was with him.

More than once I looked down at the flower still somehow stuck in my leather jacket. The bud had opened a little, a few of the petals showing a deeper pink within their folds.

We approached a section that was nothing like what we'd seen before. A glimmering gold glow surrounded the bush and trees to our right, and in the center of it, a bridge arced over a patch of rushing white rapids into a meadow.

"What is that place?"

"You can't go there, not if you want to go back to the land of the living." Strike slowed and stared into the meadow. "That is the place souls go before they make the final pass."

"Like limbo," Remo said.

I stared into the meadow. There was great beauty within it, and a sense of peace flowed out around it, beckoning me.

But all of that was secondary to what I was seeing: a figure I knew as well as I knew my own, one I thought I would never see again. I let go of Remo and was running for the bridge as I screamed for her.

"MOM!"

She turned, a swirl of skirts around her body as she faced me. It looked like her wedding gown to me. Maybe when you died you got to wear something that brought you joy? A part of me hoped that was the case. Her eyes lit up and she smiled, her whole face aglow with happiness. Happy, she was happy.

Hands and a coil of snake wrapped around me, jerking me to a stop as my foot met the first plank of the bridge.

"Drakaina, you cannot! Your soul will be forced to move on if you cross the bridge," Strike said.

I cried out, reaching for my mom, wanting to know she was okay. That she was truly happy. She ran toward me, the stalks of long, weaving grass and flowers bending as she passed. "Alena!"

Her voice had never sounded so sweet, and I held my hand out to her. She stopped on her side of the bridge, stretching her hand out to me. "Alena, what happened?"

"Mom," I whimpered, unable to draw back, straining against both Remo and Strike.

She lowered her hand and slowly nodded. "I see you, my girl. Don't fret, I'm fine."

"You were killed; it's my fault."

Her smiled slipped, and a tear fell with it. "No, it wasn't your fault. The Hydra would have sought me out. I saw the writ when I arrived here. My death would have been at her hands in a thousand variations of that day. Even if you had never become a Drakaina, I would have died at her hands. Do you understand? This was not your fault."

I couldn't help the sobs that echoed in my chest. "I love you, Mom."

"I love you too. Tell your father, and Tad, that the three of you were my world. Everything I did was to keep you safe. To try and help you find happiness." She blew me a kiss and stepped back. "Go on, now. You have a job ahead of you. Do not grieve me, Alena. You have a lifetime ahead of you, and it shouldn't be spent in tears."

I wiped at my face as she backed away from the edge of the bridge. "Wait!"

"There is nothing more to say, my girl, except this: Be strong. Be brave. Be honest. Love and do not fear your heart."

I grabbed the flower from my jacket and held it out to her. "Take it, and you can go home. We can be a family again. Please."

Her smile was sad, and in it I felt my heart break. "Alena, there is no going back. Your grandmother . . . she is wrong."

The flower slipped from my fingers. "Why, why would she tell me it was possible, then?"

My mother's eyes never left mine. "Because she wants to believe that this isn't the end. She's always been afraid of death, Alena. Always. But this isn't the end." She smiled and blew me a kiss. "Trust me, this isn't the end."

The peony floated down onto the bridge, and the wooden planks trembled, cracked, and fell into the water. I was pulled back as the vision tumbled in on itself, as my mother faded from sight and in her place was nothing but a patch of broken, dead trees, their limbs twisted with blight.

"Your mother is a smart lady," Remo said. He tucked me against his side. "Very smart."

He guided me away, following Strike farther into the underworld, because I was a blubbering mess. Everything in me wanted to turn around and run back to search for the bridge. To cross it and have the peace my mother held in her eyes. What was the point of seeing my mom if I couldn't even hug her? If I couldn't truly say good-bye?

"What you saw there is as much a threat to your success as the monsters, Drakaina. Your love for her almost did you in." Strike didn't look at me as he spoke. "Hades is no fool, he knows you are coming, and he will continue to try and stop you. It is obvious you are less afraid of the monsters than most, so he will use other things against you."

As if his words had summoned the next challenge, a slumped figure sat on a log ahead of us.

"Do not touch her," Strike said. "No matter what."

The figure looked up, but I didn't recognize her. Remo sucked in a sharp breath. "Elizabeth."

She raised her eyes, clear gray eyes that sparkled with unshed tears. "You said you loved me."

Remo's whole body jerked as if she'd stabbed him. I grabbed him around the waist as he lurched toward her. "It's not really her, Remo." Her. The girl he'd loved before me. The one Santos had turned into a vampire.

She wrapped her arms around herself and rocked, a low keen on her lips. "You did this to me. You trapped me here."

Remo shook his head. "No, I never wanted this for you."

"But you did it. Your love was a lie."

He slipped out of my hands, and I leapt forward, grabbing him around the ankles and tackling him to the ground. I crawled on top of him. "Remo, this is not true, this is not her. If she loved you, she would never say these things to you."

He breathed hard underneath me, puffs of dirt blowing up around us from his breath. Elizabeth stared at him. "You love her more than you ever loved me."

He didn't deny it, and I couldn't help the curl of warmth wrapping around my heart.

Her gray eyes narrowed, and she leaned forward. "You're going to be the death of her too. That is the way you are with the women you love. Your mother. Your sister. Me. Her."

Remo pressed his face into the ground. "I cannot leave her. Not again."

I glanced up at Strike. "Help me."

We lifted Remo and physically dragged him away from Elizabeth. She cried after us, begging for him to save her. Begging for him to hold her one last time.

When we no longer could hear her, we finally stopped. I sat on the ground beside Remo. "You okay?"

He grunted, his face coated in dirt and mud, scratches bleeding from the branches that had cut at him. "Yeah."

So, really, he meant no. But I understood. We had to keep going.

"Strike, how much farther?" I asked.

The snake opened his mouth to answer, but it was not his voice that spoke, but another I knew from my past.

"The question is not how far, but why would you really want to go there, granddaughter?"

I lifted my eyes and stared at the smiling man in front of us. "Gramps?"

The man in the long cloak and old-fashioned clothes swirled his hand out and bowed in front of me. "The one and only."

CHAPTER 16

I glared at Gramps, who I recognized only from his younger pictures, because he was hardly the old man I remembered. In fact, the resemblance to Merlin was there in the dark hair slicked back, the build of his body, and the shape of his jaw.

"You jerk! Why didn't you tell us you were a warlock?" I snapped.

He barked a laugh and touched his overlong nose, the same way Merlin did. He shook his head. "Your parents forced me to swear I wouldn't. They didn't want you and your brother to know. That whole Hera business was a mess."

I rubbed my hands on the arms of my jacket. "So why are you here now? Surely Hades knows that we've figured out his ploy; I won't be coming over to hug you."

"Oh, Hades didn't send me. Warlocks don't truly exist the same way others do when they die." He tucked both hands behind his back. "You see, I thought perhaps I could help."

I frowned, wondering if anything he said was true. "Strike?"

"Lies."

"That's what I thought."

I looped my arm through Remo's and walked away from the vision of Gramps.

"You're going to get yourself stuck here, one way or another, Drakaina," Gramps growled at me, and I had no doubt it was Hades who was speaking, not my grandfather.

I spun and glared at him, feeling the hiss roll up through my belly. Maybe the power of the Drakaina was not there in me, but the desire to snap my teeth hadn't left. "Hades, you can go stuff your head in a gas stove and light yourself on fire."

"Oooh, now she's getting testy." Gramps grinned at me, and his face began to melt like a wax candle, the skin sloughing from his face and slowly revealing the bones beneath. "How do you like me now, Drakaina?"

I turned my back on him, and Remo kept a hand on me. "Games. These are games to him, that's all."

Strike nodded. "That is true. Hades gets bored."

As we left Gramps, or the vision of him, behind, a thought spilled into a question.

"Why didn't we end up in the meadow with my mother?"

Our guide was silent a moment. "Most likely because it wasn't really your time. When it's your time, you go to the place designated for you. But if you come through early by accident, then you wander the swamps until you are drawn across the bridge. Or down the tunnel."

"The tunnel?"

I shouldn't have asked. A hole opened up right in front of us, so fast Remo and I teetered on the edge, staring down into the depths. Strike whipped around us, jerking us back, but not before I saw the leering faces, the broken and scarred skin, the eyes filled with horror and pain. I saw them as they reached for us, begging for help.

I clutched at Remo. That was where I'd end up, I knew it. The place where murderers and liars went. Okay, I was assuming that last bit. I closed my eyes, but the images remained.

I walked, hanging on to Remo with my eyes closed, trusting him to keep me safe while I tried to process what I'd seen. My future, that's what I'd seen.

"You won't go there, Alena." Remo's voice was soft, but it cut through the horror.

"You don't know that," I said.

Strike interrupted us. "We are here."

I opened my eyes. Strike coiled to a stop in front of us, his head dropping down so we were face to face. "This is as far as I can take you. There shouldn't be much between you and Cerberus from this point on, but do not touch anything you do not have to."

I peered around him to see a large chain-link fence that was hung with signs:

"Stay Out."

"Do Not Enter. Guard Dog on Duty."

"I Can Make It to the Fence in 3.6 Seconds, Can You?"

"Thank you, Strike," I said.

He bobbed his head and winked one large eye. "For my queen, I would do all I can to make sure you have the help you need. I will pass the word through our kind that you are alive and well. And that you have a new face but the same strong heart."

I reached up and ran a hand down the middle of his face, his skin smooth and cool under my fingers. "Thank you. Now go. I don't want you to take the heat for this."

Strike slithered away, disappearing into a sudden fog that swept up and around us, obscuring my vision to no more than a few feet in front of us. "Well, isn't that a bowl of peaches," I muttered.

"How bad do you think Cerberus is going to be, exactly?" Remo tightened his hold on me.

"Not a clue, to be honest." I stepped toward the chain-link fence, glad for the distraction from the pit behind us. The fence faded in and out of the fog, and I wondered if it was even all that solid. I touched the metal, using it as a lead as I made my way down the fence line looking for a gate. I made it all the way to a rock face that blocked us on one side, then went back the other way.

"There may not be a gate," Remo pointed out.

I nodded. "I know, but I'll feel like an idiot if I climb over the top and fall into a pile of stinking dog poo only to find out that there *was* a gate."

We made our way down the other end of the fence, slowly, nothing stopping us.

And that alone made me nervous. So that meant either we'd out-distanced all the monsters—which I seriously doubted—or they were afraid of Cerberus. I was guessing the latter.

I paused at a section of fence where the wire was pulled back at the corner, small with jagged edges, just big enough to crawl through. "Bingo."

I crouched and pulled the wire back, bending it easily. I held it, and Remo went through first, then I dropped down into a crouch and followed him through. I was on my knees, and Remo stood in front of me, his very nice rear end blocking my view. "See anything?"

"Alena, this is bad," he whispered.

I made myself peer around him, though my heart hammered and my body wanted nothing more than to run. I stared up, way up at the three-headed dog that stood over us, silent as a statue, saliva and blood dripping from his mouth.

Remo had understated the situation. This was far worse than bad. This was epically bad.

Cerberus didn't move, but he didn't have to in order to scare me. Neither of us really had anything to face him with. No power, no strength of a monster, only our wits.

His three heads were trained toward us, each one with a maw filled with teeth, as though someone had just kept adding teeth until there was no more room and then added a few more for good measure. I'd seen the effect once when an employee had overstuffed a cream puff at my bakery until it spilled out the edges. But I highly doubted Cerberus was anything as sweet as a cream puff. Two of his heads had short ears that stood straight up, and the middle one had no ears at all, like they'd been cut off. He stood easily over twenty feet at the back, his three heads higher yet than that, and I had no doubt he could snap us each up in a single bite. But all he did was watch us. Or at least that's what he seemed to be doing. Every once in a while one of his heads would swivel to the side, swaying back and forth . . . like he couldn't hear us. I looked at him more closely.

"Are those scorch marks on his heads?" As in lightning-bolt scorch marks. If Zeus had blasted him, maybe he couldn't hear us. "What if he can't see us when we hold still? Like T. rex?"

"That was a movie, Alena. And this is a giant dog. He should be able to smell us, right?" Remo kept his voice pitched low, but I noted that he didn't move either. We were as frozen as Cerberus. I dared to slowly lift my hand, putting it on the back of Remo's belt. Just in case I had to yank him out of the way fast. My heart hammered, sweat flowed freely down my spine, and I had no idea what to do. How to get past this big monster and how to make it all the way to Hades was beyond me.

The oversized mutt swiveled one of his heads again, tipping it as if he could almost pick up on us. There were more scorch marks down the side of his neck.

"I think Zeus nailed him. It would hamper all his senses. I think we just have to make a run for it," I said as I jerked to my feet.

"I can't run as fast as I used to," Remo pointed out, but I was already moving. I tightened my hand on his belt and bolted straight toward Cerberus. The middle head locked eyes with me, let out a snarling bark, and lunged. I dodged to one side, dragging Remo with me, as the middle head snapped where we'd stood only seconds before. I spun, like dodging Tad as we played basketball when we were kids, my back against the right head of Cerberus. I rolled with my back against his mouth, so close, and yet he missed me except for a flick of his tongue. I yanked Remo, and we were under the three-headed dog and running for the far side of the compound.

The place was a full-on junkyard with strange machinery and broken-down metal in piles everywhere.

"Let's split up, he can't take us both." Remo pulled my hand from his belt and pushed me in one direction as he headed in the opposite.

"No, we can't split up!" I yelled, but it was too late, and Cerberus was rushing between us. I held my ground; I couldn't let him go after Remo. I waved my arms at him. "Come on, dumb dog, I'm just standing here waiting on you." Cerberus took one look at me . . . and swerved after Remo.

His huge paws dug into the ground, churning up dirt and metal, flinging it every which way. He swept past me, and I did the only thing I could think of—I grabbed his one long tail and yanked it backward. I didn't know how much strength I truly had left in me, so I gave it all I had. The tail gave way at the base, tearing partially off as I pulled and Cerberus ran. He howled and spun as the pain finally reached at least one of his brains. I was flung into the air like a kite with its string snapped loose. At the peak of my flight, my hands slipped on the slick fur, and I flipped through the air . . . and landed on his back. I dug my hands into the mangy fur, realizing that his body was covered only in patches. Sections of his back were indeed burned off like Zeus had really given it to him.

I felt bad for him. "Cerberus, stop this!"

One head turned around, and he snarled at me. I realized he could actually reach me from there. I held on tighter. "Zeus shouldn't have hit you with the lighting."

He grunted and shook his head. I blew out a breath. "Look, I just need to talk to Hades. Can you let us go through?"

He shook his head again.

"Not even if I say please?"

He snapped his teeth at me, missing me by mere inches.

"I don't think you can talk him down. Not all the monsters are on our side, Alena," Remo shouted, and Cerberus began to turn back to him. It was now or never. I pushed myself to my feet and scrambled up his neck to sit behind the ears on his middle head. Or where his ears should have been. I dug my hand into the edges of the burned and charred skin and pinched hard. He whimpered and went to his knees.

"I don't want to hurt you more than I already have, dog. But I have to get to Hades. So either you are going to take us, or . . ." I had no real threat, so I left it hanging in the air.

I hoped that the big dog had something of an imagination, and it would fill in the blank with something truly horrendous. Maybe fire hydrants that attacked him, or a herd of cats that would chase him up a tree, I really didn't know. Below me, he whined and licked his lips. He tried to shake his head, but only got one flick in before I gripped harder, pinching him again. Mostly to keep my seat, but he didn't need to know that. Cerberus let out another whimper, and I dared to let go and slide down his back.

That was the mistake, though. He lunged at me the second my feet were on the ground. I threw myself out of the way, but one of his teeth caught the edge of my leather jacket, hooking me close to his slobbering mouth. I stared into his maw, thinking that I was done like an overcooked cake, ready to be tossed. But Cerberus stumbled, which threw me upward and unhooked my jacket from his tooth. I hovered in the air for a moment and then fell to the ground with a heavy thud. Cerberus whimpered, cried out, and fell back away from us, a length of pipe protruding from his chest, air and blood bubbling around it. Remo grabbed me and hauled me to my feet. "I don't know how long that will hold him. We have to run."

I struggled to put together what had happened. How had Remo lifted that big pipe without his vampire strength?

"I have muscles, Alena. I am not *really* as weak as a newborn kitten, you know." He ran beside me as we wove our way through the junkyard, dodging sharp metal and leaping over deep holes. I glanced down at one of the holes, noting the bones sticking out, the pieces of skull that had been shattered and half buried. Cerberus was not a nice dog, not a nice monster at all. I clung to Remo as we ran, left, right, left, right, trying to find our way out. We circled around a chunk of metal that looked like a downed airplane hull, and skidded to a stop. Cerberus was in front of us, on his side, struggling for breath.

He was in pain, that much was obvious, and again I felt bad, I couldn't help it. Wasn't his fault he'd been turned into a guard dog.

"Stop feeling sorry for him; it's going to get us killed."

Remo was right, but I couldn't help it. I liked dogs. "This place is like a labyrinth." I tugged him back behind the equipment and out of Cerberus's line of sight. "How are we going to find our way out?"

A flutter of wings snapped us both around. Ernie grinned down at us. "That's where I come in."

I held my arms out, and he swung into them for a hug. "I have never been so happy to see you, Ernie."

"I thought I'd find you back at the swamp, but Strike told me he brought you to the dog." He shook his head and then peered over my shoulder. "He'll be okay. He can't be killed, which means we need to get you two out of here before he pulls the pipe out and heals up." As if his words were the cue, there was a loud squelching, sucking sound of a pipe being pulled from flesh. Ernie swept up to our head level. "Come on, this way."

He flew ahead of us fast, and we ran after him, fear nipping at my heels. I kept glancing back. How long before Cerberus was on us again? We couldn't kill him, so we had to get past him. A howl of a hunting cry ripped through the air, and the ground shook.

"Faster, Ernie!" I yelped, true terror whipping my arms and legs into an even greater frenzy.

"Left, and then into the plane," he yelled back at us. "Shit, don't look back."

Oh, why did he have to go and say that? I couldn't seem to stop myself. I glanced over my shoulder. Above the piles of junk, I could see Cerberus's heads bobbing here and there as he chased us down. He was probably only twenty feet or so back, but the curves through the junk created something of a barrier.

I stumbled, and Remo grabbed my elbow, steadying me. The airplane hull came into view, and we leapt for it as Cerberus roared behind us. Warm, wet spit slammed into the back of my neck, and I fell to the floor of the plane. The world shifted, and I clutched at Remo as the plane spun as if it was falling from the sky. Heat and explosions ripped through the air around us, and I tucked my head against Remo's neck. "I love you."

If we were going to die, I wanted those to be my last words. Love might not be strong enough, but it was a reason to keep fighting, to keep on doing what we were doing and hoping for the best. Remo pulled back a little, his eyes on mine. "I love you too." His lips were on mine, and we fell through the strange sky, clinging to one another.

We landed with a thud, but not so hard that we were more than bumped apart, sliding over the interior of the plane. I sat up and brushed hair out of my eyes. Adrenaline still coursed through me, and I shot to my feet as I searched around for the next monster, the next challenge we would have to face, the next ghost from our past. But there was nothing but a flickering light from outside the plane. I held a hand out to Remo, who still sat on the floor. He wove his fingers between mine, and I helped him stand.

Ernie fluttered around us. "Here we are, Hades's house."

"Hades's house?" I shook my head. "Are you sure there are no more monsters? No more bad guys to deal with?"

Ernie shrugged and then winked at me. "Only Hades. I'll leave you to decide if he's a monster or a bad guy. It will depend on his mood, to be honest."

"Awesome, so he's hormonal, is that what you're saying?" I frowned, and Ernie laughed.

"Aren't all the pantheon?"

He had a point that I chose to ignore. With Remo's hand in mine, I stepped from the plane and took a good look at where we'd landed. The place was exactly what I would have conjured in my mind if someone had asked me what the underworld looked like. We were inside a dark, dank cave that was lit here and there with torches. Even that light wasn't enough to truly illuminate the place, or the figure that sat on the stone throne in front of us.

Hades—I mean, who else could it be—was dressed in a long black cloak with a hood that was pulled up to shade his face. I couldn't have said if he was handsome, ugly, a monster, or human, other than the fact that as he stood he was more human in shape.

"Well, well, I see you finally decided to visit, Drakaina. Tell me, how do you like the underworld so far? Is it all you could have hoped for?" His voice was a deep timbre that sounded as though it were filled with gravel.

"Please, don't act like we didn't already talk. You were impersonating my gramps, you jerk." I let go of Remo and stepped forward, finding myself more than irritated. I was downright pissed, and Hades was about to hear about it. "You knew I was coming."

"Of course I did."

"And you made it as difficult as you could."

He laughed. "Yes."

"You're an asshole," I said. Ernie and Remo groaned at the same time, whispering for me to ease off. But I was done easing off. I was done with it all. I wanted answers, I wanted to make things right, and by heaven, hell, and the underworld, Hades was going to help me.

Whether he knew it or not.

CHAPTER 17

"I've been called far worse, Drakaina." Hades didn't seem at all bothered by my assessment of him. "But it is the first time someone who has come to me for help has called me names as an opening line."

"I doubt it will be the last." I took a few more steps forward. I refused to back away from him. "You started the Aegrus virus, which means you can stop it."

"That is correct." There was laughter in his voice that I didn't like. Laughter at me. Like I'd come all this way for him to just tell me no. Well, he had no idea who he was up against.

"How do I get you to listen to me? What will convince you to stop the virus?" I knew how to bargain. I knew how to negotiate. It was just a matter of getting him to spill the beans as to what he wanted in exchange.

Hades stood and began to slowly pace in front of me, tucking his hands behind his back. "What, you aren't going to offer yourself?"

"I doubt you'd want me." I shrugged. "You have a wife that, from my recollection of the stories, you love, and she returns the sentiment."

He grunted. "The stories are rarely anywhere near the truth. Regardless. You are right, you aren't my type." He paused. "No offers of money?"

"Again, I doubt that flips your switch or floats your boat," I said.

"Interesting turn of phrase . . . ," he murmured.

"I could always have Ernie shoot you with one of his arrows, see if that gets a response," I said. Ernie and Hades grunted at the same time, and I kept talking. "But what I want is for you to do the right thing. People are dying."

"Which brings me more power, stupid snake," Hades growled. "More power means that I have more control in the world and I have more say in how things are done in Olympus. You have somehow managed to bungle your way through, surviving two heroes and avoiding a third to this point. Do you know what a pain in the ass Theseus is here? Truly."

"I have an idea," I said. "He was hardly easy to deal with when he was alive."

Hades stopped in front of me, and his hooded face drew near. There was no heartbeat I could discern coming from him, and the smell rolling off him was one of burnt wood and incense . . . the smell of death wasn't thick on him like I'd expected. I didn't slouch. "You are a business man, then? You want power, you want a say . . . Hera has offered you those things, but she isn't in control yet. Technically your brother still rules."

There was a heavy pause while that dark face, its features hidden, hovered in front of me. "True," he finally said.

"So let's negotiate. Zeus has given me the right to negotiate in his place."

"Zeus?" Hades roared and snapped his fingers. There was a poof, like a magician showing off his tricks.

And there was Zeus all wrapped up in chains, in front of me, a gag in his mouth and his eyes about as pissed as I'd ever seen them. There was only one thing I could do.

"Hey, Zeus." I waved at him, as though his situation didn't bother me in the least. Because I suddenly realized just how much the world really was waiting on me. Not just the Aegrus virus, but Zeus's life, and the future ruler of Olympus, which was going to impact the entire world. Hickory sticks, this was going to be tougher than I'd ever imagined. I drew in a breath. "You still good with me negotiating for you?" Like he had a choice. I wanted to laugh but didn't dare.

Zeus's eyes bugged out, and I nodded as though he'd given me the go-ahead. "That's what I thought. You all saw him agree?"

Ernie stared at me like I'd sprouted another eight heads and become a Hydra. Even Remo didn't seem to know what to make of me. But they both nodded, slowly, as though they weren't entirely sure what I was up to but were going to go along with it.

Hades chuckled. "Oh, I think I'm going to like you. I agree, my big brother looked like he just handed you the reins to his rule."

I cleared my throat. "Excellent. What do you want *exactly* in exchange for not only stopping the Aegrus virus but backing your older brother once more?"

Hades roared with laughter; he even went so far as to throw his hands in the air and wriggle his fingers. "Good gods, Zeus, where did you find her?"

Of course, Zeus couldn't answer.

"He didn't, Merlin did," Ernie said. "He picked her because he thought she was weak, but as you can see she is anything but."

I didn't smile at Ernie but kept my attention on Hades. "As I said, what do you want?"

I could almost feel the sands of time slipping by, feel the souls that floated toward us as more and more people died from the virus. Hades chuckled and wiped at his face with a hand. "Well, how about this? You make it so I still get an equitable number of souls that I'm getting from the virus, and we can talk."

"Well, that's just plain stupid, and you know it," I snapped. He froze, as did every other man in the room with me. I didn't care. Enough of this garbage. "I'll give you power to make what you want of the underworld. Redecorate, change the colors, change how it's run. You can be second-in-command at Olympus next to Zeus, above Hera, even."

Zeus tried to yell around the gag, but Hades just stared at me. Or I assumed he did. "And flip that damn hood off, I want to see your face."

"No, it's in my favor to remain hidden."

"Do it," I snapped, wishing I had the strength of the siren behind me still to affect people. Miracle of miracles, he flipped his hood back, much to what was his own obvious astonishment. Damn him for being as good looking as the rest of the pantheon. He didn't fit with the rest, though; he was obviously the black sheep of the family, at least in coloring. His hair was as raven black as mine, but his eyes were a bright blue that shone with power. He glared at me. "Happy?"

I shrugged. "Better than staring at a black hole. Now, back to negotiations."

"You always this intense?" He arched an eyebrow, and I arched one right back.

"No, but then I'm not usually bargaining for the life of so many people, and the fate of the world." The words were out of me before I could filter them. Hades folded his arms over his chest and stared me down.

"I like where you're going with the negotiations. But I want something more."

"What?" I asked, knowing that it was probably going to be something I regretted. Call it a feeling, but I was learning to listen to my instincts. Finally. I tugged the jacket a little at the bottom hem. Hades had a slow-growing smile that I didn't like.

"I want there to be an easier way to divorce my spouse. No more of this 'you both have to agree' shit. If I want out, I get out. I want that for all of us, and the only ones who can make it happen are Zeus and Hera agreeing."

My jaw dropped open, and Hades gave me a slow nod. "Now you begin to see the problem, when it is up to those two idiots to lead the way. They are the example, and it is by that example that we, the pantheon, live."

I spun and glared at Zeus. "Is this true?" He rolled his eyes and nodded. I stalked over to him and yanked the gag out. "Explain."

"Look, I don't want to be married to her, but it isn't up to me, I've told you that. It's in Hera's court, and it's what she holds over me. Hades knows that. Until she agrees to the divorce, none of us can be free," Zeus said.

I spun back to Hades, who nodded again. "True. Which is why I've been helping her. If I can soften her up, maybe we can all be free of each other."

Holy smokes in a kitchen on fire. My mind whirled. "Wait, so all this Aegrus virus, the infighting, all of it . . . is so you can both get divorces?"

Zeus and Hades shared a look that I recognized. A look between siblings that spoke volumes. Zeus finally blew out a sigh, and Hades grinned. "Yeah, I guess it is."

I blinked several times, horrified. This was how far the pantheon would go to get what they wanted. They'd light the world on fire and let it burn. What a lot of greedy bastards.

"So if I can get Hera to agree to this, then you make it all go away? You make sure that the virus stops killing people?" I wanted to be crystal clear on this part.

Hades and Zeus started laughing at the same time, so hard that tears streamed from their eyes. Ernie drew close to me. "You're suggesting that you can do something that no one else has managed in thousands of years. And if you remember, Hera hates your guts. Remember? She's been trying to kill you? Sending the Hydra after you?"

I did remember, but I knew something that the men didn't understand. A woman scorned, a woman cheated on and tossed aside as though she were nothing . . . I knew that pain as well as anyone. And that was my ace in the hole, the only ace I had. "Is it agreed? If I can get Hera to agree to the new system of divorce, you will stop the virus?"

Hades wiped his face. "If you can manage that, I will kiss the ground at your feet and set you above me in Olympus."

I frowned at him, and repeated myself. "Do you agree that if I can get Hera to agree, you will stop the virus and you will support Zeus again?"

His laughter stilled. "Shit, you really think you can do it?"

I held my head high. "I do."

There was silence for a moment while I waited for Hades. With obvious reluctance he nodded. "Alright. You have my word."

I turned to Zeus. "And if I do it, you are going to take the reins of the supernatural world. You are going to be Zeus again, not just some pansy Blue Box manager. You will become the liaison between us and the human world. And you won't allow the pantheon to treat the world like its playground again. Understood?"

Zeus stared hard at me, glittering with anger. "Fine. But you won't convince Hera of anything. She's a hard-nosed bitch who is out for revenge, and you are on her shit list, Drakaina."

My guts tightened at the thought of not being able to convince Hera. "I have a backup plan. One I know she'll go for no matter how much you think you know her."

Remo put a hand to my lower back. "There will be another way if she won't agree. We can figure this out."

Hades and Zeus shared another of those sibling looks again, and I glared at them both, but finally settled on Hades. "If I'm going to deal with Hera and get you what you want, you need to send me and Remo back. I can't talk to her from here."

The two brothers nodded at one another, and then Hades looked at me. "Fine. But I keep Zeus here as a security deposit. Also, I don't want him helping you. You made the negotiation, you follow through on how it's going to be done on your own. No help at all." His brilliant blue eyes sparkled with something dangerous. Like he too had an ace up his sleeve. An ace I wasn't going to like, like the bite of a rotten peach in the middle of the pie.

"Fine. Not like he's been much help anyway," I said. Hades laughed, and Zeus grunted as if I'd slapped him. I shrugged. "What do you want? It's the truth."

Hades approached, and Remo tightened his hold on me. The two men were of the same height, but Remo was broader across the chest with more muscle. Hades looked at him first. "You stuck my dog with the pipe?"

"Yes." Remo's voice was deadly intense.

"Excellent. Then I won't regret this one bit. Another piece of insurance, to make sure you put your all into making Hera change her mind." Hades grinned at me as he snapped his fingers, and the underworld around us faded into a blast of color and light.

"No!" I screamed the word as Remo was torn from me. No, he couldn't keep Remo, because what if I did fail? Wasn't it enough I'd lost my mom?

My whole body jerked as I sucked in a breath of stale air, my skin cold on the cheap linoleum floor of the hospital room. I lay in a puddle of my own blood, coagulated and thick, but still with the multicolored rainbow lights that it held within it. I sat up, and the feather Merlin had stabbed me with fell to the floor, cracked in half down the spine. I touched my chest over my heart, a tiny ridged scar the only evidence that I'd been mortally injured. A soft groan and the sound of an unsteady heart spun me around. Remo lay on the floor behind me, and I fell on him, kissing him. "You're here, you're alive, I thought he'd kept you."

Hades hadn't taken him after all. What in the world had the underworld boss been talking about, then? How could sending Remo back with me be insurance?

Remo's eyes opened slowly, and they were fogged with pain. I put a hand to his face. He was hot to the touch, and his heartbeat was unsteady, like it was out of sync . . . Wait . . . his heart?

He coughed and blood coated his lips. The first stages of the Aegrus virus clutching him close.

"Oh my God." I cupped his face and stared into his eyes. "He made you human."

CHAPTER 18

Hades's voice floated around us.

"No, I did not make him human. He was dead when he came to the underworld. I cannot send the dead back; I can only send people back alive. And in this case, that makes him rather human. I did, however, give him the virus. *That* is my insurance, and a rather tight deadline to make things happen. Your man has less than twenty-four hours before the virus kills him. Get to it, Drakaina. Find Hera and make her believe that you are serious."

Hades's voice faded, and I stared in shock at Remo. A very human Remo, who was dying in my arms. I picked him up and laid him in the hospital bed I'd been in not all that long ago. "I'm going to get Merlin. He can turn you."

"No. Deal with Hera. You can do it. I trust you." He breathed the words out and then coughed—hard enough that I heard something crack in his chest. I couldn't stop the cry that slipped past my lips. I put my hands on his and held his fingers tight.

"Remo, he can turn you, and then you won't die."

"No, you're going to stop the virus, and Hera will take it away from us all. Go." He smiled, but it was weak and his heart seemed to stumble, like it didn't know how to beat properly anymore. A small hand touched my shoulder, and I saw Ernie floating beside me. "He's right, you have to go. There is no way that you can help him by staying here and watching him die. We have to find Hera. And the only way to do that is . . ."

"Through Hercules and the Hydra," I said. I already knew that. I knew I'd have to face them, and when I faced them, Hera would show up. But I didn't want to leave Remo. I knew all too well what it was like to be lying in quarantine with no one there to comfort you. No one to hold you as you died.

"HERMES!" I yelled his name, and seconds later he zipped through the window, skidding to a stop in midair.

"What's up?"

"Get Dahlia, bring her here, and if not her, then get Tad. Or someone. Remo needs someone here with him." I clutched Remo's hand, and he shook his head.

"No, you need them all with you . . ."

"No, I don't." I wanted to smack him. Hermes was already gone, off to gather whomever he could. The night sky was dark, and Dahlia would still be up. No doubt she and Tad would come together. That would keep them out of harm's way at least.

I bent over Remo. "I can do this, but only if I know there is someone here with you."

He let out a sigh and closed his eyes. "Shit, I remember being human all too well now, and it sucks being so weak."

I bent and kissed him on the lips, a tear slipping down over my cheek. "Hang on, please hang on."

"Only for you," he breathed back, and then he was asleep. I pulled a blanket up over him and took a step back and then another. Once more I escaped the hospital room that held nothing but death in it. Only now it wasn't my death I ran from but Remo's.

"You've got a plan?" Ernie asked as he flew by my side.

"Yes, but it's not solid. It may not work."

"Oh, that's not what I want to hear," he said.

I didn't disagree. I burst out of the hospital and ran for the water. I stripped out of my clothes and tossed the leather jacket to Ernie. "Hang on to that for me." I took two more big running strides and then leapt off the rocks that overlooked the edge of a cliff. I dove into the water, shifting as I fell so I emerged on the water's surface in my snake form. I already knew I couldn't wait on the ferry, if it was even running this late at night, which I doubted. I swam hard for the other side of the sound, my eyes on the lights of Seattle. I didn't know where to find Angel and Hercules, but I knew what would get their attention. And for Remo I would do everything I could to bring that attention down on me.

The water sluiced around me, and a coast guard boat swept up beside me. Poseidon waved. "Heard you're taking on Hera. I can't say I'm rooting for you, but . . . get her, Drakaina."

I bobbed my head, glad he wasn't attacking me this time at least. I emerged from the ocean and made my way up over the loose sand and rocks and onto the docks. Screams erupted all around as I slithered forward. Sure, I wasn't moving as fast as if I had a vehicle, but I wasn't really all that worried. What I wanted was attention, lots and lots of attention. The first major intersection I came to, I slithered out into the center of it and coiled up in the middle, completely blocking traffic. Was it the best idea I'd ever had? Probably not, but then again, it was the only idea I had, and all that mattered was that I saved Remo. No matter what I had to do.

Humans hurried out of their cars while I stayed silent and still, waiting. Cameras clicked, and I saw more than one person using their phone to take a video of me. I held still, wondering how long it was going to take to get Hercules and the Hydra to show up.

Ernie was there suddenly, puffing hard. "Snake, shit, you can really move when you want to. So now what? We wait?"

I nodded, and he flew up to sit on the top of my head. A cherub on top. A cherry on top. I shivered, and my skin rippled down the entire length of my body, casting sparkles of light and color every which way. I sat there, waiting, and I could feel the time slipping by. I could feel Remo's death beckoning him and could almost hear Hades's laughter. I wanted to cry with the frustration of it. Twenty minutes passed, and I knew they weren't coming. I let myself shift down into my human form. The people around me rushed forward, and I cringed, waiting for them to hit me. Except they didn't. One woman wrapped her coat around me. "Oh, my dear, you must be freezing."

Another person, a man, held open the door of his car. "Here, it's warm in here."

"Why are you being nice to me?" I whispered, shock and uncertainty making me hesitant to take what they offered.

"Because you are looking out for us. You're like our . . . our very own Jedi facing down Darth Vader," a young man said from the left of me.

I looked at him. "Seriously?"

"Okay, well, we could call you our very own Batman, but he isn't supernatural. Just a billionaire with nice toys."

I cleared my throat. "Thank you, all of you."

I held a hand up to Ernie, and he dropped not only my jacket but the rest of my clothes down to me. "Thought you might need everything."

He had a good point. I quickly dressed. "Thank you, all of you, but I have to go."

"Where? Maybe one of us could give you a ride?" the young guy said, and while I wanted to believe he was helping me only because he saw a pretty woman, I had a feeling it was more than that. He wanted to be a part of whatever was going on. Whatever he saw as an adventure, and he had no idea how dangerous it was.

"No, I have to go alone. I don't want you to get hurt." It was only then I saw how few people there actually were. For a main intersection, the place was downright deserted. In a city of over six hundred thousand people, we should have been swarmed with cars backed up, people shouting and yelling, police and ambulance sirens. Yet there was a total of a dozen cars, and maybe twice that many people. I tightened my jaw. This was the virus running rampant—it was clearing the streets of life.

A new idea swept over me, and I knew it was probably my only chance. "Ernie, you know where Hercules has holed up, right?" One way or another I was going to face the hero and the Hydra.

He nodded, his face serious. "Yes."

"Then we will go to him."

The people around me cheered, but I couldn't be happy, not when I knew what I was going to do. Or at least try to do. Death should never be cheered for.

A cop car pulled up, and a police officer stepped out, and for just a moment I thought it was Jensen. For once, it wasn't, but that didn't mean my plan changed.

I ran over to the cop car, and the police officer's eyes widened. "I know you."

"Bully for you. I need your car. Give me the keys."

"I can't do that."

I stared him in the eyes, flexing my siren abilities. "You can and you will. Give me the keys."

He tossed them to me and stumbled back. There was no obsessive love in him; I hadn't made him love me. I'd made him do what was right, what he already knew was right. I took the keys and slid into the driver's seat. "Ernie."

"I'm here. You've got a better plan now. I can see it on your face."

"Zeus was supposed to meet with those who were supporting him at his office; that's what he said back at the cabin. They may still be there, and I need them. This is more their war than anyone else's." I turned the key over in the ignition and slipped the car into reverse. I hit the pedal and spun the steering wheel. The tires squealed, and the smell of burning rubber filled the air. I flicked it back into drive and hit the gas. We shot down the mostly empty street. Ernie leaned over and flicked on the lights and the siren.

"I always wanted to do a ride along." He smiled at me, and I managed to give him a quick, albeit wobbly, smile back.

"Ernie. Tell me I can do this."

He sobered up instantly. "If anyone can, it will be you. You've defied the odds so far; I can't imagine this will be any different."

I clutched the wheel, driving as if I truly were inside *Gran Turismo*. Tad would be proud of me. I blinked several times, thinking of the way my mother had looked in the underworld. "I saw my mom there."

"You mean . . . back there?"

"Yes, she wasn't being hurt. She seemed . . . happy. And she didn't want me to bring her back," I whispered.

"It has nothing to do with you." Ernie moved so he sat on the dash, facing me. His wings were backlit by the flashing lights. "Look, your mom had been unhappy for a long time, stuck between protecting her husband and two kids, pretending to be one thing, while truly being another. It's a shit way to live. I should know. I have to pretend to be working for two different sides all the time. I've never been happier than the last few days once I sided with you, Alena. And as for your mom, I bet it's the same. A release, freedom in a weird way, even if it means she loses out in other areas."

"But why wouldn't she want to be with us?" The cry slipped out of me, and I bit down on my lower lip. "No, don't answer that. I can't deal with it right now."

He answered me anyway. "It's not you she doesn't want to be with, Alena. It's the world and the fear she's lived with for so long. She probably doesn't realize she can have her family and her freedom. Or she could have."

I drove onto the highway and really pushed the gas pedal, staring hard through my tears. I wove the car around the few other vehicles that were there. Again, so few that I would have known something was wrong even if I didn't know about the virus going viral. It wasn't long before the Blue Box was there in front of us. I pulled into the parking lot, driving right up to the front doors. I pulled over and flicked the siren off, but I left the lights flashing. I took the keys and tucked them into my pocket.

"I've never seen Blue Box so empty," Ernie said.

"Everyone is sick," I said as I strode through the doors, surprised they were open at all. Not because of the lateness of the hour, but because there had to be a fair number of employees that hadn't shown up to work. There had to be . . .

A greeter waved at me. "Welcome to Blue Box, deals of the day in the meat department."

Meat department. I saw the sign, and my stomach rolled with hunger. I'd not eaten much the last few days.

"Where is the manager's office?"

"Back of the store, behind the women's lingerie section."

Of course it was. This was Zeus we were talking about after all. I hurried toward the meat department first. I grabbed three packs of steaks and a package of hot dogs. "Ernie, grab me some milk."

"Okay." The uncertainty in his voice would have made me laugh another time. As it was, I was on a time limit. I ripped the packaging off the steaks first and crammed them into my mouth. My teeth cracked the T-bones, and I swallowed the steaks in big, bloody chunks. The hot dogs were next, mostly because I could eat them as I walked. Ernie caught up to me, carrying a jug of chocolate milk. I took it, cracked it open, and tipped it up to my lips. The few people in the store stared at me with wide eyes as I chugged the entire container.

"Shit, you really were hungry." Both his eyebrows had disappeared into his hairline.

I tossed the empty container to one side and headed to the section where the shoes and lingerie were. "I'm going to fight, and I need all the energy I can get."

Ernie bopped in front of me, nodding. "There may be no one here; the pantheon on Zeus's side may not have shown up at all."

"True, but I doubt it. I think they would try and make things happen even without Zeus. I think Smithy will organize them." At least, that was what I was hoping for. I passed by the shoes and the lingerie section, then hit the swinging doors that led into the back storage room. To my right was a set of stairs, and I hurried up it, not bothering to be quiet. At the top, there was a single door, and I didn't knock. Just turned the handle and pushed my way in. And pushed was the right term. The room was loaded with people. At the front of the room was Smithy, and his eyes shot to mine. "Alena! You're alive?"

"For now," I said and shoved my way to the front of the room. I took a good look around. Yaya was there, or at least I thought it was Yaya. The woman I'd called grandmother for so long stared at me from a face as young as mine. Again the doubts surfaced about her motives, and I had to push them away. One problem at a time. "I need to get to Hera."

"That's what we're all discussing," a woman said, and I turned to see Artemis watching me, her body bristling with weapons. "Hera has made it clear that she will not be coming out of hiding anytime soon."

A surge of anger flushed through me, and I struggled not to shift right there. Breathing carefully, I got the urge under control after a few deep breaths. I looked around. Everyone had peeled back from me and had pressed up against the various walls. I wanted to laugh. I blew out a breath. "I think—no, I know—this has to be a full-on assault. I will meet the Hydra and Hercules, but I need the rest of you to actually stand with me."

"You want us to fight for you?" a man from the back slurred, his eyes not entirely focusing on me. I struggled to place him for about three seconds before I recalled his name in the recesses of my early learning. God of wine. Of course we would get him on our side. "No, Dionysus. I don't want you to fight for me. I want you to face the pantheon that Hera has brought to her side. I will face the monsters; you keep the rest from attacking me."

"And the vampires?" Yaya asked, arching a delicate dark-brown eyebrow at me. "They are completely out of control without Remo or Santos guiding them, though that young one, Max, is making an effort."

A bakery full of smoke and burnt cookies when there was a line of customers waiting outside couldn't have been more stressful, though it was close. I went through my options quickly in my head. There wasn't a lot I had left to me.

"I need the vampires held off; they can't be brought into this. I will deal with them if I survive." I stared hard at her. "You and your priestesses got any juice left in you?"

She grinned, a slow spreading of her lips that made me think I wouldn't want to cross her, even if she was my yaya. "That we do."

"Great. Get the last of the SDMP together, and they can help you with the vampires." I glanced at Smithy, and he nodded.

"I'll put in a call to Oberfall. He'll help," he said.

I looked back to my yaya, who seemed fiercer than I'd ever recalled her being. "Keep them off me until I can deal with Hera."

My shockingly youthful grandmother gave a salute. "General."

Someone at the back raised her hand and pushed forward. It was the satyr and healer Damara. Her horns glittered in the fluorescent lights. "What about the rest of us who aren't actually part of the pantheon?"

I thought for a moment. "Triage. Do what you can to keep the casualties down. Get the humans and Super Dupers who don't want to be a part of the fight out of the area."

She nodded. "Done."

I looked around the room, seeing all the faces. Seeing they were looking to me to make it happen. They thought I could take out a goddess. A sudden wave of anxiety flushed through me, but before it took root, I pushed it away, forcing it back. "No more hiding. We do this and bring Hera to her knees. If I . . . do this right, you will all be free to divorce those you want to."

Behind me, Smithy jerked as if I'd punched him in the gut. "Why would you do that?"

I didn't look at him. "Because it is the only thing I could do to convince Hades to stop the virus. It's a boon for all of you, though." I did look at him then. "You can be free from the bonds that have held you all for so long, if you want."

They seemed stunned, so I kept talking. "Ernie, you said that you knew where Hercules and the Hydra are holed up?"

He nodded and lowered himself to stand on the table. "Yes."

I was ready, I could do this. "Then take us there."

CHAPTER 19

It didn't take long to mobilize everyone. The pantheon had their own ways of traveling, and I sent them all off first. As the room emptied, they touched me, wished me luck, and in general said their good-byes. Artemis gave me a nod, as if I should know what she was getting at. I just nodded back.

Panacea was the last to leave, and she took both my hands in hers. "You have a bit of a healer's touch, Alena. You are not all monster and power and rage. Remember that." She leaned in and kissed me on the mouth, surprising me, and then she was gone.

Okay, so Panacea wasn't really the last one in the room. "Why are you *really* doing this?" Smithy said.

"My family, Remo, my life. I want it back, Smithy. Hera is not going to stop, which means either I die or I find a way to thwart her. I can't keep living like this. Running, fighting, trying to find a life, trying to find peace when around every corner someone I love is threatened." I thought about Remo lying in the hospital bed, my heart breaking. What would I do if I lost him?

Smithy put a hand on mine. "He's dying?"

I nodded and pulled my hand away. "I love him, and I can't save him if I don't do this."

"You could die trying to stop her."

"Then at least Remo and I will be together." I looked up at him in time to see a shot of pain rush over his features.

"I remember a time I loved like that," he said softly, "and I have known that desire again recently."

I shook my head. "No, we have had that discussion."

"I know. But I hope you remember that if your life is on the line, Remo wouldn't want you to die just to be with him. Life is precious, Alena. Even after all these years, I still feel that way." He leaned in and brushed his lips across mine, in the same way Panacea had done, though his touch was far less platonic. Even so, the flicker of desire I felt was nothing like the way I felt with Remo. The fleeting feeling was more of an acknowledgment of what almost was—what could have been.

Smithy left the room, and I leaned on the table. "Ernie, you ready?"

"You got it. What do you need me to do?"

"Have your arrows ready; I may need you to shoot someone. But it will be a last resort, okay?" I stood and took a deep breath. This was it; I was going to battle, and I was probably going to die. Funny enough, the second I let myself just accept that fact, the fear and terror slid away from me, like sloughing a skin, and I was able to breathe. I was able to see things clearly.

I jogged out to where the police cruiser still sat, lights flashing. The greeter waved at me as I hurried by. "Thank you for coming to Blue Box!"

I stepped outside and froze in place. Because all my plans just shot out the window in a single wicked smile from nine Hydra heads.

Hercules stood in front of Angel the Hydra. He was dressed in the same black armor that was a blend of old school and modern. Leather bulletproof vest, a helmet that looked like something the SDMP wore, and several weapons at his side, two of which were guns. The one I kept my eye on, though, was his sword strapped to his back. I knew from experience that a hero's weapon could damage me—badly.

"Drakaina. We end this now."

I nodded. "Hercules, this doesn't have to go down this way. Hera doesn't care about you. She had Hades imprison your father."

His face darkened. "My father rarely has time for me, so why would I care about his capture?"

"He didn't know that Hera was manipulating you." I felt the need to try to make this right, as much to keep him from attacking me as because I understood what it was to always want someone to love you. "You won't make her believe in you. You will never be good enough for her to call you her son. But you are a good man. I believe that."

His face darkened further. Ernie leaned in close. "Maybe don't go that route. With a woman, yes, but a man being told he's being an idiot when he has a sword strapped to his back—not so much."

Oh dear. So much for familial bonds. I stepped around the car, and the Hydra let out an echoing hiss across all nine of her heads. I refused to change tactics. I knew I would have to eventually, but maybe I could talk Hercules down. Maybe I could do with him what I couldn't do with Cerberus. A thought lit me up.

"You are nothing more than a dog on a chain to Hera." I paused. "And I don't think you are a bad guy, or you wouldn't have helped me dig my mother out of the bakery." I swallowed hard past the sudden lump. Hercules looked away from me.

"I gave her my word I would stop the monster ravaging the world." He bit the words out.

"It isn't me," I said. "Surely you can see that it isn't me? She's using your desire to please her."

He put a hand over his eyes. "What would you have me do? Turn on her?"

"No. Just don't fight me," I said, hope blooming in my chest. "I . . . I need to speak with Hera. I need to convince her that she doesn't have to do this. She's killing people; the virus is wiping out the humans at a rate that in no time will leave the world decimated."

His jaw twitched. "I can call on her. She will come."

The hope that had bloomed withered and died as the Hydra swept a head toward Hercules. "Watch out!"

But I was too late. She slammed into him and sent him flying through the air, at a speed I knew would take him out of the fight for a good amount of time.

Ernie shot high into the air. "I think you should shift now."

I silently agreed.

I called up the Drakaina in me with a mere thought, and the shift took me faster than ever, coursing through my body. As I emerged from the shift, the Hydra was already charging me. I ducked out of the way, and she dug her claws into the asphalt, spinning her body around to face me. She roared. Spit flew from all nine mouths, splattering my body. I coiled around myself, tucking my body away from her claws as she reached for me. I knew from our previous encounters that with her nine heads, claws, and wicked teeth, she outmatched me. But my venom . . . my venom could do her in. If I could get my fangs in her. I hissed at her, a rumbling sound that reverberated through my entire body and gave her a good look at my fangs as I swayed from side to side.

She paused for a moment, all her eyes narrowing at once, and then she shook herself and launched toward me.

I let her chase me backward, forcing me across the mostly empty parking lot. She charged me, all her heads stretched in my direction. I knew what I had to do, I just had to wait for her to give me an opening. I stopped at the far edge of the asphalt where the trees met the edge, and I flattened myself to the ground. She shot over me, and I slithered between her front legs. She clamped down on my tail with one of her mouths, crushing through the skin and bone. But I was already in place. I coiled myself around her, loop after loop, all the way up her nine necks so that all her heads were pinned together like a gothic flower bouquet.

Her one mouth still held my tail, and I squeezed her until she let it go with a pop.

With someone else, I would have tried to talk her down. But she'd killed my mom. With glee. On purpose. She had killed her own family and gotten away with it.

Anger snapped up through me as hot and sweet as melting chocolate and much more deadly.

I struck hard, as fast as any lightning bolt from Zeus. I dug my fangs deep into one of her necks and pumped my venom into her body. She jerked and tried to claw at me, but I had her wrapped up good, pinning her entire body down. She writhed and snarled, her jaws clamping open and closed repeatedly as she bit at the open air. Over and over, there was nothing she could do. I held on for all I was worth, knowing it was just a matter of time.

I listened for her heartbeat as I kept my mouth tight on her. Which is why I didn't see the blow coming. I was hit hard on the back of the head, hard enough to knock me away from the Hydra and loosen my coils on her. My vision spun, and I struggled to get my bearings.

Angel took advantage of my momentary distraction, and all nine of her heads clamped down on me at once, teeth digging through the flesh and bone, and I reared my head back in pain, unable to stop her. She had me stretched out like a piece of pasta being rolled in a long line. I blinked several times, fighting to see who had hit me. Hercules had come back, that had to be it. Damn him for not seeing the truth.

A soft, feminine laugh rolled through the air. "Oh, you think Hercules got you? You think that because I am the goddess of love, I can't fight? Stupid snake." Aphrodite strolled into view, her face sharp with hatred. How I had ever thought her beautiful I had no idea. The reality was she was as hideous as any of the monsters I'd met in the underworld. I hissed at her, which flicked some of the venom off my fangs, and managed to splatter it on her. She screamed and clutched at her face as she spun away.

The Hydra turned her heads as Aphrodite burned under my venom. She dropped me to laugh, and I hit the ground hard with a thump that resonated through my entire body. Pain ripped through me, but I pushed through it and made myself put some distance between us.

It was only then that I saw the parking lot set out in front of me. On one side stood Smithy, Panacea, Artemis, and the other members of the pantheon who were with Zeus. On the far side was Hera, her hair and skirts flowing around her as beautiful as ever, and her crew, which included Hermes. And Hades, of course, but it was Hermes that hurt me. He saw me looking at him and shrugged. "Sorry, got to go with the winning team, Drakaina. And we can all see it isn't going to be you." Well, that at least explained why I could never get ahead of Hera, why she always seemed to be that one step in front. Hermes had been playing both sides . . . I should have at least suspected.

I turned away from him and flicked my tail forward, catching the screaming Aphrodite with the broken tip despite the hurt of it, and sent her toward our side and right into her husband's arms. I didn't care what happened to her; I had bigger problems. Angel circled around me, her heads weaving back and forth, forward and back. I struggled to keep my eyes on all of her heads.

Ernie dove in beside me and whispered in my ear. "Time, you just need time. The venom is working. She's slowing down."

All well and good. I twitched my head to send him away. Time wasn't on my side, that was the problem. If it were just a matter of time, I could survive anything. But the reality was that the toxins from her fangs were working in me too. I could feel them making me want to lie down and close my eyes. Angel shot forward, and I didn't duck or dive. I opened my mouth and took one of her heads completely inside of it. My body coiled, convulsing around her as I pulled her closer. The eyes on the other heads widened in tandem as she realized what I could do at the same time I did.

I was going to swallow her whole.

While a part of me recoiled at the thought, the Drakaina in me approved.

She can't hurt you inside of you. Your stomach acid will break her down in seconds. Already the head in you is dissolving.

I knew I had only one shot at this. I whipped my body around, twisting and writhing as I fought to get a hold on the big monster. No longer was she on the offensive as she scrambled to get away from me, fighting to put distance between us. I opened my mouth, and the stump of a neck slid out, limp, hanging down, dripping green blood.

I shot forward, grabbing another head and yanking it toward me, my jaw unhinging as I worked it around her and partially swallowed it. Just far enough to let my stomach acids burn . . . The remaining seven heads came at me, driving teeth into my head, ripping chunks of flesh off. The pain was intense and shattered my confidence that I would make it out alive. But I didn't stop what I was doing.

I let go of the now-headless second stump and grabbed a third, and then a fourth, and a fifth. I was winning, but it was at a cost that I wasn't sure I would survive. Her claws dug into me, holding me as much as I held her. We were tangled around one another in a death match that was going to end only when one of us stopped breathing.

Blood flowed around us in a river of color and pain that swept through the parking lot.

"You've almost got her, Alena. Then we win!" Ernie yelled from what felt like a very long way away. I swayed where I was, staring down the last head of the Hydra. Her body and face sagged with pain, yet as we locked eyes there was nothing but hatred in hers. Hatred and my death. I grabbed her around the neck, got my mouth over her final head, and dragged her into my throat. I tightened my hold on her body as it jerked, her claws raking my sides with one final protest of her death. Slowly, her final heartbeat gave a thump, and then there was nothing but silence.

I let her go and slumped sideways, unable to even pretend to keep my own head up. I looked down the length of my body. I was missing huge chunks of flesh, and I knew the lower part of my tail was broken, the bones snapped clean in half. Spots where her claws had raked me oozed the rainbow blood that glittered on the asphalt. Her toxins flowed through me, and the sound of my heart slowed, beating painfully.

I lay down. I had done the first part, but now I needed to finish it.

Into my range of vision swept a woman in white—Hera. I'd seen her only once, at the stadium after I'd finished off Achilles. But I would have known her anyway. Her cold beauty, the queenly presence she maintained. She was a goddess through and through. She stopped in front of me, obviously not afraid of me in my current state. I couldn't blame her. I wasn't sure I could even lift my head, never mind actually strike a blow at her.

"Drakaina, it seems that you and I are destined to meet on the field of battle. So come at me, snake. Let us see your power in all its glory against a goddess of the pantheon." She flicked her hand, and a sword appeared. This couldn't be happening. She wasn't serious, was she?

"Even you know that isn't fair, Mother."

Hera spun to one side. "Hercules, I'm surprised you made it back in time to see the finale."

He glanced at me and gave me a slow nod. "This has been a long time coming. You want to fight? Then you can fight me."

The pantheon around us oohed, like an awestruck crowd at a Backstreet Boys concert. Across the way, Panacea pushed her way through the crush of people. Hercules drew Hera's attention away from me, and Panacea had her hands on me. "I can heal you a little, but it will take much of your strength."

I nodded, and warmth flooded through me. I closed my eyes, wanting only a moment to rest, a moment to take in the lack of pain rushing through my body. Only I barely got a moment before the crowd cried out, and I forced my eyes open. Hera stood over Hercules, a sword through his belly. "You see? You are not the fighter you believe yourself to be."

"You would kill me, then?" He gasped, one hand around the edge of the sword. It had to be cutting into his palm, but he didn't pull back. She shook her head. "No, but I can't have you meddling." She yanked the sword out, and he gasped again. She spun it around and hammered it into the top of his head. He fell backward with a thud onto the asphalt.

I raised myself up and swayed where I was.

Hera sneered at me. "Even half-healed, I can take you, snake."

I stared at her, thinking about all the things I had to say, none of which could be done in this form. I let the Drakaina go and slowly shifted down to my human form. Naked, standing on a half-healed but still-broken foot, gashes and bite marks all over my body, I faced her. "No more death. Please."

She laughed. "Oh, you think you can talk me out of this? Hades warned me that you would try."

I shot a look at Hades, who shrugged. "I want to see if you're as good as you think you are," he said.

Why, oh why, would he make this harder? Because he was an elephant butthole, just like the majority of the pantheon. I wrapped my arms around myself. "You are killing humans; you aren't making them love you. They fear you, and you've only made them love me more because I stand between you and them. If you keep killing them off, the only member of the pantheon with real power will be Hades as he collects their souls."

From above my head came a soft sound of agreement from Ernie. "Excellent point, Alena."

Hera's eyes glittered as she stepped toward me. "I will kill you, and they will see you for the monster you are. And don't worry about Hades. He will never rule."

Hades grunted as if she'd slapped him.

I kept my eyes on her. "You keep saying that, but it isn't true. All the humans will see is a goddess who was supposed to protect them turn into the monster. The roles have reversed, but it doesn't have to be that way."

"You cannot convince me." She rushed forward with a thrust that sent her sword through my right shoulder.

I cried out and fell back, but spun upward again to face her, resolute in my next words. "If I let you kill me, will you stop this? Will you stop the virus and give Zeus his damn divorce?"

The crowd around us gasped, and her eyes widened. "Is that what you think this is? A divorce squabble?"

"That's what Hades said." I pointed at him, noting that Zeus was now beside him, still wrapped in chains, mind you, but there.

Her shoulders tensed, and Hades tried to step back into the crowd, but Zeus blocked him. Not that Hades could get away from Hera's gaze. Her whole body stiffened, and she took a step toward him before stopping herself and swinging around to me. "Your words are rather good at distracting me, Drakaina. I will have no more of it." She took a few steps backward, as if giving me room.

Smithy waved at me, getting my attention. "You have to shift. You can't take her like this." Like this? Like what? I was missing something, I had to be.

I kept my arms wrapped around my body, and a last desperate thought coursed through me. I lifted a hand to Ernie, and he shot close to me. I whispered to him, "Get as many people infected with the virus here as fast as you can. Take Smithy and the others and get them to help."

His eyes were full of worry. "You will be alone."

I nodded. "I know. Go."

He was gone in a flash, and I didn't watch to make sure he did as I asked. I didn't need to. I trusted him.

I wasn't sure I had it in me to shift again, but in my belly, I knew Smithy was right. Again, I was faced with either bending my morals or dying. Life was worth fighting for, I knew that. I called the shift forward and let it take me. My snake form reared up, high above Hera, but only for a split second.

Hera's form grew, rising up until she was the same size as me. This was what Smithy had meant, then.

A giant woman to face a giant snake. Oh dear, this was not going to go well. I pulled back, readying to strike, when she swept forward with her sword, which had also unfortunately grown in size. I fell backward, twisting to spin around until I faced her again, now from flat out on the ground. I wasn't going to be fast enough. I could feel it in my blood and muscles. The toxins and then the healing from Panacea had taken too much out of me.

Hera smiled down at me, her hair spooling out all around her on a breeze I couldn't feel. She looked every inch the warrior goddess, and I knew that fighting her would only end with one of us dead—most likely me. I flicked my tail out and slammed it into her legs, throwing her off balance. She stumbled sideways toward the Blue Box and barely caught her balance at the doors. The few humans left there cried out and stared up at her in horror.

I gathered the last of my reserves. This was like the last dessert at a bake-a-thon gone terribly wrong—I had to just hold on long enough to get through to the finish line. I coiled back, rising up higher than I ever had before, until I was almost completely on the back quarter of my tail. I was nearly twice my normal height as I slithered forward, moving as fast as I could. Hera spun up with her sword, and her eyes widened as she had to look up at me.

"Why won't you just die?" She pulled her arm back for a swing, and it was my opening. I shot forward with the last of my reserves driving me. I coiled around her body and arms, squeezing her until she dropped the sword. Her body shrunk, like a deflating vanilla soufflé disappearing into my coils. I wasn't going to lose her—not this time. I didn't know if I could, but I thought about being smaller, shifting down to a comparable size.

Behind us, Ernie cheered. "Go, Alena, go! You've got her on the run."

"Little shit," Hera snarled. But I was following her in size, so as she finished her downsizing I was still there, wrapped around her, squeezing her tight, staring into her eyes. Something passed between us, and for a moment I saw myself. I saw a woman scorned, tossed aside like she was nothing, unloved by the man who should have stood by her forever. It cut through me as sharp as any weapon.

I shook, shifted, and stumbled away from her, shaking my head. "I can't."

The crowd around us sucked in a collective breath, and I slowly turned. Hera had her sword pointed at my neck, but she didn't thrust it, didn't swing it. "Why can't you? You are a monster, you're designed, created even, to kill and maim."

"I . . . my husband cheated on me when I lay dying in my hospital bed. He used me for my money, he used me because I was a fool in love with him, my eyes closed to his faults."

Her eyes narrowed, and I swallowed hard. "I know you don't want to think this is about a divorce, that this isn't about you and Zeus . . . but I would hate him too. And you know what? If you'd come to me first, I have no doubt I'd be on your side of the field. Because I understand what it means to be hurt by the one you love the best, the one who held your heart and crushed it in his unfeeling hands."

She didn't move. It was as if my words had frozen her. Her lips parted. "And what does it mean to me that we suddenly understand one another? You want to be friends?" She laughed and stepped back. "You are a fool. The pantheon doesn't work that way."

I kept my eyes on her. "Maybe I just want to help make things right. Maybe I want to see if you truly have the best interest of the world in you. You want to rule? Well, maybe you need to show some compassion. End the virus."

I glanced at Ernie and nodded. From behind me shuffled those still able to walk but sick with the Aegrus virus. "You can save them, Hera," I said. "You can be their hero."

The crowd oohed, but Hera didn't move, her eyes half-closed, her body still.

Those who were sick stumbled toward us, crying out for her to save them. That they would love her forever. Her eyes opened wide, a flash of pity in them. Hera slowly raised her sword, pointing it at Hades. "I will end the virus."

The sick humans cried out. She glared at Hades. "Do it, Hades."

"Are you sure? I think she's just trying to make you do what—"

"Hades!" we both yelled at the same time. He grimaced, nodded. "Fine."

The humans stopped moving, and a flash of green light flickered above their heads, flowing down like pixie dust, coating them. Within seconds, they were cheering. Healed. I closed my eyes, praying that Remo was just as healed.

I shivered where I stood, and Hera stared at me. "Now what?"

I shrugged. "Divorce Zeus, but take half of everything. Including control of Olympus." I gave her a small smile. "Make him pay for what he's done, but hurt him, not the rest of us."

She snorted, shook her head, and then looked over the parking lot. "And the pantheon? Would they split down the middle?"

"Not my issue," I said. "I just want the virus stopped, and I don't want to be stalked by your heroes anymore. Go kick Zeus's ass. I'm tired."

I sat down on the asphalt, then lay back so I could stare at the sky, the dark color fading into nothing as I waited for whatever the fallout would be. Not caring about anything . . . but then I jerked upright.

"Remo."

CHAPTER 20

The time it took to get back to the hospital on Whidbey Island seemed to be counted in years instead of hours.

I wore clothes Panacea had given me, a long white dress that was pinned at the shoulders with two large discs engraved with snake heads. Smithy went with me, and Poseidon gave us a ride in his coast guard boat, though he grumbled the whole way. I gripped the edge of the boat as it zipped across the water, bouncing on the waves. Ernie sat on my shoulders, clinging to my hair.

"We'll get there in time, we have to," he said.

"You're sure Hades turned him back into a vampire?" I asked Smithy again. Maybe for the tenth time. Because I couldn't believe it.

Smithy nodded, his face somewhat green in the growing light of the oncoming morning. "Yes. When he reversed the virus, everyone went back to the way they were before." He leaned over the edge and vomited into the spray of water. I turned away from him. The sun was at my back, warming my bare skin even as we hurried.

The sun was up. How was I going to save Remo if he was burned to a crisp? Fear clutched at me, driving me the rest of the way when I would have otherwise fallen to my knees, passed out from sheer fatigue.

The boat pulled up to the docks, and I was climbing the ladder before Poseidon had properly moored. At least that's what he yelled at me while I scrambled off the boat. Barefoot, I ran toward the hospital, shocked when I saw the bodies still there.

"Ernie," I whispered.

"No, don't think like that. Hurry." Ernie pushed me, and I stumbled forward. I broke down the front doors and ran for the stairs. The stale air of the closed-off hospital, the faint scent of antiseptic, cleaners, death, unwashed bodies. I closed it all off as I bolted up to the tenth floor. To my room. I slid to a stop in front of the door, suddenly unable to push it open. As if I were that girl again, sick and dying, unable to save herself.

Only now it was my heart that was sick and dying. Whatever lay on the other side of the door would either save me or be the shattering of my heart. With a half-hitched sob in my chest, I put a hand to the door.

"You can do this," Ernie said. "You're not that girl anymore."

I pushed the door open and walked in, making myself look around. There was no one in the room.

"No one came to be with him?" I did a slow turn. "Of course not. I sent Hermes." I put a hand to my head and flicked my tongue out, scenting the air. There was a hint of cinnamon and honey . . . and other vampires. The more I breathed, the more distinct smells I picked up on. Ten, maybe even twelve.

"The vampire council is how many?"

"Baker's dozen," Ernie said.

I nodded, feeling it in my bones. "Ernie, they have him."

His eyes were filled with worry as I crawled into the bed and lay down where Remo had been. I breathed in his scent and closed my eyes. I couldn't save him if I was weak. I couldn't do it without sleep. "Watch over me," I whispered.

Ernie answered in the affirmative, but it wasn't him I called to. With my eyes closed, I saw my mother, I saw her smile and nod. "I will watch over you, my girl. Sleep." And I let myself slip into the abyss that spoke my name.

I woke up to a hand on my shoulder shaking me.

"Alena, are you alright?" Tad's voice cracked. "Tell me you're alright." And then he pulled me up while my eyes were still closed so that I was enfolded in his arms. I hugged him back and pressed my face against his chest. "I'm . . . no, I'm not okay, but I'm going to be."

I pulled back a little from him. "Dahlia and Sandy, are they okay?"

He nodded. "They're at Mom and Dad's place." The pain in his eyes, the look in his face. I knew without him saying it.

"The vampire council is there." I spoke the words as a statement, not as a question.

He nodded again, and his voice cracked. "They're hurting Dahlia and Remo. And Dad . . . he can't stop them, he's not strong enough after turning people who had the virus."

I stood and took a breath, then another, feeling my body shake off the last of the sleep. "No rest for the wicked."

"What are you going to do?" he asked, his eyes full of uncertainty and fear. "Alena?"

I smiled, and while it was tiring, and a bit hard to make my lips turn up, I meant every word.

"I'm going to save them."

We stood a few houses down from the front of my parents' house, the midnight hour still a long ways off despite the darkness. A cold, wet gale had blown in off the water with us, and I was soaked through. I looked around, seeing the eyes of vampires here and there, watching us. "Anyone want to come with me while I will still let them?"

A few crept forward, and I was surprised when it wasn't Remo's vampires, but Santos's. Lee was at the lead. "We've been waiting for you to show up. We aren't strong enough to take them on our own, boss. But we've been watching, looking for an opportunity."

I arched an eyebrow. "Why?"

He shrugged, his words matter-of-fact. "You said if Remo wouldn't take us, you would. He denied us, so we are yours. And we have something for you."

From his back he pulled a flask. I backed up so fast I was twenty feet away between one breath and the next.

Tad got in front of me and snarled. "You bastard."

Lee held up his hands, his eyes wide. "No, no. We did a switch. We took the fennel oil from them. What they have in there is diluted honey. It was the closest we could get to the right consistency of the oil."

I slowly regained my composure. "Why not just use olive oil?"

He shrugged. "Didn't have any on hand."

Tad beckoned him forward. "Let me see it." He took the flask from Lee and spun the cap open. I could smell it even as far away as I was.

"Ernie, take it to Smithy. Tell him to get rid of it."

Ernie saluted and scooped up the flask and was gone in a flash of wings and feathers.

There were maybe fifteen vampires who stood waiting for some sort of instruction from me.

"I want you to stay here. You'll hear me if I need help." Confidence flooded me. Not the cocky, I'm-going-to-win-and-everyone-hear-me-roar type. More the I've-been-through-enough-crap-to-last-a-lifetime-and-I'm-going-to-make-sure-said-crap-happens-no-more kind.

Not one argument slipped out of their mouths, or Tad's. I walked up to the front of my parents' house alone and let myself in.

Dahlia and Remo were laid out on the table, side by side, blood all around them. Their eyes were closed and their chests still. That didn't mean they weren't going to be alright again eventually, though; they were vampires after all.

A hand shot out from my left to grab my neck. I reacted faster than even I knew I could move. I grabbed the hand, twisting it around until the arm snapped, and I kept on pulling until it came off. I held the vampire's arm in one hand and his neck in the other. I didn't look at him, couldn't.

Vampires shot from every direction, and I broke bones, snapped backs, and removed limbs as though I'd been doing it my whole life. All I could see was Remo and Dahlia, hurt, dying, at the hands of these monsters.

In a matter of minutes, they were all incapacitated, groaning, injured badly enough that they wouldn't get back up.

I called out into the house. "You really do not want to upset me today."

"I see, then how about we do things the hard way?" slid a voice from down the hall as a vampire dragged my father's limp form in his hands.

"Alena, go," my father whispered. That was the last straw, the final grain of sugar that tipped the scales.

I tossed the vampire in my hands behind me, feeling the Drakaina's power pulse through me, stronger than ever before. No, that wasn't true. The power had always been there. I was just finally ready to fully embrace it as my own.

The command in my voice was thick and heavy as mud-pie pudding. "Let him go."

My dad was dropped like a hot potato, and the vampire in front of him trembled. I lifted an eyebrow as he took a step. "Freeze."

His limbs seemed to turn to stone, and he shook even harder. "Impossible."

I strode toward him. "Rules are going to change, or I will do to you what I did to the rest of them, only I won't be so kind with you." I tipped my head toward the vampires I'd dropped.

Whatever hold I had on him slipped. He snarled and flung an open flask at me. I didn't stop moving, trusting that Lee had been telling the truth and he had truly swapped all the oil for honey. The sticky sweet scent of the thinned-out honey spread over my face and slid down my neck. I licked my lips. "Nice, but it isn't going to save you."

He moved as if to run, and I was on him with a single leap. We crashed to the floor, and I pinned his arms down. "Oh no, you aren't going anywhere. You hurt the ones I love the best."

"They aren't dead," he said.

"You hurt them," I repeated, tightening my grip on his wrists. "New rules, you understand?"

He stared at me, his eyes filled with a mixture of hatred and fear. "What do you want?"

"You will allow vampires to cross-species date, marry, or cohabitate as they please."

He grimaced. "It won't work."

"It will work for those who want it bad enough." My voice was silken smooth, deadly even to my ears, and I drew his face close. "You will not interfere in Remo's life ever again, and you will not return to his territory. Ever."

"We are the council, it is our job—"

"Ever." The word rumbled with a hiss that started deep in my chest.

He was silent. My fangs dropped, and I leaned in close to his neck. "Do you agree?"

"Fuck you."

I felt the movement behind me. I rolled to the side, bringing his body with me. A long wooden stake was jammed between his ribs, right through his heart. I stared past him at a vampire I did know. Max, Remo's second-in-command. He nodded at me.

"What are you doing?" I yelled.

"About time you showed up," Max said. "They won't negotiate. There is only one way to deal with them." He pulled the wooden stake out of the vampire and drove it into another's chest.

I pushed the now truly dead vampire off me and stood as the house flooded with Remo's gang. They scooped up the council members one by one and carried them out of the house. I'd killed two, and the rest were easily taken because of the injuries I'd inflicted. I heard the screams, I saw the wooden stakes. I ignored it as best I could, knowing I was going to have nightmares about this night. I went to Remo and Dahlia. I lowered a fang and sliced it through my wrist. I held it over Dahlia's mouth first, as she seemed further gone. Her face twisted after the first few drops, and then she groaned and sat up.

I moved my wrist over Remo's mouth and waited. I touched his short hair, running my hand over his head. "Remo, please don't leave me again."

I glanced over my shoulder to where Tad was checking on Dad. "How is he?"

"Banged up, bitten, but otherwise okay."

A hand reached up and touched my face. I stared down into Remo's now-open eyes and smiled. "Hey, Sleeping Beauty." I said, and promptly burst into tears.

EPILOGUE

Three weeks later we had a party at my house in Seattle.

To say it was strange would be an understatement. The theme was a mixture of anniversary, funeral, and triumph. I made the red velvet cake my mom had wanted. Dad cried when he talked about her, about how much she really had wanted both Tad and me to be happy. Tad kept his arm locked around Dahlia's waist, his eyes saying it all. He was happy.

Yaya was there, but she insisted we call her Flora from now on, seeing as she no longer looked like a yaya. Max had locked on to her and was currently following her around the room, asking about being a priestess of Zeus. I flicked my eyes up to Ernie, who was sitting on the top of the bookshelf in the living room.

"You keeping your arrows to yourself?" I asked.

He grinned. "Don't need to use them; all of you are doing just fine. Finally."

I rolled my eyes but couldn't help the smile. Hercules had even come to the party, though he stood off to one side. He had healed up fast from the wound Hera had inflicted on him—Ernie said it was because he was half-immortal.

Smithy had declined the invite. Aphrodite needed him, as she was slowly healing from the venom burns.

The pantheon was in upheaval, but Zeus and Hera were working together, and they had already reached out to the human government on behalf of the North American Supernatural Community. Or NASC. Ernie had snickered at the acronym.

"Next thing you know, we'll be wearing T-shirts with that on the chest."

I had a feeling he might be closer to the truth than he wanted to know. I was impressed at how fast Zeus and Hera had pulled things together. The north side of the Wall had been cleaned up in a matter of twenty-four hours, the pantheon put to work dealing with all the issues laid out, from sanitation to medical treatment to the SDMP. It was an impressive feat, even I could give them that. Though it only proved everyone had been right. Zeus was primed and ready to be a leader again; he'd just needed a gigantic shove in the right direction.

Sandy approached me from the kitchen, her arms loaded with platters of baked goods and fruit. "I think this is a bit much." She wobbled, and I helped her set them down on the dining table.

"You've seen Tad eat, yes?"

"Right." She laughed and shook her head. Her eyes flashed when Jensen walked in, tucking his hat under one arm. I pushed her in his direction.

"Can you show him around?"

"Sure."

Ernie snickered and pointed two fingers at his eyes and then to me. I did the same back at him.

There was a knock on the door, and my cousin Samantha put her head in. "Hey."

I smiled at her. "Come on in."

She cleared her throat. "I brought a date, is that alright?"

I nodded. "Of course." I should have asked her who it was first.

She opened the door farther, and Roger walked in behind her. My eyes narrowed, and I strode forward as a hiss whispered past my lips. "You have some nerve. You think I'm going to let you hurt my cousin too? Break her heart?"

Roger held up his hands. "I'm sorry. I am."

I glanced at Samantha. Her eyes were wide and a bit glossy with unshed tears. "You do care about me."

I snorted. "Of course I do. You are family, even if you are a goblin. But if you are serious about Roger, you'd better keep a short leash on him."

She grinned. "I'm good at short leashes. Consider him a pet project."

They laughed, and I shook my head. Not my love life. I locked eyes with Roger as they headed into the house. He'd tried to kill me, left me to die, and cheated on me. He deserved a goblin for a girlfriend. She'd bite his manhood off and eat it for lunch if he so much as looked at another woman. And by the way he all but clung to her, they'd already had that conversation.

A set of hands wrapped around me from behind, and Remo's signature scent rolled over me. I leaned back into him and wove my fingers through his, a sense of belonging and love filling me up.

There were no words between us; there didn't need to be. We were together, and that was all that mattered. He was now the leader of the North American Alliance of Vampires—NAAV. Another acronym Ernie laughed at.

"You ready for your big announcement?" he murmured into my ear.

"Hmm. Yes."

He kissed me on the cheek and then gave me a wink. "And after the party, what do you want to do?"

"Break in that new bed of mine." I winked back at him, slow and seductive. "But only if you are feeling . . . up . . . to the task."

His eyes widened and then narrowed. "Don't tease me, Alena."

I crossed my heart with one finger and walked backward away from him. "I would never tease about that."

I waved at Sandy, and she hurried over to my side. I took her hand and squeezed. Merlin watched from the corner of the big room, his eyes hooded. He'd been invited because he was family. I was surprised he'd showed up, actually. He had been working with my dad, helping him get better with his magic the last few weeks. I suspected his true motives but hadn't been able to question him on anything yet.

I looked at Sandy. "Ready?"

She nodded, a grin plastered on her face.

"If I could have everyone's attention," I said.

All sets of eyes turned to me—family; friends who were like family; and those who'd been with me all the way from being a timid mouse of a baker, trapped in her own life, right through every battle, every hero I'd faced, every side of myself I'd had to come to accept.

Emotion flowed up through me, and I struggled to breathe, never mind speak around it. Finally I pulled myself together. "Thank you, to all of you. For standing by me when it would have been far easier to walk away. For letting me find my wings—"

"You ain't got wings, or is that something you haven't showed us yet?" yelled Max from beside my—Flora.

I rolled my eyes. "Manner of speaking, smart-mouth."

Everyone laughed, and I took a deep breath and dove back in. "Sandy and I . . . we're going into business together. We're going to start two bakeries. One here in Seattle, and one on the north side of the Wall."

The laughter died, and I knew why. The Wall was supposed to come down, but if I was putting a bakery there . . . "There is a reason. There are a lot of Super Dupers who aren't safe to be part of the general populace yet." I thought about the silly werewolf who'd tried to play with the protestors, how close he'd come to infecting them with the werewolf virus without even meaning to. "Not now, and maybe not ever. I want to . . . give them something that is normal until the Wall can come down in every aspect. I want them to feel like they are still a part of this world and not truly cut off. Sandy will run the bakery there. And I will run the bakery here in Seattle, but we'll help each other."

Really, the job of running two bakeries was going to be through-the-roof hard, but I was excited. A number of the vampires who'd tied themselves to me turned out to have a knack for baking, and they'd agreed to work the night shifts for the bakery across the Wall.

"What are you going to call it?" Ernie called from his perch. He knew darn well what the name was, he just wanted me to spill it.

I smiled. "Hisses and Honey."

Merlin slid out of the house when everyone was congratulating his great-niece. He shook his head and strolled down the street. That she'd come so far . . . he wasn't surprised. It was why he'd picked one of his own family members in the first place. Contrary to what he'd told everyone else, he'd chosen Alena because he'd seen the iron core in her along with her huge ability to love. That was where her power lay, and he'd known it from the beginning.

A soft set of footsteps didn't turn him around; he knew who it was. "Good-bye, Flora."

"You stop right there. You're up to something. I know you, Merlin. You haven't changed from that snot-nosed little brat who stuck tacks in his friends' shoes when they weren't looking."

She caught up to him, and he forced a look at her. He could see why his brother had fallen under her spell. Of course, that romance had fizzled out long before Jack met the human who he would marry and start a family with, but she was undeniably enchanting. Her hair was a deep brown and her eyes close to ocean blue, and she had a lovely, curving figure. Lucky for her to have tied her life force to the belief in the gods. Lucky indeed. He raised both eyebrows. "I'm up to nothing."

"Where are you going?"

He grinned and turned away from her. "I have clients to see. Your son-in-law is taking over my practice here."

"He is?"

"You think I was training my nephew just for shits and giggles? Like his daughter believed of herself for so long, he's stronger than he thinks." He snorted.

She was quiet a moment. "What are you really up to, Merlin?"

He smiled. "You know, there are other Walls, Flora. I could use a hand in taking them down." He paused and glanced at her. "That is, if you're up for a challenge?"

She stared at him, the rise and fall of her chest going at a rate that told him she was going to say yes before she ever did.

Within hours they were on a flight across the world, headed for a place he'd sworn he would never return to. A place far deadlier than the one they'd just left.

"You really think we can get the Wall in Europe to fall? Where would we start?" she asked as they flew over the north Atlantic Ocean. "It's been up longer than all the others."

He nodded, a smile on his lips. "We start at the farthest tip of it, and push it over like a domino."

She glanced at him. "Jankkila? You want to go to Finland first?"

He nodded. "That I do."

"And you really think you can do this?"

With a grin he leaned back in his seat. "Of course I do. I *am* Merlin after all."

ACKNOWLEDGMENTS

This one is for all the women out there who thought they weren't strong enough. For the women who found their spines and stood up for themselves and realized, in doing so, they had far more worth than they could have ever imagined. For the women who broke free of tradition in order to give their children wings. You inspired this trilogy, and helped me to create Alena. Thank you.

ABOUT THE AUTHOR

Shannon Mayer is the *USA Today* bestselling author of the Rylee Adamson Novels, the Elemental Series, the Nevermore Trilogy, A Celtic Legacy series, and several contemporary romances. She started writing when she realized she didn't want to grow up not believing in magic. She lives in the southwestern tip of Canada with her husband, son, and numerous animals. To learn more about Shannon and her books, go to www.shannonmayer.com.

Sign up for Shannon Mayer's newsletter:
http://www.shannonmayer.com/tut8.